To Chloe,

Best Wishes,

GLIMPSE

CARSON BOSS

LifeRich Publishing is a registered trademark of The Reader's Digest Association, Inc.

LifeRich Publishing books may be ordered through booksellers or by contacting:

LifeRich Publishing
1663 Liberty Drive
Bloomington, IN 47403
www.liferichpublishing.com
844-686-9607

Because of the dynamic nature of the Internet, any web addresses or links contained in this book may have changed since publication and may no longer be valid. The views expressed in this work are solely those of the author and do not necessarily reflect the views of the publisher, and the publisher hereby disclaims any responsibility for them.

This is a work of fiction. All of the characters, names, incidents, organizations, and dialogue in this novel are either the products of the author's imagination or are used fictitiously.

Any people depicted in stock imagery provided by Getty Images are models, and such images are being used for illustrative purposes only.
Certain stock imagery © Getty Images.

ISBN: 978-1-4897-4520-0 (sc)
ISBN: 978-1-4897-4519-4 (hc)
ISBN: 978-1-4897-4521-7 (e)

Library of Congress Control Number: 2022921209

Print information available on the last page.

LifeRich Publishing rev. date: 12/01/2022

CONTENTS

ACKNOWLEDGMENTS

I would like to express my gratitude to the hundreds of students I have had the privilege of teaching the scriptures to over the past few decades. Your willingness to learn and apply the principles taught by our Savior and his prophets and apostles was truly inspirational to me.

I would also like to thank my wife, Tara. Her belief in me, my writing ability, and the story I wanted to tell inspired me to sit down and finally finish it.

To my children and grandchildren, I hope this effort inspires you to keep learning and honing the talents God has given you to help others.

I would like to thank my extended family and friends who have supported this endeavor by reading and offering constructive feedback that helped me fine-tune this work. Special thanks to Natalee Cooper (author of *A Heart's Design*), Amy Spalding, and Kevin Johnson.

INTRODUCTION

The concept of good versus evil is a universal theme that's permeated all aspects of belief and thought. It goes back to our first parents, who had to deal with Cain slaying Abel. The wickedness of man has been chronicled for thousands of years and seems to be more rampant than ever.

But what is behind this wickedness and how can it be overcome?

Fortunately for us, God has provided the answer. The scriptures are a blueprint for how to avoid the fiery darts of the adversary. This can be done by putting on the whole armor of God, as spoken about by Paul (Ephesians 6:11–17). It is our charge as followers of Christ to stand for righteousness by helping our family and our neighbor come unto him.

Mark Banks was taught these principles by his grandparents from his youth. These principles helped him to overcome some difficult events early on. Now he will need to use these teachings, his gift of the spirit to contact those beyond the grave, and wise counsel from trusted advisers to try to stop an evil force from hurting the ones he loves and all of humankind.

CHAPTER 1

THE ASSIGNMENT

"What was that?" Jeremy asked Mark, positioning the camera hanging around his neck directly in front of him.

"What was what?" Mark shot back, trying to keep his gaze steady between two headstones.

Jeremy snapped several pictures that briefly illuminated a large section of the cemetery with each click. "I thought I saw something move in those dark shadows between us. Did you see it?"

Mark didn't say anything and watched as Jeremy dropped his camera to his chest and began rubbing his eyes with both of his palms. He could tell his best friend since the third grade was losing focus on their assignment and wasn't sure how much longer he would last.

"I don't know if I'm too tired, hungry, or bored, but this has to be the dumbest assignment the professor has given us," Jeremy said, pulling the camera over his head and slamming it into its bag.

"Whatever." Mark turned back to the area he was focused on and began taking pictures.

Jeremy continued to make snide comments for several more minutes until Mark decided he'd had enough.

"Look, if the professor is right about what he has been teaching us this semester, we should be able to capture some evidence of spiritual energy tonight. Plus, it was your idea to come to this cemetery in the first place."

His comments stopped Jeremy's verbal assault, but he could hear him muttering under his breath, loud enough to let him know he wasn't happy.

Mark agreed it was a bit unusual for this to be the first field assignment that Miles Windham, the professor of their Spiritual and Psychic Phenomenon class at the University of Maryland, would require. But he wanted to take the class seriously, even though it was an unpublished elective and not worth any credit toward graduation. He also wanted something to show for his efforts after canceling some plans to attend the Terrapin football game and its accompanying parties.

"I can't feel my hands, and my memory card is full. Let's get out of here," Jeremy said in a raised voice toward Mark.

Mark glanced over and gave him a death stare. "Shut up and let me focus." He quickly turned around to face the other direction and steadied his camera on an illuminated headstone that had a beautiful carving of an angel. Her soft features and a warm smile radiating in the light of the moon made him recall what the professor had explained the day before that got him so excited about their assignment.

"It will be a harvest moon tomorrow night," he'd said, "and the spiritual world will be at its peak. I want you to visit a local cemetery of your choice and take several pictures. Focus your cameras on the darkest possible areas, and make sure to use your flash. Hopefully, some of you will be able to capture a glimpse of a deceased soul by capturing their orb of energy. There will be no better time than tomorrow."

Even though there were a few cemeteries closer to the University of Maryland campus, they had decided to make the forty-minute drive to visit the Historic Congressional Cemetery. Jeremy had done some filming there for one of his classes his junior year of high school and had talked Mark into making the journey.

Mark had found out from doing some research on his phone before they left that the earliest headstones dated back to 1807, and it was one of the most famous cemeteries in the nation.

He couldn't wait to bring the photos he was taking to class the following week to see if any of them turned out. He had seen several demonstrations by the professor that his equipment did not lose resolution when enhancing objects several times the normal size.

Mark's train of thought was again interrupted by Jeremy fiddling around with his camera and letting out loud sighs. He knew Jeremy was nearing his breaking point.

"I told you we needed to grab some food before we did this. The sound of my stomach growling is creeping me out."

Mark didn't comment and snapped several more pictures.

"I'm beginning to question why I even agreed to take this class with you in the first place. We're not even getting any credit for it. Wasting our Saturday night looking for orbs. What's an orb anyway?"

Mark knew he couldn't focus on the assignment until he addressed his question.

"Look, J, there's a lot more to this class and these assignments than getting credit for them. If you would take notes in class, it might help you remember what the professor's main goal is for us attending the class and what an orb is."

Mark lowered his camera deliberately and turned to face him.

"An orb is a soul's energy that can sometimes be captured on film. It's their way of letting you know they're nearby. The professor said once you begin to pay attention, or acknowledge them, they might reveal more of themselves to you."

Mark looked at Jeremy and could tell by his blank expression that his explanation did not have the effect he had been hoping for.

"What is there to acknowledge? I didn't see the images the professor was talking about in those pictures he showed us yesterday. The orbs could've been water drops or dust on his lens," Jeremy said in a challenging tone, moving closer to Mark.

Mark's mind raced back to the dozens of white circle images that the professor had shown them from his travels to different parts of the country. He thought several of them showed obvious features of men and women.

"You don't know what you're talking about. That shot he took next to that church in Virginia clearly showed a young lady's profile. Then there was that one he took at Gettysburg that showed the outline of a young soldier. How could you not see them? You must be blind as a bat."

3

Mark winced after his bat statement and smiled quickly before turning away, hoping to avoid an argument. It was too late.

Jeremy fired back with a little more force. "Are you kidding me? I didn't see my grandparents in little round balls; I saw *them*. To send us out here trying to see anything other than someone's actual spirit is a joke."

Mark could tell Jeremy was not going to back down after he mentioned his grandparents. He decided not to escalate their argument further and continued taking more pictures.

His was glad his tactic worked when he noticed Jeremy returning to his original spot out of the corner of his eye.

Mark had learned through trial and error over many years how to diffuse an argument with Jeremy.

Their friendship had been forged through several shared experiences. One of them was seeing their deceased grandparents soon after their passing.

Mark's mind raced back to the words the professor shared with them after their first class.

"The whole reason I have so much hope for both of you is the similar experiences you had earlier this year," he'd said. "Dreaming about a loved one visiting you after their death is very common and often deals with a person's loss mechanism in the brain. But knowing you're awake while experiencing your events with multiple senses, from what you both described in your admission letters, is something else. I'm glad you both accepted my invitation to take this class. I hope you will achieve the ability to make tangible contact with a person who has passed on to the other side before this semester is out. Only then will you begin to realize why you were given your gifts."

Mark had no idea what the benefit of this type of contact would be for him but felt he owed it to himself and his grandfather to find out what it was.

CHAPTER 2

LACK OF FOCUS

With their agreed-upon time for visiting the cemetery nearing its end, Mark hoped to take some more pictures uninterrupted, but Jeremy wouldn't let him.

"Here's a congressman, and here's another. How many congressmen are buried here anyway?"

Mark turned to notice Jeremy zigzagging in between a few large, box-shaped headstones and rolled his eyes. "I have no idea. Please stay over there if you're done taking pictures."

Jeremy started calling out football plays while dodging headstones and using his camera like a football.

Mark tried to stay focused and steadied his camera on another dark area just behind the headstone he had been standing in front of.

Jeremy ran past him and bumped his shoulder.

"Dude, touch me again, and I'll lay you out," Mark shouted, his blood boiling.

"Chill out," Jeremy said, walking back slowly while keeping an eye on Mark. "If it gets us out of here faster, I'll leave you alone. How is the flash of a camera supposed to capture their energy again?"

Mark couldn't tell if Jeremy was trying to placate him by asking the question or if he wanted to know, but he decided to answer him, nonetheless.

"Focus on the headstones where the moon's light shines the brightest, and then take pictures of the darkest area surrounding it, using your flash. If they are nearby, the light from the flash will be absorbed by their energy and will show up in the picture. The professor said if we practice looking for them enough, we might be able to see that energy without the use of a camera."

His comments got Jeremy to hold still, but the questioning continued.

"If I couldn't see the images that you saw in the professor's pictures, how does he expect me to see anything by just staring into a dark space?"

Mark thought about his question for a moment, trying to find the best way to respond. Suddenly, an explanation popped into his head.

"Remember looking at those 3-D magic eye pictures all the time when we were kids? They only had a bunch of small images on them at first, but as you relaxed your eyes, the larger picture would start to form?"

"Oh yeah. I remember that hidden picture of Storm from the *X-Men* you had. I almost went blind staring at that thing," Jeremy said, raising his eyebrows up and down.

"It's the same technique here. You and I have talked a lot about seeing something out of the corner of our eyes. Then when we look in that direction, it's gone. We must get to the point where we don't chase that image but stay focused on that spot until the image appears."

Jeremy nodded in agreement and started to stare at a spot directly in front of him.

Mark felt good about his explanation and was happy that Jeremy understood his impromptu analogy.

"I still don't know what seeing a ghost is going to do for us."

This time, Jeremy's choice of words irritated Mark.

"They aren't ghosts, J. I get sick of the other kids in our class using that term. To me, it's disrespectful. I'm sure we have better things to do after we die than going around haunting people."

Jeremy recoiled. "You're right. I guess I'm just frustrated that we haven't figured out anything regarding our abilities after taking this class for over a month now."

Mark settled down. "Don't be so quick to give up. Let's see what happens with being here tonight." Mark picked up his camera items and moved farther away from Jeremy to avoid more questioning.

He made his way over to another well-illuminated headstone that had a large sculpture of Mother Mary, with her hands pressed together in prayer. Her expression looked down at Mark like she was beckoning him to come up and face her.

Mark relaxed and began to focus on the dark area surrounding her image. For the first time during their visit, he was starting to feel a presence. He slowly moved his camera just to the right of the headstone, feeling like something was drawing him there.

He had started to take a few shots when he was startled by a rustling of leaves behind him that made him spin around.

Instead of Jeremy, he was surprised to see two shadowy figures coming toward him.

CHAPTER 3

UNPLANNED INTERRUPTIONS

Mark had a hard time recognizing the approaching figures due to the moonlight shining from behind them, making their faces unrecognizable.

"Hey, Mark. I thought we might find you here," said a familiar voice.

Mark thought he recognized the voice but had a hard time placing it in this setting. "Yeah? Who's there?"

"It's us. Stacie and Paul," said a young woman coming close enough for him to recognize.

Before he could comment, he was startled by Jeremy, who had moved up next to him with his arms in a karate pose.

"I was about to run over here and drop both of you when I saw you sneaking up on Mark." He quickly dropped his arms to his sides. "You're lucky that I'm so weak from hunger and don't have the energy."

Mark was relieved to see them both.

Stacie Wonders was Mark's former girlfriend and had been instrumental in helping him deal with his grandparents' death right before their high school graduation.

He was surprised when she showed up at his Spiritual and Psychic Phenomenon class since she had never revealed any spiritual event to him.

They had mutually decided to just be friends in college, but Mark had a hard time turning off his feelings for her, especially when Paul was around.

Paul Donovan, or P-dog as he was known by his friends, was new to their friendship circle, due to him following Stacie wherever she went. Mark didn't know if his negative feelings toward him stemmed from jealousy or if he just didn't trust the guy.

"Of all of the cemeteries close by the campus, you two picked this one?" Mark asked, his heart rate returning to normal.

"You know that this cemetery is famous for sightings of the undead," Paul said in an ominous voice for effect. "I'm surprised we're the only ones here. I thought a few more from our class would be here."

"It doesn't surprise me. All the normal kids are partying it up after the football game instead of hanging out in cemeteries," Jeremy said, moving over to Paul and playfully putting him in a headlock.

While watching them tussle, it bothered Mark that Jeremy had taken to Paul so easily. He moved over and pulled them apart, forcefully knocking them both to the ground.

Jeremy laughed it off and quickly jumped to his feet. "We've been out here for two hours, and the only thing I've experienced is cold and hunger. It is so hard to focus when I'm suffering from hypothermic starvation."

"Have you two had any success with the orb hunt?" inquired Stacie while helping Paul to his feet.

"Not sure yet," Mark said, holding up his camera. "It's hard to see if I captured anything by looking at my screen. I noticed some intense light on that statue of Mary, and I got a few shots in before you two showed up."

"I think Professor Windham is getting crazier with these assignments the more the semester rolls along. I took his class to learn more about the reason we had our experiences during his class hour. I don't want to waste many more nights in a cemetery when I could be studying for other classes that give me credit," Stacie said, a little irritated.

Mark tried to ease her frustration. "I thought his lecture this past week was one of his best. The thought of being able to train yourself to see others after they've moved on is awesome."

Paul put his arm around Stacie and pulled her close to him.

"I agree with Mark, Stace. If we can learn to master contacting dead people now, that could open the door to other dimensions and give us *absolute power*," Paul said in a thundering voice.

Even though Paul was joking, Mark thought he made a good point regarding opening the door to other dimensions, and he was about to expound on that topic when a large beam of light blinded his vision.

"You kids need to gather your stuff and leave, now."

CHAPTER 4

A KEY DISCOVERY

A burly man in tattered overalls had moved up behind Stacie and Paul, holding a flashlight in one hand and a shovel in the other.

Mark and his friends quickly banded together.

"Don't you know there's a city ordinance for being in cemeteries after dark?" the man asked gruffly.

With his heart racing for the second time in a matter of moments, Mark looked around for any comments, but his friends remained silent.

"We didn't know of any ordinance. We are all students at the U of M," he said, hoping that their college status would buy them some leeway.

The man stood there for a moment, sizing them up and down with his flashlight.

"You look too young to be college students, but then I can't tell how old kids are anymore. The older I get, the younger they look."

Mark purposely laughed at his statement, hoping to break the tension, and the man's mood lightened a bit. He dropped the shovel to the ground and clicked off his flashlight.

"What are you doing here on a Saturday night anyway? If I was in college, I would be at a party, not a cemetery." The man stroked his scruffy beard.

Mark didn't know if he should divulge the true nature of their visit or not and kept silent about it.

Stacie moved past Mark and flashed a huge smile at the man. "You wouldn't believe us if we told you." She laughed playfully while putting her hand on the caretaker's shoulder.

Mark recognized what she was trying to do. He had seen this side of her many times when they were dating. Whenever someone put her in a stressful or uncomfortable situation, she would use her sweet smile and flirtatious nature to charm whoever it was.

The caretaker's countenance changed immediately.

"If this is a truth-or-dare kind of game, these aren't my kind of odds, with only one girl in the group," the man said with a chuckle.

"I agree. If it was, I would be with a greater number of girls than this," Mark said in agreement.

After more awkward silence, Mark could tell by the man's posture that he was not going anywhere until he knew what was going on.

"Well, you guys shouldn't be out here. We don't want people disrupting the gravesites."

Stacie jumped in again. "We have the assignment to visit a cemetery for one of our classes, and we just happened to run into each other at this one. I'm Stacie. This is Paul, Mark, and Jeremy. And you are?"

"Pete," the man said, reaching out his hand. Mark shook it, and the others did the same in turn.

"Nice to meet you. If you are here for an assignment and attending U of M, you must be students of Professor Miles Windham."

Mark looked at his friends', amazed Pete was able to discern that from the small amount of information they had provided.

"It's nice to see we're not the only class that he has done this to," said Jeremy.

"Not the first and not the last," said Pete, chuckling again. "He's a strange fella."

Mark thought the same thing about Pete. "You know him then?"

"Yep. I've been here twenty years and have seen hundreds of kids wandering this cemetery getting freaked out. Most of the time around Halloween. But if I see kids taking pictures or just spending time by themselves around a full moon, it's usually his students. That's why I do my rounds on these nights. One of his students, a girl, just up and vanished last year."

Mark noticed a look of deep concern cross Pete's face as he looked past them toward a specific area in the cemetery.

"A girl?" Stacie asked.

"Yes. She came here by herself quite often. Then one night she just disappeared."

"Disappeared? Can you give us a little more detail?" asked Jeremy.

"I only talked to her once. She mentioned she would be visiting the cemetery quite often and asked if it was all right. Since she came alone and always sat in the same spot, I thought no harm could come of it and told her she could."

The caretaker paused and started scratching his beard again.

"One night, I was cleaning out a water line and noticed her sitting in her usual spot. After an hour or so, I noticed she hadn't moved at all. She looked to be in a trance or something. When I went to my truck to get something, I turned to see if she was still there, and she was gone. I thought maybe she had fallen behind the large cenotaph she was sitting on. I walked over to see if she was okay, but nobody was there. The only thing I found was a notebook and a pencil."

"She must have left while you were in your truck," said Jeremy.

"Did you ever see her again?" Mark pressed.

"Nope. Haven't seen her since. I thought she might have left while I was looking away, but I don't see how I could've missed her. Her car was still there when I left for home that night. I thought of calling the police, but what would I have told them? When I came back the next morning, the car was gone, so I suppose she showed up later to get it. I still have her notebook though."

Mark's imagination started to fire off in many directions, and the most disturbing thought that kept surfacing was maybe Pete was some psycho who had stolen the girl's car and buried her body somewhere in the cemetery.

He glanced over at Stacie and could sense her uneasiness. She slowly moved closer to Mark, away from Pete.

"I can take that notebook to class with me next week and ask the professor about her," Mark offered.

"Sure. No reason why I need to hold onto it. I figured she might return for it, which is why I didn't chuck it. It's in the work shed. I'll be right back. You kids stay right here."

Pete picked up the shovel and swung it over his shoulder almost hitting Paul in the face. Then walked off.

Mark looked around at the others and could see they were lost in thought about what might've happened to the girl.

He thought about leaving while the caretaker was gone, but the intrigue of who the missing girl was, and obtaining her notebook kept him from suggesting that to the group.

Although the professor hadn't mentioned other students from prior classes by name, he had personally told him and Jeremy about another student who was able to break many barriers between this life and the next. He wondered if this girl was that student.

"Pete is a freaky dude. He's probably seen a lot of weird stuff, working here all these years. I can think of a hundred jobs I'd rather have than working in a cemetery," Paul said.

"Do any of you have any idea who this girl might be?" asked Mark.

"I don't remember the professor mentioning anything strange happening to another student, but Jeremy's right. I'm sure glad we're not the first ones to be asked to do this," said Stacie.

While they waited for Pete to return, they all agreed that Mark should be the one to ask the professor about the girl since he seemed to be the teacher's pet. None of them wanted him to wait until next Friday's class to find out who she was, so Mark agreed to try to meet with the professor between his classes on Monday.

When Pete came back with the notebook, Mark moved in front of the group and practically pulled it out of the caretaker's hand in eagerness.

"There's no name on it. But I'm sure the professor will know who it belongs to. You kids are more than welcome to stay if you want—and good luck with your assignment. Just don't mention my name if anything weird happens. I don't want to be pulled into anything supernatural," he said with a smile and walked off.

Mark anxiously opened the notebook while the others gathered over his shoulders to see what was inside.

CHAPTER 5

THE NOTEBOOK

Mark began to scan all the entries that filled up the first page. They were written much like a diary and contained numerous dates and observations. There were also small sketches of headstones and a crude map of their locations. It didn't take him long to notice the initials "M.B." written toward the top right corner, assuming they were hers. He thought it a strange coincidence that he shared the same ones.

A bolded entry written near the center of the first page caught his attention.

Joy, peace, and tranquility.

While scanning the entries page by page, he noticed how positive they were at first, but they became darker in tone toward the final page. When he looked down at the last entry it gave him chills.

Get out of me!

Stacie reached over Mark's shoulder and turned back toward the beginning.

"Look at how her writing style has changed. It's like different people are making entries toward the end. Sort of like a shared diary."

Mark noticed what Stacie meant while thumbing back through it. The early entries were written in nice penmanship, but it eventually turned into harsh block lettering toward the end.

"Looks like she came here a lot, judging by all those dates," said Paul.

"The caretaker did mention that he had seen her a few times," Jeremy said in agreement.

"I also noticed she mentions talking to someone named Abby early on," Mark said, pointing to the girl's name. "But Pete said he always saw her alone."

"Maybe she was referring to a friend or someone who was taking the class with her. The entry here makes it sound like she knows her pretty well and looks forward to learning more from her," Jeremy said, pointing to another entry farther down the page.

"At least you have a name you can run by the professor," said Paul.

Stacie put her hands on Mark's shoulders and squeezed tight. "You're going to take this to the professor on Monday and not forget?" she said with a hint of distrust in her voice.

Mark looked at her with a blank stare and didn't respond on purpose.

"Maybe I should take it to the professor." Stacie attempted to pull the notebook out of his hands, but Mark playfully bit at her arm to keep her at bay.

Mark had forgotten a handful of their dating milestones when they were a couple, and Stacie liked to throw in his face how forgetful he could be. "I won't forget, Stace. We're not in high school anymore," he said with a smile.

Stacie gave him a wink and then reached out and took Paul by the arm. "Okay then. I've got to get lover boy back to his crib. How long are you two going to hang around here?"

"Not long if I can help it," said Jeremy.

"Just a little bit longer," responded Mark.

He watched Paul put his arm around Stacie and pull her close as they began to walk off. He knew Paul did it to get under his skin, and it worked.

"We'll catch up with you at church tomorrow. Don't do anything you'll regret," commented Mark in all seriousness.

"I can't say I won't try," Paul said, turning toward Mark and Jeremy with a big smile.

Stacie pulled Paul along by the collar of his sweater. "In your dreams, you perv."

Mark stood there watching Paul with contempt until they returned to Stacie's car.

He looked over and saw Jeremy grinning at him. It must have been obvious for his best friend to pick up on the fact that he still had feelings for Stacie even after months of trying to convince him that he was over her.

"I think those two make a great couple," said Jeremy, looking off in their direction.

"Whatever. P-dog is a player and not Stacie's type. If Stacie falls for all his Romeo crap, then they deserve each other."

His heated reaction to Jeremy's prodding surprised him, and he opened the notebook again quickly. "Can we get back to the notebook?"

After reading in silence for a while, another entry toward the end caught Mark's attention. It read, *What is happening? How did they find me?*

The intrigue of who this girl was and what she had experienced continued to grow within him with each passage he read.

"Take a look at this. I wonder who *they* are," Mark said, pointing to the statement.

"Maybe *they* are other students," Jeremy suggested.

"Could be. I will meet with the professor first thing on Monday and see if we can track down this girl. Maybe she can tell us what we can expect from this class going forward. I know I haven't seen anything out of the ordinary tonight, unless you count our run-in with creepy Pete."

"Amen to that," Jeremy said, slugging Mark on the shoulder before walking back to his spot to get his stuff.

While Mark was gathering his equipment, it dawned on him that he didn't want to leave without checking out the area where Pete said the girl had vanished from. The spot he had pointed to happened to be very close to where he was.

Before he could check it out, Jeremy returned quicker than expected. "I'm heading to the car. Hurry up so we can get some food. It's almost ten, and I'm dying of hunger."

Mark nodded in agreement and purposely took his time gathering his items to give Jeremy time to leave. Once he was far enough away, Mark made his way over to the cenotaph he thought Pete had pointed to and sat down on the cold stone.

He had learned before they arrived that there were dozens of these large, box-shaped headstones called cenotaphs at this cemetery, which indicated a well-known congressman was buried elsewhere but deserved a monument there anyway.

The moon was a little higher in the sky now and was illuminating everything around him. He began to look around in all directions to see if he noticed anything unusual about the area.

He glanced up at the moon and was admiring its brilliance when he got a distinct feeling someone was watching him from behind. He whipped around and looked in the direction of the car to see if Jeremy was coming up behind him, but there was no one there.

He began to take note of all the statues looking down around him. *No wonder you feel like you're being watched.*

Just then, a gust of wind blew open the notebook he had sat beside him. The girl's entry of *Joy, peace, and tranquility* jumped off the page again. He decided to concentrate on those words and ignore his feelings of paranoia.

As he thought about them, it suddenly dawned on him that he had written those exact words in his admissions letter when describing how he felt the night his grandfather visited him. He concluded she must have had a similar event happen in her life, leading her to the professor's class.

The wind picked up again, and he caught a faint smell of vanilla floating through the air. He stood up and followed the fragrance over to an opening between the two cenotaphs that were directly in front of him. A snap of a twig beneath his foot made him look down.

Nestled between them was a small, obscure gravestone that was barely noticeable. He reached down and cleared some leaves from it. He pulled out his phone and turned on the flashlight to see what was engraved.

Abigail Turnbow
1853–1873
"The unexamined life is not worth living." —Socrates

After reading the quote, he realized it summed up his reasons for being at the cemetery perfectly. He had always been one to question everything he was taught, to learn more about it. Then he would arrive at his conclusion about whether it was true. He rarely took someone's word for it.

He contemplated why the young woman had the quote on her gravestone and the reason her life ended so soon. Realizing he was lost in thought for quite a while, he turned to notice Jeremy was now lying on the hood of his car, waving for him to hurry up.

Again, he gathered his items to leave when the smell of vanilla hit him so strongly it took his breath away, and he staggered backward.

Looking around again, he saw no one. But the smell made his stomach roar with hunger. He began to think Jeremy was right. Maybe his hunger was making him imagine things.

With everything in hand, he began walking toward his car when a beam of light moved past him to the right. It made him look back in the direction of the area he had just left. The light stopped and illuminated the area between the two cenotaphs.

Am I seeing an orb with my own eyes?

"Come on, dude, or I'll break in through your car window. I'm freezing," Jeremy yelled from the parking lot.

Mark began to quickly assess the pros and cons of staying much longer. The largest of the cons was Jeremy. Mark knew he would freak out if he saw him take his camera back out of its bag, and he did not put it past his friend to break his window.

He stood there in limbo, looking back and forth between Jeremy and the ball of light. After a few glances toward the light, it slowly vanished, much to his disappointment.

Mark couldn't believe all the interruptions he had experienced in one evening and vowed to come to the cemetery alone next time.

CHAPTER 6

ROADBLOCK

Mark didn't need his alarm clock to wake him up Monday morning. Jeremy's snoring took care of that at 4:00 a.m., and he couldn't go back to sleep thinking about the events of Saturday night.

He knew he couldn't miss out on the opportunity to meet with Professor Windham before his other classes. The professor had told him on several occasions he was usually the first in and last to leave and to stop by any time.

There was one positive Mark found in waking up before Jeremy. Time to shower. It took him a few weeks to learn that if he woke up much past eight, he never had time to shower due to Jeremy taking so long.

It had been more difficult than Mark had anticipated in getting used to living with Jeremy and all his strange habits. Even though he had spent a decent amount of time with him over the past eight years, it was a whole different story living with him day in and day out.

But in the end, he figured it was better to room with someone he knew than to get used to a total stranger, and he was determined to make the best of it.

Mark slipped out of their room quietly and began making his way to the professor's classroom on the other side of campus.

It was a crisp fall morning, and Mark couldn't tell if the chills he was experiencing were from the cold air or his anticipation of their meeting. He broke into a slight jog in hopes of stopping his teeth from chattering.

Upon entering the Public Health building, Mark made a beeline to the professor's office. The building was eerily quiet this early in the morning.

When he entered the classroom, he was relieved to see a light coming from under the door to the professor's office. He made his way down and poked his head in to find him reading at his desk.

The professor looked up, startled, but quickly noticed it was Mark and waved him in with a smile.

"Hello, Mark. I hope you enjoyed your assignment on Saturday night, and I'm anxious to see if you captured any images," he said, closing his book. "Also, if you were worried about missing the football game, we were blown out by the Mountaineers, so you didn't miss anything."

"Figures," Mark said, sitting down on one of the comfortable leather chairs the professor had at his desk. "The assignment went well, and I hope some of my pictures turn out. I figured that about the game. Our defense is horrible this year."

Mark slid his backpack off his shoulder and set it down on the adjacent chair.

"I didn't want to wait until our class on Friday, so I thought I would swing by and tell you what happened, if you have some time."

"Something happened then?" the professor asked, intrigued.

Mark thought about revealing everything he could to the professor but decided most of it could wait until Friday's class discussion. He decided, for the sake of time, to just relate to him the part about the notebook so he could find out who the owner was.

He reached into his bag, pulled out the notebook, and placed it on the desk in front of him.

"Professor, a few of us from class met the caretaker of the Congressional Cemetery, and he told us that he had run into a few of your students over the past few years. But there was one girl from last year who visited a lot and then ended up disappearing one night."

The professor eyed him and then the notebook, back and forth several times, with an unusual expression. Mark paused, waiting for the professor to say something, but he remained silent.

Mark continued. "The caretaker mentioned he went over to check to see if she had fallen, and all he found was this blue notebook." Mark turned it around and slid it toward the professor. Then he opened it and pointed at the initials on the first page of entries. "I was wondering if you could tell me if you remember a student with these initials last year."

The professor slid it toward him and examined the notebook for a moment, without saying a word. His face began to show more concern the more he read, but he remained silent.

"Do you know what might have happened to her?" Mark asked, attempting to get him to comment.

Again, there was awkward silence.

Mark had not seen this side of the professor before. He usually had lots of things to say about everything.

When the professor reached the end of scanning the entries, he looked up at Mark abruptly.

"Mark, I'm sorry, but I've got to prepare for a lecture for another class. Do you mind leaving the notebook with me, and I will see if I can remember who it belongs to and let you know on Friday?"

Mark was taken aback by his request and stammered his reply. "Sure … I guess."

Mark grabbed his backpack and noticed the professor's mood seemed to lighten when he stood to leave.

He felt like the professor knew who it belonged to but didn't want to tell him.

The professor stood up quickly and shook his hand. "Thanks for understanding. Until Friday then."

The professor placed the notebook in his briefcase and rushed past him with a hurried smile.

Mark stood there disappointed about losing sleep over such an anticlimactic encounter.

He left the office dejected, knowing he had a long week of wondering ahead of him.

CHAPTER 7

UNUSUAL FEEDBACK

The week did go by painfully slowly for Mark. Both Jeremy and Stacie continually peppered him with questions he couldn't answer, which made the waiting even more excruciating.

He was hoping to catch the professor before class started that Friday but had a hard time finding the SD card that he had taken out of his camera, and they barely made it on time.

The class began with the professor asking for everyone to pass up their SD cards.

Mark's anxiety over the owner of the notebook was quickly replaced with curiosity about the images he might've captured. He and Jeremy had viewed their pictures by hooking their cameras up to the small TV in their room but were unable to notice any distinct images in the photos that could be an orb.

He took it upon himself to gather the cards from his classmates and walked them up to the professor, placing his SD card on top.

The professor took the cards and counted them. "There are only six cards, but I count eight of you."

Mark glanced around the room and saw Stacie shooting him a look of desperation. He remembered he hadn't seen her or Paul with a camera on Saturday. Without missing a beat, he turned back toward the professor and explained that all four of them worked on the assignment together.

The professor simply smiled and moved over to his projector.

Mark was relieved that the professor didn't ask any follow-up questions.

"While I get this set up, I want all of you to quickly write down on a piece of paper one unusual experience that stood out to you from this assignment. Then pass them forward with your names on them," said the professor while working on the projector.

Mark reached into his folder to get out a piece of paper. He couldn't help but notice Stacie and Paul flirting with each other, apparently unaware of what the professor had requested.

"Hey, you two, the professor wants you to write down an unusual experience you had on Saturday."

"Meeting Pete was about the extent of it for me," Stacie said quickly and then turned back to Paul, expecting Mark to write it down.

Paul leaned over. "I told her the only cool thing that happened to me on Saturday night was the kiss she planted on me when she dropped me off at my dorm."

He now regretted covering for them earlier.

"I doubt the professor wants to know that." Mark's adrenalin made it come out louder than he wanted.

Stacie pushed Paul back with her arm, embarrassed. "It wasn't even that big of a kiss, you jerk. I only let you to get you out of my car."

She turned back to Mark. "How about you? Did anything worthwhile happen after we left?"

Her question sparked his memory regarding the perfume he smelled. "Not until just before Jeremy and I left. Which reminds me, were you wearing a lot of perfume Saturday night?"

"I don't think so. Why?"

"The wind kept kicking it up. I thought it might've been yours."

"It wasn't mine," Paul said, leaning forward and looking for a laugh.

"What did it smell like?" she asked, without acknowledging Paul's comment.

"Vanilla, if I had to pick the most obvious smell."

"I usually don't wear perfume before going to cemeteries, and I definitely wouldn't choose a vanilla perfume," Stacie said in disgust. "Write it down and see what the professor says."

Mark was going to mention their meeting with the caretaker, the notebook, and the strange light he saw, but he decided to bring those up with the professor when he had the chance to talk to him in private. He decided to do what Stacie said and wrote down the account regarding the perfume instead.

They all passed their papers forward, and the professor eagerly collected them and began to look them over. Mark was eager to see what Jeremy wrote about and if any of the other students had experienced anything unusual.

Mark noticed the professor looked like a kid at Christmas opening presents. His face lit up with each one he read. After a few minutes, he stopped suddenly and looked straight at Mark.

"Mr. Banks, would you like to explain a little about your visit and your sensual experience with the class?"

A few of the students laughed at the way the professor phrased the request, and Mark looked around, embarrassed, not knowing how to begin.

The professor clapped loudly to get everyone's attention back on him. "Class, you recall in week one I discussed with you the importance of the five senses and how each one of them can be enhanced, from time to time, when dealing with things of a supernatural or spiritual nature. I believe Mark experienced one of these events involving his sense of smell."

The professor turned his attention back to Mark.

"You have no idea how close you were to contacting someone on Saturday night."

CHAPTER 8

SENSORY RECALL

Mark looked around the class. Every eye was upon him, waiting for him to clarify what his supernatural experience was regarding his sense of smell. He took his time omitting other details in his mind and decided to stick with the basics of their visit.

"We got to the Historic Congressional Cemetery, or HCC as we like to call it, around eight. The moon was so bright that we had to keep moving to different locations to find pockets dark enough to use our flash. We just took turns taking pictures, and nothing out of the ordinary was happening except for the sound of Jeremy's stomach growling."

A few students laughed while Jeremy acknowledged the comment with a parade wave.

Stacie leaned over toward Mark. "Tell them about the notebook and that Pete guy we ran into."

"Not now," he whispered and then turned back to the class.

"Just before ten, we all decided to head back to campus. I was gathering my equipment near a large cenotaph I had been sitting on."

"A what?" one of the students interrupted, looking confused.

Before Mark could explain, the professor jumped in.

"Cenotaphs are large sandstone boxes where many important people in Washington were recognized but not necessarily buried. Usually congressmen. The cemetery has dozens of these types of headstones. Many of them were painted white to make them illuminate at night, but many people thought they were unattractive, so they discontinued using them by the later part of the nineteenth century. Go on, Mark."

"Well, I was getting cold and a little paranoid being there by myself. I was standing over a headstone of a girl who died when she was only twenty. The wind picked up, and I smelled some strong perfume."

"Describe exactly what it smelled like. This is important," said the professor excitedly.

"Well, it smelled like vanilla, with a little bit of citrus. It was like the person was standing right by me."

The professor clapped his hands loudly.

"Yes. Thank you, Mark. I want to stress the importance of what Mr. Banks experienced. Most of the time, people with your gift see a loved one or acquaintance after their passing. That's why you're a member of this class. A handful of you communicated audibly with that person. But Mr. Banks's experience with his sense of smell is unique. I'm surprised this woman did not attempt to reveal herself to you in physical form. Are you sure you didn't see anything?"

Mark fought back the urge to bring up the ball of light. "No. Nothing else."

"That's unfortunate. She was most likely ready and willing to make herself known to you."

The professor's comments made him realize he may have missed his opportunity, and he shot Jeremy an irritated look.

Mark could tell from the whisperings and looks of those around him that they did not understand what the professor was talking about. Even Stacie and Paul were looking at him with questioning looks.

Mark looked at the professor and shrugged his shoulders.

The professor gave Mark a wink.

"It sounds like most of you don't understand, so I want to do an experiment with everyone. I'll be right back." He retreated to his office.

Mark had no idea where the professor was going with this, and no one said a word until he returned with a small tray of spray bottles.

"I want you all to come down to the front row so everyone can participate. I usually do this experiment for one of my other classes, but I think it pertains to our discussion."

While the students were making their way down to the front of the classroom, Mark purposely sat in between Stacie and Paul to make sure Paul didn't derail the experiment.

"I want you to remain silent and close your eyes while I spray these fragrances one at a time. I want you to lock on to the first memory that comes to your mind. You don't have to share them out loud. Just let the smell transport you to whatever place and time it can. Here's the first one."

Mark closed his eyes and heard the professor pump one of the bottles four or five times.

He breathed in the smell of peppermint. The smell immediately took him back to Christmastime when he was a kid. He could see a mental picture of the trays of peppermint bark he would help his grandmother make. He would usually eat so much it would make him sick. He noticed the smell brought both comfort and nausea at the same time.

The professor waited a few minutes for the smell to clear and the chatter to calm down. Some students couldn't help but share their memories out loud.

"Okay, okay, here's the next one."

The heavy scent of roses wafted through the air.

Mark was instantly transported to his aunt Ruth's house in Baltimore. When they would visit for an occasional Sunday dinner, she would give him and his sister a giant bear hug. Her rose-scented perfume was so strong it would take multiple washes to get the smell out of his clothes.

"How about this next one?"

The strong scent of lemon cut through the air.

Mark could see his grandpa's old mahogany work desk. When he played hide-and-seek with his sister Cassie, that was his favorite place to hide. The desk always reeked of the lemon-scented Pledge his grandmother used to clean it.

"Now, get ready for this one."

Mark inhaled a big whiff of vinegar, and his nose began to burn. Several students groaned.

The smell conjured up a funny memory of salt and vinegar potato chips. Jeremy's dad was a bigshot lawyer who Mark idolized growing up, and they were his favorite kind of chip. Mark thought it was a rite of passage to like everything that he did, so one day when Jeremy's dad offered him some, he kept eating them until he became physically ill. He hadn't eaten one since.

"Last one."

Mark opened his eyes enough to notice the professor burying his face in his arm while he sprayed.

The awful smell of skunk started to permeate the classroom, and everyone groaned out loud. Mark buried his face in his hands.

The professor quickly chided the class. "Come on, class. Focus on the smell. Where does it take you?"

Mark's mind wandered back to a beach in Virginia that his grandparents took him and his sister to every summer. It seemed like there were more dead skunks on the way to the beach than there were people. They referred to it as skunk beach.

"Now, how many of you were able to recall a memory with all five of those smells, by raise of hand?" asked the professor.

Mark raised his hand and was surprised to see every other hand up.

"I imagine it didn't take you long to come up with a memory. That's because our sense of smell can create an instant recall of another time and place. I think we will operate with the same senses that we do here after we pass on. The vanilla fragrance that Mark smelled on Saturday was most likely the favorite fragrance of the woman who was trying to reach him when she resided here—her spiritual calling card, if you will."

"Mark, you're probably glad her perfume of choice was not skunk scent," Paul said, mugging for a reaction from the class, which he got.

Mark could tell the professor was growing tired of his interruptions.

"Mr. Donovan, did you notice anything on Saturday? You haven't mentioned much of anything to contribute to the class today."

"All I know is that I was with an angel from this dimension," Paul said, shooting a romantic glance past Mark at Stacie.

Mark noticed the professor roll his eyes.

Stacie threw her pencil at Paul and barely missed Mark's face. It ricocheted off Paul's shoulder and landed at the professor's feet.

Stacie hid her face on Mark's shoulder out of embarrassment. Without thinking, he leaned over and kissed the top of her head like he had so many times before, much to the surprise of Paul and Jeremy.

Mark couldn't believe he had just done that and was happy when the professor clicked off the lights and an image of the cemetery popped up on the whiteboard.

"Let's turn our attention to your pictures from Saturday night. Shall we?"

CHAPTER 9

SNAPSHOT ORB

Much to Mark's delight, his shots appeared first. He glanced up at the wall clock and realized they had only about fifteen minutes left in class. The professor began to advance the pictures he had taken quite rapidly, and he was worried something would be missed. Suddenly the professor stopped.

"What have we here? Judging by the brightness of this orb right here, it appears this student captured a magnificent orb. Whose is this?"

Mark raised his hand.

"It would appear that Mr. Banks had an all-star Saturday night."

Mark noticed a large, white, circular object just to the right of the Mother Mary headstone where he first felt a presence. He was amazed to see how bright the orb was when using the professor's equipment.

"So, what is an orb again?" asked the professor while scanning the students for a response.

A few of the students took turns answering the best they could, but Mark could tell none of them seemed to remember what the professor had taught them the previous week. Even though he had the answer down pat from explaining it multiple times to Jeremy, he decided not to comment to save time. His attention remained solely on the orb.

While the students were talking, Mark let his eyes relax. With each passing second, he began to see the side profile of a young woman appear in the orb. The more he relaxed, the clearer her features became. He was just about to comment on what he saw when the professor started to address their responses.

"All of your comments have some validity. But to put it in more simple terms, an orb is our soul's photo identification. It is simply the first and most common manifestation we can get from those who have moved on."

"Is the next life like moving onto another dimension?" Mark asked, remembering Paul's comment about dimensions from Saturday night.

"Good question Mark. I believe there are dimensional elements with each phase of our soul's progression. If you recall, we discussed a little bit about the ten purported dimensions theorized by some of the greatest minds using the superstring theory during our first discussion. I believe there are several tie-ins we can discuss at another time."

After a few more clicks, the professor stopped on another slide. "Here's another fine specimen."

Mark let his eyes relax again when he noticed it was the same image of the young woman in even greater detail. This time, the orb had moved to the other side of the headstone.

Mark looked around at the mostly blank stares of his friends and classmates. *Does nobody else see her?*

The professor was about to advance to the next slide when he couldn't contain himself any longer. "Professor, does no one else see the profile of the young woman in these shots?"

"You don't say," said the professor, stepping back further from the whiteboard to get a better view. Within a few moments, a large grin crossed his face. The professor motioned for Mark to come forward. "Please come and show us what you are seeing."

Mark moved to the whiteboard and waited a moment for his eyes to adjust to the brightness. He grabbed a black dry-erase marker and began to outline the features he was seeing. It took him a moment of stepping back and forth to get the different vantage points of her profile. By the time he was done, everyone in the room gasped in amazement at the detail that was right before their eyes. Satisfied with his drawing, he sat the marker down and returned to his seat.

"Very good, Mr. Banks. We now have the profile of the young woman who was trying her best to reach you."

The professor clicked off the projector and turned on the lights to reveal the picture of the woman Mark had traced.

"Now we know what she looks like and that her favorite perfume contains hints of vanilla."

Mark was happy to realize the evening was not spent in vain.

The professor spent the rest of the class pointing out the characteristics of legitimate orbs versus pictures that contained only specs of light refraction or dust particles that could often be confused as orbs. Mark noticed that with each slide he stopped on, it was easier for him and his classmates to identify the differences.

When the class ended, Mark felt validated in the assignment his friends thought was a waste of time. They all huddled around him to share their excitement. A few of the other students patted Mark on the back before leaving.

After the other students had cleared out, the professor approached Mark and his friends. "I want to thank you for taking this assignment seriously. I feel the others in the class learned to not be so skeptical of these exercises going forward. Often, orbs are passed off in most photographs, but if people took the time to look, they would be surprised at how detailed they can be. Their world is very close to ours, and we must all understand that everyone who passes on gives off energy. You can notice it if you slow down and train yourself to do it."

A shot of guilt passed through Mark again, realizing that he should've gone with his first instinct to turn around and go back to where the light had stopped.

The professor moved in closer. "Contrary to what many of my colleagues will teach you here at this university about there being nothing after this life, we all continue living after death. It is my opinion that our souls continue to advance in light and understanding while moving from one phase to the next."

Mark was deep in thought, processing what the professor had just told them, when it dawned on him that he needed to bring up the subject of the notebook. But the professor had moved back to the front of the room to gather his equipment before he could bring it up.

Mark looked at his friends. "I don't know about you guys, but I'm sticking around to get to the bottom of the notebook."

CHAPTER 10

GROUNDWORK

Mark loved when the professor took the time to impart additional knowledge to him and his friends. The fact that he had shared some personal feelings about the afterlife assured Mark that he might be in the mood to talk more about the notebook.

Mark's friends huddled around him as they approached the professor. Before Mark could open his mouth, the professor turned and asked his friends if they had smelled the same fragrance at the cemetery, and all of them commented they had not.

The professor then turned his attention solely to Mark and put his hand on his shoulder. "Mr. Banks, I can't believe how close you were, but you had too many distractions for her to appear."

Mark shot a disappointing glance toward all of them this time.

"It is better if you are isolated when making contact for the first time. I'm surprised all of you decided to go to the same cemetery."

Mark could see a look of apology on Stacie's face.

"Professor, we wanted to ask you about the notebook Mark brought to you on Monday," Stacie said, changing the subject.

Mark could see the professor's surprised look with the change of direction in the conversation.

"Did you ever figure out who it belonged to?" Jeremy asked.

"That's right. You all would've seen it. Yes, one moment." The professor hurried to his office and returned clutching the notebook.

"If you remember who she is, we could return it to her," Mark suggested.

The professor just stared at the notebook for a few moments and then looked up with a look of regret. "It belonged to a student by the name of Marianne Bawley. She was far and away one of the most spiritually gifted students I have ever taught." The professor then paused, trying to recall something else.

Mark was more than happy to get the name from him and was about to thank him when the professor continued.

"About halfway through the first semester last year, her whole persona began to change, and she stopped coming to my class altogether. I never found out why."

"I think something horrible happened to her," said Jeremy. "If you notice her writing in the notebook, it seems to change for the worse around the same time frame you mentioned her leaving the class. The entries all seem like she is seeing or experiencing some amazing things early on, but by the end, her entries get very dark."

Mark was impressed by Jeremy's assessment.

Before he could comment, Paul jumped in. "Did she refuse to do any of your assignments or give you any reason why she would want to quit?"

Paul's question took Mark by surprise. He didn't know he had a serious bone in his body.

"I would have to pull out my class notes from last year and let you know. My memory isn't what it once was. I know she wrote about some amazing things that happened during her first few field assignments, and I know I kept those. It's my hope all of you will be able to have a better experience with this class than she did."

"Do you think we have her ability?" Mark asked.

The professor looked at the four of them one at a time, with a look of confidence. "Like I mentioned the first day of class, the only reason you were invited to participate in this class is all of you have experienced a visitation that science can't explain. If each of you experienced an event without even looking for it, just think of what you could learn with more focus. That is why this class was created and why I am allowed to teach it under the auspices of the psychology department. It is my goal to identify and then train students with your ability to reach their utmost potential. Imagine what these spirits could teach us that could help mankind make a smoother transition to the next life."

"I like talking to you, Professor. I feel I'm special every time," said Paul with a wide grin.

"Mr. Donovan, you are special indeed."

Paul just kept smiling, not realizing the offhanded burn from the professor, which made Mark and the others laugh.

"Let me pull out what I have kept, and I will let you know what I find. In the meantime, keep trying to implement the techniques I have been teaching you and see what happens. I have a good feeling about all of you, so don't give up on this class. Keep working on it, and we'll chat next week." With that, he handed Mark the notebook and went back into his office.

Mark stood there for a moment, feeling gratified that the professor had placed so much trust in him and his friends. He could tell by the confident looks on their faces that they felt the same way.

"Let's meet over at the McKeldin Library around lunch and look Marianne up in the student directory. Hopefully, she's still enrolled here," Mark said.

When they exited the building, Mark walked in silence with Stacie to their next classes, which happened to be in the same building.

"I wonder if she'll even talk to us. It's pretty apparent she was not happy with anything by the end," said Stacie.

"I agree. But she must have some words of advice for us, good or bad. Maybe we can get her to tell us about her experience that got her invited to the class. At least we have that in common."

Mark realized after he made that comment that Stacie had never told him the whole story about what she experienced.

"I don't mean to pry, Stace, but when are you going to tell me about what happened to you?"

After an awkward pause, she stopped and gently grabbed Mark by the arm. "I've only ever shared my events in that letter, so I could get into the class with you. That was hard enough. Until I fully understand why it happened, I would prefer not to talk about it. But I promise to tell you someday."

Seeing that the subject made her uncomfortable, Mark backed off the subject and gave her a quick side hug before entering the building.

"That's cool. After Saturday night I feel it's only a matter of time before we find out why we're all in there. I'll see you at the library."

CHAPTER 11

A SHOT IN THE DARK

Mark sat in his other two classes before lunch, with his mind darting back and forth between any clues Stacie might have given him regarding her spiritual event and if they would be able to find Marianne in the student directory.

After only a few months of college, it was becoming abundantly clear that it was hard for him to properly focus on his other classes. His generals seemed so boring in comparison with what he was learning from Professor Windham. He felt he was just starting to scratch the surface and couldn't wait to apply the techniques more often.

Mark bolted out of his last morning class and sprinted toward the library.

When he reached the McKeldin fountain, he was stopped in his tracks by the familiar scent of vanilla in the air. He felt a slight tingle on the back of his neck. Within seconds, the feeling became so powerful he felt lightheaded and sat down next to the fountain, looking around excitedly. He didn't know if something supernatural could happen in broad daylight, with the courtyard being packed with students, but he tried to steady himself by relaxing just in case.

His view was drawn to the right when he spotted a young woman with striking features walking toward him. He began to blink rapidly, wondering if she was living or dead. Her blond hair was the most brilliant white he'd ever seen. When she got closer, he noticed her pale white skin. The large sunglasses she wore, and her red lipstick made her look like a ghostly movie star. No one else seemed to notice her.

She seemed to move effortlessly through the crowd, and he expected her to disappear at any moment.

Mark stood up to move closer and tried to get in her line of sight. When she went past him, he smiled at her. She didn't even notice him and continued heading toward the library.

Since she was heading in the same direction, he fell in close behind her. Catching a whiff of her perfume, he wondered if she was the young woman in the orb he had captured. He knew he needed to reach out and touch her to know for sure. He sped past her to get in a better position.

He stood his ground on the sidewalk opposite the oncoming group of students, forcing them to get in a single line.

When she approached, he was about to brush up against her shoulder when he was blindsided from behind by a body blow that knocked him off balance. He fell to the grass just off the sidewalk.

"What is up, my ghost-hunting brother?" the voice said. Mark laid on the ground in a daze, trying to get his bearings.

He slowly stood up and glanced in the direction of the girl, but she was gone.

Mark turned around to notice Paul standing there grinning.

Feeling anger surge through him, he grabbed Paul by the shirt, pulling him close. "Paul, I'm going to rip your head off." He stopped short of using more colorful language because his grandparents had spent years helping him clean it up.

Soon after his parents' divorce, at the age of ten, he fell into a nasty habit of letting foul language flow when he was angry. His grandparents stressed to him that cuss words were a lazy way to speak, and he would get further in life by not using them. This was asking a lot of a kid growing up where he did. But after breaking the habit, he liked the attention not cursing brought him in high school. No matter how hard his classmates tried to bait him, he would stop and think before letting a curse word fly.

Instead of slugging him, he put him in a headlock.

"Easy," Paul said, pushing his head away from Mark's tight noose. "Who were you looking for anyway?" he asked, looking past Mark toward the library.

"I thought I saw ..." Mark stopped midsentence. He didn't want to waste time explaining the girl to Paul, not knowing if she was real or not. "I thought I saw Stacie. They're probably in there waiting for us."

Mark looked in all directions for the girl when he entered the library but could not locate her. He couldn't believe she had disappeared so quickly.

Stacie and Jeremy had been waiting on a bench near the entrance and hurried over to them.

"It's about time you two showed up," Stacie said, a little miffed at their delay.

"You just can't go a few hours without seeing me, can you?" Paul said, leaning in for a kiss from Stacie.

"Whatever." Stacie pushed his face away. "What is up with you, Mark? You look ticked."

"Never mind," he said, looking for a computer. The others joined in the search.

"There's one," Jeremy said, walking toward an open station.

Mark cut in front of him and sat down first.

He quickly located the student directory and typed in *Marianne Bawly*. The hourglass popped up and after a few seconds came up with the words *No Matches Found*. Mark looked to the others for ideas.

"Try her last name with an *i-e* instead of a *y*," offered Jeremy.

Mark typed the change and hit enter. The same message popped up.

"Maybe Bawly is with an *e-y*," Stacie interjected.

Mark typed in her suggestion, and the name *Marianne J. Bawley* popped up on the screen. Mark sighed with relief. "Nice job, Stace."

He clicked on the name, and a little more information popped up.

"It looks like she is a chemistry major and lives in the commons. That's not good," Mark said, disappointed.

Sitting on the south end of campus, the University Common Apartments took up a huge amount of real estate and consisted of six massive dorm buildings. Mark knew it would be a monumental task to find her there.

"Instead of asking around there, why don't we check with someone at the chemistry building and see if they can look up her class schedule for us," suggested Jeremy.

"Not a bad idea, J. We could just say one of us found her notebook and want to return it," offered Stacie.

Even though none of them were chemistry majors, that option seemed like the better of the two to Mark, and they all agreed to go check it out.

On their way over, each of them took turns talking about what might've happened to Marianne the night she disappeared. They were eager to meet her.

When they reached the chemistry building, they agreed it would look too suspicious if all four of them went in together to inquire, so they settled on Mark and Stacie.

"Let's go find our mystery girl," Stacie said, grabbing Mark by the arm and pulling him into the building.

CHAPTER 12

ON THE HUNT

Mark noticed a young lady sitting at a student services desk looking quite bored. They both made eye contact, and she gave him a pleasant smile.

"Excuse me," Mark said in his friendliest tone. "My friend and I were trying to find out the next class that Marianne Bawley might have here. I found her notebook on the ground outside, and we were hoping to get it back to her."

"Sorry, but I can't give out someone's class information. If you want to leave it with me, I could look up her contact information and get it to her."

Stacie moved in front of Mark. "It looks like it contains some personal information, so we wanted to give it to her in person to keep others from reading it."

The girl's facial expression changed to a cold stare directed at Stacie. "Well, if it's so personal, why did you two read it?"

Mark knew they had been caught and didn't know what to say.

"Thanks for nothing," Stacie said with a curt smile. She walked away from the desk, beckoning Mark to follow.

Mark was disappointed they'd been shot down so quickly. "Now what?"

After a few moments of discussion, they decided to try another area of the building. Turning down an adjacent hallway, they stopped at the first classroom they came to. Mark spotted a student in a lab coat working with some liquids and knocked on the door. The young man looked up and waved them in.

Mark noticed him give Stacie a long look, and he pushed her forward.

As if on cue, she turned on her charm. "Excuse me, but I'm trying to find my friend Marianne and get this notebook back to her before her test today. I forgot which class she had, and she is not answering her cell phone. Could you help me?" she said with her most flirtatious grin.

The young man was taken aback by her sweet nature and nearly spilled the contents of the beakers he was holding.

"Sure. That would suck if she needed her notes for her test. What is her name again?"

"Marianne Bawley. That's l-e-y."

"I'll need to use the computer in the office to look her up, but I'll be right back." The young man made his way into a small office toward the back of the classroom, turning back to smile at Stacie a few times.

Mark looked around the room nervously, hoping a teacher wouldn't show up and blow it for them.

Stacie grabbed the notebook from Mark and started thumbing through it while they waited. Mark leaned over Stacie's shoulder and started looking at some of the entries with her. Looking at the changes in her writing style made Mark wonder if she might have multiple personality disorders that he was learning about in one of his other classes. He was lost in thought when the young man returned.

"It shows she has a class at two p.m. in room 206, directly above us. If you want to leave it with me, I'll make sure she gets it. I could call you and let you know once it's delivered," the young man said hopefully, looking right at Stacie and not even acknowledging Mark. He could tell the kid didn't get many cute female visitors in his lab and was enamored with her.

"No thanks, cutie. I'll just swing back in a bit and give it to her. I need to talk to her about some other stuff anyways."

"Let me know if you ever need anything else," the young man said, disappointed his plan to get her number had backfired.

When Mark and Stacie emerged from the building, Jeremy and Paul ran up to them, nearly knocking them over.

"We were getting nervous out here. What took you so long?" Jeremy asked with excitement.

"Relax," Mark said, backing Jeremy off. "We had to ask a few people to get the information, but she has a class at two. Since I'm the only one without a class at that time, I'll swing back with the notebook and give it to her then." Mark grabbed the notebook out of Stacie's hand.

"Since I was the one who got her information, you better give me a call tonight after I get off work and let me know what happens." Stacie gave him a serious glance.

"I will. I promise to call you later."

Stacie and Paul turned and left, but Jeremy was still standing there. Mark knew why.

"J, I'll see you back at the hole when I'm done. You'll be the first to know what happens." That was all Jeremy needed to hear and Mark gave him a fist bump.

Mark decided to go back into the building and hang out in the study area near the entrance.

Even though it was lunchtime, he had butterflies in his stomach from the apprehension of meeting Marianne. Food was the furthest thing from his mind.

Sitting down in one of the oversized chairs, Mark began to reflect on his first semester of college. He marveled at how fast time was flying by since his high school graduation. Even though he had experienced tragedy earlier in the year, he began to reflect on the positives in his life to that point.

He was rooming with his best friend. His former girlfriend, who he now realized he still had feelings for, was still involved in his life. He wasn't that far from home, which made it easy enough for him to visit his mom and sister most weekends. He also didn't have to work. The money his grandparents left him was more than enough to pay for his schooling, living expenses, and car payment.

Occasionally, he would get a little envious that Stacie and Jeremy had jobs they liked, but by not working, he was able to carry a few more credit hours. His goal was to get through school quickly and not waste any more money than he had to.

Mark glanced down at his phone for the time and noticed it was almost two. He decided to go up to the classroom and ask the teacher if Marianne was in that class, just to make sure the information they had received was correct.

When he got to the classroom, he noticed a stocky teacher in a lab coat with his back to him, putting out some vials on one of the desks.

Mark opened the door and approached him cautiously from behind, trying not to startle him. "Excuse me."

The teacher turned abruptly to face him. "Yes?"

Mark could hardly keep from laughing at his appearance. His hair was a complete mess and completely gray. He had thick bottle-type glasses that made his eyes look like they were three sizes larger than usual, and a wiry mustache covered his lips like a giant caterpillar. To Mark, the guy looked like a cross between Colonel Sanders and Einstein. It was all he could do to keep his composure.

"I was wondering which workstation Marianne Bawley would be sitting at for class today. I have her notebook that I was going to leave for her."

The teacher eyed Mark up and down through his thick glasses, which made Mark start to laugh on the inside. He wondered if all the chemicals this guy had been subjected to could be the reason for his appearance.

"She sits in the second workstation toward the back door," he said, pointing in the direction with his short, stubby index finger. "Are you, her boyfriend?" he asked, looking at Mark unamused.

The question took him back a little. "No, just a friend."

"Good. She is always texting someone during my class, and I figured it was a boyfriend of some sort. I was going to tell you to leave her alone during class."

Suddenly the teacher reared his head back and sneezed so hard it sent his glasses flying into some of the vials he had set up on another table, knocking a few of them on the floor in the process. Mark lost his composure and began to laugh when the teacher tried to stop the vials from falling on the floor with his body contorting in a lot of unnatural ways.

Feeling sorry, Mark took the time to help him pick them up.

On his way out of the classroom, the teacher asked if he was going to leave the notebook, but Mark pretended not to hear him. He knew he couldn't turn around and confront him without breaking out in laughter again.

After collecting himself outside the classroom, he decided to wait at the end of the hallway until the class started. He could then look through the glass panes in the doors to see Marianne.

CHAPTER 13

POSITIVE ID

Mark waited for all the students to file in while pretending to look at the notebook. He listened for the teacher to begin class before moving up to look in. Instead of starting at the back door, he wanted to look from the front to see if he could see her face.

He glanced through the opening but could not see her. The angle of her table was obstructed by the layout of the room, and he could only see the student at the end of her table.

He moved to the back door and looked through. From this vantage point, her station was too close to the wall, and he still couldn't see who was sitting there.

You've got to be kidding me.

Mark knew the only way to see who was sitting in that spot was to crack open the door and peek his head in. He waited until the professor had finished his instructions and was busy moving around the class helping the students with their assignments.

Upon opening the door, his heart dropped when he noticed the girl against the wall had pure white hair just like the girl he had seen earlier by the fountain. The top of her head was all he could see with the other students blocking his line of sight. He knew he would have to go to the front door to know if it was her for sure.

He went back to the front door and stuck his head in. Getting a good look at her face assured him that the girl he followed earlier was Marianne Bawley. He closed the door quickly, with his heart racing.

He was glad to see she was real and that he didn't miss another opportunity. But he knew he had smelled the same perfume that he had at the cemetery and wondered what the connection was.

Not wanting to miss the chance to talk to her, he decided to wait at the top of the stairwell until the class was dismissed so he could try approaching her there. He knew none of his friends would be able to interrupt him if he approached her inside the building.

When the class ended, Mark watched with apprehension while a procession of students passed by. But there was no sign of her.

He made his way back to the classroom again and noticed her helping to put some lab materials away while talking with the teacher. Mark couldn't quite hear what she was saying, but he could hear the teacher's deep voice. The sound of it made him laugh, just thinking back to their previous encounter.

Moving closer to the door, he could hear the professor telling her someone had stopped by before class to give her a blue notebook.

When the professor stopped talking, he saw her whole body go rigid.

The professor disappeared into his office, and she turned around enough for Mark to see her face. She just stood there staring toward the front of the class with a worried look.

Happy he had not missed his opportunity, Mark decided to wait near the entrance of the building, knowing he could not miss seeing her there. He ran down and sat on one of the chairs that faced the doors.

Nerves got the better of him while he waited. He began to roll and unroll the notebook repeatedly.

When she rounded the corner at the bottom of the stairs, their eyes met. Mark forced a smile and began to stand up. He noticed her look down at the notebook in his hand. Without looking back up at him, she quickly exited the building.

Mark had to dance around some students mingling just outside the entrance. She was walking surprisingly fast, and he had to break into a jog to catch up with her.

"Are you Marianne Bawley?"

CHAPTER 14

A STERN WARNING

Mark could tell she pretended not to hear him. She picked up her pace even more and continued to head up Stadium Drive. Doing his best to keep up, he tapped her on the shoulder to get her attention.

"Look," she said, whirling around. "I don't know who you are or what you want, but please leave me alone."

The look on her face let Mark know that she was in no mood to talk to him, and he could tell he didn't have much time with her. He hastily held the notebook up in front of her. "I'm sorry to bother you, but I found this notebook, and I think it belongs to you. I just wanted to give it back to you."

Mark could tell his comments seemed to relax her a little bit. She took off her sunglasses and looked directly at him and then down at the notebook in his hands.

"Where in the world did you get it?" she asked, eying it in disbelief.

Mark could sense she was very uncomfortable seeing it again.

"My friends and I were at the Historic Congressional Cemetery last Saturday night, and a worker gave it to us."

She looked at Mark suspiciously and then took it from him and began to thumb through it like she didn't believe him.

While she looked, Mark was taken aback by her natural beauty. Being so close, he was able to confirm his initial thought that her skin was almost lighter than her hair. She had piercing blue eyes that made him feel a little awestruck when the light caught them.

She turned and began walking at a normal pace while continuing to read. Feeling that her initial coldness toward him had abated, Mark decided to walk with her.

"Since I'm heading in this direction, is it all right if I ask you a few quick questions?"

"No, I don't like hanging out in cemeteries anymore if that is where this is going," she said, giggling softly.

Her lighthearted response caught him off guard.

"As I said, my friends and I were there for a while last week for our Psychic Phenomenon class. This caretaker guy named Pete said he noticed you visiting a few times, and after one of your visits, he found the notebook. I'm sorry to admit this, but we read some of your entries, which is the reason I wanted to talk to you."

Mark expected her to jump on him for invading her privacy, but instead, she calmly stopped and turned to face him.

"You were at the cemetery for Professor Windham's class?" she asked with a hint of sarcasm.

Mark was happy she was starting to engage him in conversation even though he could tell her defenses were still up.

"Yes. I showed the professor the notebook, and he remembered you. He called you one of his most gifted students but wasn't sure why you left his class."

"Gifted," she said with contempt. "That guy has no idea what's going on or what he's messing with. He invites kids into his class and gets them all excited and hopeful that they have a gift but doesn't say anything about the awful things that can happen when they tap into it. If you want my advice, I'd drop his class before it's too late. Stick with classes that will do you some good here and now."

Mark was surprised at the seriousness of her tone and her warning.

"If you don't mind me asking, too late for what?"

"Look, I've got another class, and I don't have time to get into it." She turned and began walking away again.

"I'm sorry if I made you feel uncomfortable, Marianne."

Mark retreated and walked behind her to give her some space when it dawned on him that some of the students walking nearby started to notice him shadowing her. Not wanting to give them the impression he was stalking her, he deliberately slowed down and let her walk off.

Even though their encounter was not what he was hoping for, he figured he had returned the notebook and gotten her opinion regarding the class, and he knew where to find her if he ever needed to accidentally run into her again.

Just as he was turning to head back to his dorm, he noticed Marianne turn around and walk back towards him.

"Look, if you want, we can talk later tonight. It's not fair for me to warn you and then not tell you why."

Mark quickly thought of the most recognizable spot to meet on campus.

"That would be great. Why don't we plan on meeting at the sundial at eight, if that works for you?" Mark asked, trying not to sound or look too excited.

"That works. I need to study at the library tonight anyway. I'll see you then."

CHAPTER 15

MEETING PLANS

When Mark entered the dorm room that he and Jeremy had eloquently nicknamed "The Hole," Jeremy's rapid-fire line of questioning began.

"How did it go with Marianne? What did she say? Is she a psycho, or is she hot?"

Mark noticed the empty cans of Mountain Dew scattered around his bed and knew it was the caffeine racing through his friend's body that was causing his angst.

"Relax. I have a date to meet her tonight at the sundial, and she said she would answer all my questions about our class and what happened to her." Mark laid down on his bed and put his arms behind his head with satisfaction.

"I must go with you. You've got to take me with you," Jeremy pleaded. "Stace and P-dog have been texting me like crazy, wondering if I'd heard from you." Jeremy held up his phone, showing Mark the string of texts.

"I don't know," Mark said, hesitating at the thought of bringing anyone else. "I had a hard time getting her to open up to me. Plus, she was the one who wanted to set up the meeting with me. I don't know if bringing you along would be wise. If you go, I'm sure Stacie is going to want to go."

Mark grabbed Jeremy's phone to take a closer look at the texts from Stacie and Paul.

"Did she tell you anything about the notebook?"

"Not really. She seemed kind of ticked that I had it. But her mood changed after I gave it back to her."

Jeremy stood up and grabbed his phone back, a little miffed. "You just gave it to her? Are you insane?" He reached over and slugged Mark on the leg.

"Yeah. It was hers anyway."

Jeremy sat down on his bed and looked at Mark in disbelief. "She's not going to meet you. She has the notebook now and was only saying that to get it. I wouldn't have given it to her until I got all my questions answered."

Mark could tell Jeremy's emotions were getting the better of him. He leaned up on the edge of his bed and confidently looked Jeremy right in the eyes. "She'll meet with me. I'm sure of it."

"Wait a minute. You wouldn't be this confident unless something happened between you two. Did you two hit it off?" Jeremy asked with a big smile.

Mark knew that his confidence gave Jeremy the wrong impression, even though he couldn't deny his instant attraction to Marianne. He knew he wouldn't be able to keep it from Jeremy long, so he went with it.

"Dude, if you saw her, you would be blown away by her. I mean, she looks like a model." Mark could tell his admission startled Jeremy.

"Are you kidding me?" Jeremy asked, looking at him with one eyebrow raised.

Mark decided to keep going. He didn't care if Jeremy believed him or not.

"Her hair is soft and white, and her skin is even whiter. She looks like an angel that fell from heaven. There was a connection between us. I know for a fact that she wasn't setting up our meeting just to get rid of me."

"Wow, you're falling for her. Remember the notebook. That girl probably has three or four personalities rolling around in that head of hers. I would've gotten my questions answered and then cut her loose."

Mark knew that his friend's distrust of women stemmed from his horrible relationship with his mother. She had run off to pursue a relationship with Mark's father when Mark and Jeremy were in the third grade, and he still hadn't forgiven her. This made it hard for Jeremy to form any lasting relationships with the opposite sex.

Mark pulled out his cell phone to take the discussion in a different direction.

"I'm going to call Stacie and tell her that she can tag along from a distance if she wants. But I'm going to tell her not to bring Paul. He's blown enough chances for me lately."

"How about me? I know how to blend."

"Fine. You can come too, but I want to show up first, just in case she's waiting. You two just stay out of sight until I cue you when it's safe to come over. Deal?"

"Deal. But I bet you a steak dinner she doesn't show."

"You're on," Mark said fist-bumping Jeremy to seal the deal.

CHAPTER 16

THE SUNDIAL

After reaching Stacie and setting up the plans for that evening's meeting, Mark was worried about losing the bet to Jeremy—not for having to pay for a steak dinner if he lost but for missing out on the chance to get to the bottom of what Marianne had experienced.

Marianne had displayed a whole range of emotions when he met with her earlier. But it gave him hope that she was the one who had approached him about the meeting, and she seemed genuinely concerned about his well-being.

Stacie showed up at their dorm room at half past seven, and the first thing Mark did was confirm she hadn't said anything to Paul about their plans. He knew he would lose it if Paul got in the way again. They worked it out that Stacie and Jeremy would sit on the opposite side of the dial until Mark cued them to come over. He would stretch out with both arms above his head, and they would then walk by, pretending they happened to be there by coincidence. Because she hadn't seen his friends, Mark felt confident she wouldn't assume anything fishy.

Mark led the way to the sundial, which was in the middle of a large, open area of campus situated in between the McKeldin Library and the

Omicron Delta Kappa Fountain. Upon arriving, he made a quick pass around the dial but did not see Marianne.

A cold breeze was blowing steadily, and Mark began to shiver uncontrollably. He stuffed his hands deep into his jacket pockets and began pacing back and forth, trying to generate some body heat.

He glanced over and saw that Jeremy and Stacie were in place and then looked down at his watch. It was eight o'clock. He began scanning in every direction, but there was no sign of her.

With each passing minute, the sight of a girl coming in his direction would catch his attention but only end in disappointment.

Come on, Marianne. Don't dog me.

He kept thinking that Jeremy was right. He knew he should've kept the notebook until their meeting. It was the only bargaining chip he had.

He looked over at Jeremy and Stacie and could see they were busy talking and not even looking in his direction. He was a little ticked off they had apparently already decided that she wasn't going to show.

Glancing down at his watch again, he noticed she was now fifteen minutes late. He knew he couldn't hang out there much longer in the thin jacket he was wearing.

Another ten minutes went by before Mark decided to call it quits. When he approached Jeremy and Stacie, Jeremy began to rub his stomach.

"I'll take mine medium rare with extra butter," said Jeremy with a satisfying grin.

"I can't believe she didn't show," Mark said, looking around one last time with false hope.

"That's girls for you. They give you hope and then pull the rug right out from under you," said Jeremy.

Stacie slugged him in the shoulder, taking offense.

"You should've gotten her number or dorm number or something," Stacie said, doing little to lift his spirits.

"You were right, Jeremy. Looks like I will have to stake out the chemistry lab again," Mark admitted in defeat.

"At least you know where to find her." Stacie put her arm around Mark's waist and laid her head on his shoulder, sensing his disappointment.

"You want me to pay up now," Mark said, noticing Jeremy had already started searching for restaurants on his phone. "You want steak at this time of night?"

"I'm not the one who lost the bet, so I make the rules. Longhorns is still open," Jeremy said, truly enjoying the moment.

Walking to his car, Mark wondered what could have happened to her. He knew her intention was genuine when they discussed where to meet. He had received a blow-off smile from girls before, and hers was not one of them.

The thought of approaching her after her chemistry class again reeked of desperation, but Mark knew she had some important information that could help him.

He had nothing to lose.

CHAPTER 17

ADDITIONAL INSIGHTS

Mark had a hard time going to sleep that night after his missed opportunity with Marianne. He tried repeatedly to clear his mind, but just when he would start to doze off, Jeremy would mumble something in his sleep, and his mind would start racing again.

The first few months of his freshman year had flown by, and although he could have saved some money by attending a college closer to home, it was becoming abundantly clear he was meant to be at the University of Maryland.

Even though he enjoyed certain aspects of his other classes, the Psychic Phenomenon class with Professor Windham was the most interesting class he had ever taken. Every lecture contained bits of insight that made his mind race with possibilities he had never considered.

The discussions regarding the different dimensions were some of his favorites. He had never really put a lot of thought into what other dimensions might be like but remembered seeing a program in high school on Einstein's theory of relativity that proposed the concept of multiple dimensions, and it fascinated him.

He leaned over to look at the clock, and it showed 1:00 a.m.

The late hour would've bothered him if it was on a school night, but it was Saturday morning, and he hadn't planned anything with anyone. He allowed his mind to wander back to what the professor taught regarding dimensions during their very first class.

"After Einstein's work, scientists began to use the concept of four spatial dimensions, the first being length or width, the second height, the third depth, and time is the fourth dimension.

"As you students might have learned in previous science classes, we live in the third dimension and gradually become accustomed to it the older we get. Length, height, and depth make up our perception of our current dimension. I propose to you that our soul is progressing through multiple phases that are like dimensions. Each one brings with it more knowledge and understanding that increase exponentially.

"To make a point regarding the differences between dimensions, let's discuss what a ball would look like to a soul, say in a second dimensional state, which lacks depth.

"When it approaches them, they would only see a red line at first, not a round object. It would get larger the closer it got. When it was right next to them, they would see a perfect circle lacking any depth. Then, when it passed them, it would get thin again and disappear altogether. They would only see the ball in length and height.

"In turn, if we saw a soul from this second dimension, it would look very one-dimensional because of the laws that bind it there. Before that soul can move to ours, it would have to gain all the understanding from its current state for it to effectively learn to function in ours.

"In the like, we need to understand all we can in our current state and master its possibilities and limitations to have any shot of understanding the abilities you could have by accessing the next state or phase before you die."

Mark found it fascinating that the current state of his soul was not the beginning but a continuation of additional light and understanding. He thought about the examples the professor used to explain how a person can be taught to see and understand things that others cannot, using certain techniques.

"Let me give you an example of what I'm talking about regarding how close our next phase is and how you can shorten the learning curve to access and understand it. I have some techniques that I hope to teach you in this class.

"Years ago, some psychologists did a study where they raised a kitten from birth in a room with only horizontal lines. After its eyesight developed, it was suddenly released into a room with tables and chairs that had vertical lines. The kitten would run right into the legs of these objects, even though they were right in front of it. The kitten could not cheat its reality by seeing them suddenly but had to learn, over the next little while, to see those vertical lines and understand they were there.

"Another study was done with a child who was born to sightless parents. If he remained solely in their care, he would end up being blind even though he had sight. The child had to be taken from his parents for periods while his eyes were developing because the parents could not focus directly on the child. He would spend time with other family members, who had their sight, so he could learn how to focus on them and other objects to see them properly.

"It takes focus for us to truly understand all the aspects of our state. Right now, you can only think in terms of length, height, and depth. But I'm here to tell you that you students have a chance to shorten this learning curve to the next state, or dimension if you will, which is time.

"When you are close to death you are slowly introduced to the next state, so you don't run into table legs, if you get my meaning. But imagine how much further ahead you would be if you could learn to see and understand what those legs or limitations are now, before you make your transition.

"There is a superstring theory out there that holds that the universe began in ten dimensions, but something happened that made the matter flow into four dimensions. The other six dimensions remain a mystery.

"I'm here to tell you that some people throughout history could see and access more states than just ours. They were able to shorten the soul's learning curve. I believe some of you in this class can learn this ability."

Mark remembered that this possibility had blown him and Jeremy away. He felt privileged that the professor had recognized this possibility in him from what he had written in his admissions letter.

CHAPTER 18

ACCESS GRANTED

Mark reached over, opened the bottom drawer of the small nightstand next to his bed, and pulled out the letter he had written to gain admission into the psychology department. He felt the need to review the letter to make sure he didn't forget any of the aspects of the event that started everything in motion.

To whom it may concern,

Thank you for the opportunity to write to you and express my desire to obtain my college degree within the Psychology Department of the University of Maryland. I appreciate your consideration.

What has led me to your department?

Like everyone, my life has had many challenges that I have had to overcome. But there are a couple of experiences that I've had that I hope will show my purpose for reaching out to you and why I believe I can be an asset to your department and some help to others.

I was born and raised in a lower-income suburb of Baltimore and currently live there with my mother (Deborah) and little sister (Cassandra). I would say my life has been filled with more ups than downs, and I've always tried to be a glass-half-full kind of person.

The first event that shaped who I am today was my parents' divorce when I was ten years old. It's not like I didn't see it coming. They argued about everything all the time. Looking back, it had a detrimental effect on how I chose to create relationships around that age, usually through arguing to prove a point.

My dad was in and out of jobs and felt a lot of stress in trying to provide for our family. This was the main point of most of my parents' arguments. There were some good moments with my dad before he left. We attended a lot of sporting events together, which was fun. However, he would usually use them to try and push me toward playing them when I just wasn't interested. This frustrated him, and I know it hurt our relationship.

He took a new job when I turned nine that required a lot of traveling. Soon after starting it, he came out and told my mom that he was leaving her for another woman.

I should probably mention the woman he ran off with is the mother of my best friend, Jeremy Kozlowski, who is also applying to get into this department. We weren't close friends growing up, but we spent many days talking about what happened, which helped lay the groundwork for our friendship.

After the divorce was finalized, my mom had a nervous breakdown and became a heavy drinker. She began to neglect my sister and me. This is when my grandparents on my mom's side stepped up and began to take care of us.

My grandpa Charles and grandma Ruth were our saving grace. When things got tough at home, my sister and I would go over there to escape. Luckily, they only lived a few blocks away.

My grandfather was tall with huge hands and was a great basketball player in high school and college but never pushed sports on me the way my dad did. He was very involved with politics and very knowledgeable when it came to history. He had noticed I was also interested in the past and learning all I could about it. He would pepper me with all sorts of questions to test my knowledge. If I didn't know them, he would always take time to answer them thoroughly. He would also impart a piece of wisdom I could apply to my life with each response.

My grandmother was petite. I was taller than her by the third grade. She had way more energy than me, which made her fun to be around. She made sure I knew how to cook basic meals and would help me shop for lunch food so I could prepare my sister's when we were home.

Even though my grandparents were strict, they were the perfect role models for me. They constantly reminded me that my job was schoolwork and pushed me to get good grades. They constantly stressed the importance of a college education and expected me to earn a degree.

It was at this point, at the age of ten, that I saw what can happen to those who experience major challenges in their lives and how you can choose to overcome them or let them overcome you, as they did for my mom.

I knew I had to be strong for my sister and become the man of the house. I did my best to help my mom out and tried not to put too much blame on her for the way she treated us. I'm happy to inform you that she has sobered up and has worked steadily over the past few years. My relationship with her has grown even closer since my grandparents died earlier this year.

The second major event of my life was their passing, and this is what brings me to your department. I'm hoping to understand more about a very significant experience I had with my grandfather.

A week before my high school graduation from Fredrick Douglas High School, in May, my grandparents died in a carbon monoxide accident at their home. This was the lowest point of my life.

My good friend Stacie talked me into showing up for graduation, even though it was the furthest thing from my mind. I had given up on my dreams of going to college. Without them around, I felt it was pointless. But the experience I had the night of graduation changed everything.

I had just finished my prayers and was looking for guidance on what I was going to do with my future. I remember looking down the hallway from my bedroom through a stream of tears when I saw an opening of light appear in the middle of the hallway that looked like a large white box. It grew larger and larger when I noticed a man coming from the other side. It was my grandpa, Charles. He walked right out of it and into my room with a big smile on his face. Even though he looked a lot younger, I knew it was him. He sat down next to me on my bed.

I couldn't believe what was happening and wiped my eyes many times, expecting it to be a hallucination. He asked me why I had so many tears and called me Jack. Jack was a nickname he had given me because I was always bouncing all over like a Jack-in-the-box. He was the only one who called me that.

I finally calmed down enough to speak to him. We had a long talk about what I was going to do with the money they left me and that I should pursue a college degree. He told me that I always had a way with people and could understand and sympathize with the struggle's life can throw at them with what I had experienced.

Once he felt I had the direction I needed, he stood up and said that was all the time he had for our visit. He put his hand on my shoulder, and I felt a surge of joy, peace, and tranquility shoot through me. The feeling seemed to fill my mind with the clarity I needed regarding my future.

Before he left, I asked him how my grandma was doing. He said she loved me and wanted to visit me but couldn't reach out to me quite yet. Then the opening reappeared in the hallway, and he walked back through it.

I know I wasn't imagining it or dreaming. I could feel his hand on my shoulder. I could even smell the aftershave he would wear. I looked at the clock, and our conversation had taken almost three hours.

I immediately ran into my sister's room and woke her up to tell her about it. I assumed she would just think it was a crazy dream, but she said she sensed that our grandpa was nearby and could feel his love all around her. I know there are classes within your department that could help me more fully comprehend what I experienced.

My wish is to help others overcome life challenges and help them understand the spiritual events in their life that can guide them on their path.

I hope you help me with this journey by allowing me to pursue a degree in your department.

Sincerely,
Mark Banks

The words *joy, peace,* and *tranquilly* that he had typed in the letter stood out again.

He knew it wasn't a coincidence that Marianne had used the same words in her notebook. There was a bond he felt with her after only one encounter. He just needed her to realize it too.

CHAPTER 19

BREAKTHROUGH

Mark looked up the days Marianne's chemistry class met and decided to wait until Wednesday to run into her again. He didn't want to appear too desperate.

That Wednesday, instead of waiting at the entrance, he chose to wait in front of the building. When Marianne appeared, she was in the middle of several students walking toward him. He waited until she passed and then made his way through the group to move up alongside her.

Before he could say anything, she glanced over at him. "Oh, it's you."

Mark was disappointed her defenses were back up but decided to push the awkwardness aside.

"Hey, Marianne. I'm sorry I must have misunderstood where we were going to meet on Friday night. I thought we were going to meet at the dial at eight, right?" he asked, trying to get her reason for not being there.

She pulled him to the side, away from the other students walking by, and waited for them to pass.

"Look. I didn't forget," she said flatly, looking at him with little expression.

Mark felt like he was reliving their first encounter all over again. He knew he was walking on thin ice and tried to say something to lighten her mood, but he couldn't think of anything.

"What do you know about the purpose of the class you are taking from Professor Windham?" Marianne asked, much to his surprise.

He knew he couldn't reveal to her that he thought it was the best class he had ever taken, so he decided to play it cool.

"It's okay, I guess. Professor Windham is a little strange, but he seems to believe what he's talking about."

Mark noticed her body relax a little after his response, and he was glad he had kept his opinion to himself.

"Let me guess. In your admissions letter, you wrote about some strange event in your life that you can't understand, and suddenly you get invited to his mystery class. Then you sit in this class for the first few weeks, and Professor Windham goes on about how special you are and what select company you're in. You get a bunch of strange assignments that you do rather blindly, not knowing why you are doing them. Am I right so far?"

Mark was amazed at how accurate her description was and nodded in agreement.

"That's his arrogance," she said, beginning to pace in front of him, agitated. "He has no idea what he is getting his students into. He talks like he knows how amazing making contact would be, but he has no idea that the bad outweighs the good the further along you go."

Mark noticed her cheeks getting flushed with anger the more she talked. He knew he needed to change the subject.

"I'm starving. Would you like to go grab a quick bite?" he asked with a warm smile, pointing in the direction of the campus cafeteria.

To his surprise, she took a deep breath and agreed.

They walked together slowly, talking about some of their other classes. Mark found it refreshing that she could be very conversational when he steered clear of mentioning anything about the professor or his class.

After getting a couple of personal-size pizzas and drinks, Mark talked her into eating outside so they could have a little more privacy. Mark sat and listened quietly while she began to tell him about herself.

He learned she had initially started at the university on a cheerleading scholarship but hurt her knee during a football game last fall during one of their stunts. She had to give it up because it hadn't healed properly. She had grown up in Virginia, and her parents relocated to DC when her dad got a job for the United Nations during her senior year of high school. However, she decided to finish up high school in Virginia, living with her aunt and favorite cousin, who happened to be the same age.

When she finished, Mark decided to give her a little background on his past since she had been so forthcoming. He noticed her keeping a steady gaze directly on his face, and she wasn't even touching her food. Since he had her attention, he went into detail about what happed with his grandparents and his grandfather's visit. He even made her laugh a couple of times, telling her about Jeremy and their odd friendship.

Her laugh and the way her face lit up when she smiled made his heart pound faster.

When he finished, he realized he was just sitting there smiling at her, which made her blush and turn away. Mark began to eat his pizza that was now cold to fill the silence.

"When you went to do your cemetery assignment, what made you pick the HCC instead of a closer one?" she asked out of the blue.

Mark was happy she was turning the conversation back toward the class.

"Jeremy knew about it, and we were up for a little drive. We figured there wouldn't be many of the students willing to drive out there, and we could have the place to ourselves. Plus, the professor said there would be an orb fest that night."

"Orb fest. That sure is a loose way of saying it." Marianne reached out, grabbed his hand, and laughed again.

A bolt of electricity shot through Mark's body with her touch.

"Who gave you my notebook again?" she asked. She released his hand.

"I think I mentioned we ran into a guy who worked there. He said he had found it by one of the cenotaphs you were sitting on."

She looked away for a few moments, as if she was trying to remember, and then turned back to him with a look of confusion.

"Mark, I did not just leave that in the cemetery that night. I threw it in a trash can that was in the parking lot before I left. I haven't been back there since. When you showed up with it last week, it took me off guard. I've been trying to put everything that happened behind me."

Mark didn't know if it was Pete who had misremembered how he obtained it or if it was Marianne, but he had more pressing questions on his mind.

"Speaking of the notebook, when my friends and I were looking at it—"

"How many of your friends saw it?" Marianne asked, cutting him off, her eyes wide open in surprise.

"Well, besides my roommate, Jeremy, who was with me, my friend from high school, Stacie, and her friend Paul. They showed up out of the blue that night."

"Mark. Not all those entries in that book are from me."

"What do you mean?"

Marianne looked at him and took a deep breath. "Before I get into that, I feel I need to give you a little background first. I loved the professor's class for the first few months. The things the professor was teaching were so interesting and seemed to answer some of the questions I had surrounding my experience with my cousin."

Mark noticed her fidgeting more and more with her pizza box and could sense her discomfort. He waited patiently for her to continue.

"I had gone to the HCC a couple of times by myself during those first few assignments, and I never got nervous being there. Each time I walked the grounds, I felt such peace and clarity. It's hard to explain. I was practicing the relaxation exercises the professor was teaching when it finally happened on my third visit."

Mark jumped in. "By *it*, you mean you made contact?"

"Yes. I contacted someone from the other side." She paused, looking deeply into his eyes for a reaction.

He could sense she was waiting for him to question her or not believe her. He simply smiled and nodded his head for her to keep going.

"Mark, it was the most amazing experience I have ever had. Even more amazing than the one I had with my cousin."

"Wait, the experience with your cousin happened first?" Mark asked, leaning forward, enthralled.

"Yes. I should probably back up even further and tell you about that. It was that event that got me into the professor's class in the first place."

CHAPTER 20

SHARED PATHS

Marianne paused, trying to find the right way to begin. She reached over and grabbed his hand again, squeezing it tighter than she had before.

"Mark, just like your grandparents, my cousin was killed in a car accident a few days before my high school graduation. Her funeral was the day before graduation. That night, I was sitting on her bed, looking out the window at the moon, just thinking about her."

She paused. Mark could see her eyes begin to tear up. She used her other hand to wipe some away as they fell.

"I was just thinking about her laugh and holding her pillow in my arms. Smelling her shampoo on her pillow overwhelmed me, and I thought I was going to pass out. I was about to lie down when I noticed a small, round light outside our window that looked to be floating in the woods behind the house. I thought it was someone with a flashlight at first, but the more I watched it, the more I realized there was nothing behind it."

Mark could feel her hand getting sweatier in his and placed his other hand on top.

"I threw on a sweater and followed the light right into the woods. I lost it here and there for brief moments. But when I reached a large rock that we would sometimes hang out on, it stopped moving. Suddenly, the light grew larger and larger until my cousin was standing right in front of me. I didn't even know what to say for what seemed like an eternity. I just looked at her, wondering if she was real or not. She smiled at me and started talking to me like nothing had happened to her. She told me about the events surrounding her accident and how peaceful she felt when she moved to the other side. It was so surreal. I finally settled down, and we talked for what seemed like the whole night. We talked about so many different things. Toward the end of her visit, she said I had a gift and not to waste it. Then the light started gathering all around her, and she was gone."

She pulled her hand away from Mark's and wiped her tears with both hands.

Mark was amazed at the similarities in their stories. It took him a moment to even think of something else to say while she collected herself.

"Thanks for telling me that, Marianne. Your cousin sounds amazing. If you don't mind me asking, was she the one who contacted you in the cemetery? Is her name Abby?"

Marianne gave a surprised glance. "No, my cousin's name is Crystal. Abby is the girl from the cemetery. How did you know about her?"

"You mentioned her a few times in your notebook."

"That's right. The night I contacted her, I was drawn to an area at the end of a long row of cenotaphs, and I ended up just sitting on one of them. One of the headstones next to them had a beautiful sculpture of an angel on it, and her hands cast a strange shadow down in between two cenotaphs directly in front of me. When I got up to look closer, I noticed a small grave of a young woman."

Mark's mind was reeling now, realizing that Abby was short for Abigail Turnbow, whose grave he had ended up standing over during his visit. He could feel his mouth drop open in astonishment.

"What's wrong, Mark?"

He quickly composed himself and closed it. "Nothing. Please go on."

"I noticed a light dancing just above her headstone. I stopped moving and focused exactly on the light. Within a matter of seconds, standing right in front of me was a beautiful young woman. Since I had already experienced a visit like this with Crystal, I didn't want to waste any time getting some of my questions answered about the next life, and I jumped right in. She was very patient with me and answered a lot of them. She also acknowledged the rare gift I had been given to be able to see her. She told me about a plan that had been put into motion that would have a horrible effect on mankind and that she would need my help to stop it."

Mark could not believe how far Marianne had gotten with all her experiences and could not fathom how she could just shut them all out. He hoped she would explain why and remained quiet but attentive. He was thrilled when she kept going.

"Things went well with our first couple of visits. She would give me instructions on what I needed to be on the lookout for and how I could help. On my last visit, I went back to meet her to get some important directions, but I did not feel the peace as I had before. That's when I met them."

Marianne paused and began to rub her shoulders with her hands to keep warm. Mark took off his jacket and put it around her, keeping silent.

"I was waiting for Abby when I heard her voice tell me to get out of there. Before I could do as she said, several dark figures emerged from the shadows all around me. I heard one of them ask me what I was doing there. I knew I shouldn't answer and kept quiet. Suddenly I could feel the image enter my body and take control of it. I couldn't believe the dark thoughts I was writing down in my notebook. The figures kept coming in and out of me, one by one, for what felt like hours. All of them used my hand to write down what they were most angry about."

Mark watched as her body shivered several times. She paused, looking up at the sky for a few moments, and then continued.

"I prayed for my release, and the Lord must have heard my prayer. When I came to, I was lying on the ground, too weak to move for quite a while. I made it back to my car and noticed the last couple of pages of my notebook contained threats and warnings of what these beings were going to do to me if I continued to help Abby."

When she finished, she buried her face in her hands and began to sway toward Mark. He opened his arms, and she fell into him.

"Are you okay, Marianne?"

She sat back up quickly. "Yes. I get overwhelmed sometimes and feel faint. I couldn't believe that Abby did not intervene on my behalf. After that experience, I left the professor's class and never went back. Sometimes

I would feel Abby's presence, but I chose not to allow our connection. Within a few weeks, she stopped trying to reach me."

Mark just sat there dumbfounded. Marianne abruptly stood up and walked over to a nearby trash can to throw away her half-eaten pizza.

He picked up their books and threw his box away. They began to walk in silence.

Mark couldn't imagine what it was that took over Marianne's body like that, and it scared him. He considered asking more about the figures that he assumed must have possessed her but felt she had been open enough for this visit.

To break the silence, he ended up changing the subject to that of their families. Without realizing it, he had walked with her back to her dorm, which wasn't too far from his.

He reached for the door to open it for her. "Thanks for talking with me, Marianne. You have given me a lot to think about, and hopefully you don't think I'm some creepy stalker anymore."

She took hold of his hand and leaned into him.

"Not at all. Thanks for listening to me. I didn't realize it would feel so good to get some of this off my chest. Please promise me you'll be careful."

"I will. I promise."

"If you have any other questions, feel free to call me." She took out her phone and texted Mark her number. Then to his surprise, she leaned up and kissed him gently on the cheek before entering her building.

For the first time in quite a while, Mark realized he was starting to have romantic feelings for someone other than Stacie. She had shared a lot of information and given him much to think about moving forward. He couldn't wait for their next encounter.

CHAPTER 21

SPIRITED DEBATE

Mark hurriedly made his way to his dorm, excited to tell Jeremy everything he and Marianne had discussed. The number of different subjects they covered surprised him, and he wanted to tell Jeremy while they were fresh in his mind.

"Hey, lover boy," Jeremy said with a suspect grin when Mark came through the door. He was immersed in a video game and didn't look up. "Did you two plan your honeymoon or what?"

"You have no idea." Mark yanked the game controller Jeremy was holding out of his hands and turned off the machine.

"Oh no. You are falling for this girl, aren't you?"

Mark thought he had chased Jeremy off the subject after his first visit with Marianne by playing up his attraction, but because of the bounce in his step, he knew Jeremy could sense that he was indeed falling for her.

"Dude, you kissed her, didn't you?" Jeremy asked, clapping his hands loudly a few times.

"No, we just talked." Mark avoided mentioning that Marianne had leaned up and kissed him on the cheek so he could get to the point of their conversation.

Without allowing Jeremy a rebuttal, Mark jumped right to the part of her story regarding her visit from her cousin, who Abby was, and how often she met with her.

However, he decided to leave out the part about the shadowy figures until he was able to get more information. It would be difficult for him to put into words all the physical and emotional changes he noticed in Marianne while she was telling him about that experience. Bringing it up would also lend more credence to Jeremy's opinion that she was crazy.

When Mark finished catching him up, he made the mistake of mentioning where she was from.

"You're in love with a girl from the South?" Jeremy asked in disbelief, sitting up on the edge of his bed.

"Not this again." Mark stood up and walked toward the door like he was going to leave, hoping Jeremy would take the bait and refrain from starting another argument.

Jeremy did not buy it. "You know what southern women can do to you."

Mark turned just in time to see Jeremy make a gun gesture toward his head and fire.

Realizing there was no use running, Mark felt he should take the challenge head-on and returned to his bed to face Jeremy. It was time to put his friend straight on a subject that had dogged their relationship ever since his dad and Jeremy's mom had moved out to California together.

"Virginia is not the South, J. I'm not going to let you start bagging on Marianne just because your mom was from the South."

"I'm just saying you've got to watch out for southern women. They have lots of baggage." Jeremy leaned in closer to Mark, challenging him for a rebuttal.

"You say that a lot, but where's your proof?"

Without missing a beat, Jeremy's eyes lit up. "You remember those girls we ran into on that school trip to DC our junior year who were from Virginia? That one, Stephanie, came onto you like crazy and wouldn't stop calling you but never set anything up with you. She was playing you and almost broke you and Stacie up. It was me who had to explain to you what she was doing and save your relationship with Stacie. Then there was that girl that worked with us at Dominos from South Carolina. She almost stabbed you with a pizza cutter when you rejected her."

Mark had forgotten about the girl they worked with. "True, but you can't typecast a whole group of women just because your mom was from Kentucky. Marianne is not your mom."

"Is she religious?"

"We didn't get into religion. But if it helps you sleep at night, she was wearing a cross necklace. Case closed," Mark said, leaning back on his bed and picking up his history book, assuming the conversation was over.

"All I'm saying is it's a whole different mentality down there. And in case you forgot, or haven't started studying geography in your book there, Virginia was a slave state. That makes Virginia a southern state. I would stick with northern girls if I were you."

Jeremy grabbed the controller with an air of satisfaction and began to play his game again.

Not ready to concede, Mark grabbed the remote to the TV that was behind Jeremy and turned it off.

"Just because your mom decided to run off with my dad does not make everything from the South evil. The fact your mom was raised in Kentucky doesn't stop you from eating tons of KFC, does it? Plus, she was born in DC anyway."

"Great point. I would say DC is more like the South. You know they have a strange accent that we can always pick out. Southern girls always act nice and innocent at first but end up hurting you in the end."

"My dad was equally guilty for his role in what happened, but I don't sit and bag on everything from Philly. I still eat cheesesteaks, watch *Rocky*, and cheer for the Eagles. Let it go."

Mark tossed the remote at Jeremy, hitting him in the arm.

Jeremy shrugged it off. "I just worry about you, bro. That's all." He grabbed the controller and clicked back on the TV.

Mark was happy the debate was over, knowing how hard it was to win an argument with Jeremy.

Soon after Jeremy's parents split, his father was buried in grief and focused on his work as a trial lawyer. Jeremy had picked up many argument tactics from his dad that made him a shrewd debater. This neglect left Jeremy, who was an only child, to fend for himself most of the time, and he was used to getting his way. It took Mark many years to figure out how to deal with Jeremy's stubbornness and win-at-all-cost attitude.

Turning back to his reading, it was difficult for Mark to concentrate on the Sons of Liberty chapter with his mind wandering over to his conversation with Marianne.

He now knew the name of the girl who was trying to contact him and began to wonder if she wanted him to pick up where Marianne had left off.

There was only one way to find out. He would have to visit the cemetery alone.

CHAPTER 22

A NEW PERCEPTION

Mark decided Saturday would be the best time for him to escape to the cemetery again without any of his friends coming along. The Terps were playing a late game at home, and he was pretty sure they would all want to go to the game and not spend another game night in a cemetery.

He told them the reason he couldn't go was because of some issues he was having with his mom that needed to be worked out; she wanted to meet him for dinner. Since they all knew about his history with his mom, they didn't try to talk him into going to the game.

Mark made sure he left before Stacie and Paul got to their dorm to get Jeremy. Stacie had a habit of talking him out of things.

"Dude, you guys have fun at the game. I'll probably be back late, so don't wait up," Mark said while walking out the door before Jeremy could answer.

The hour-long trip to the cemetery went painfully slowly. He kept vacillating between positive and negative thoughts. On one hand, he wondered if he had missed his opportunity and if it would end up being a wasted trip. On the other, he knew the similarities of events he shared with Marianne were not just happenstance.

When he pulled into the parking lot of the HCC, he just sat in his car, scanning the grounds for a few minutes to make sure no one was around.

There was no full moon, and the cemetery looked dark and cold.

He reached into the back seat, grabbed his hoodie, pulled it over the thick sweater he was already wearing, and started making his way through the cemetery.

The air was noticeably humid and damp. He hoped the approaching storm his phone warned him about would not blow in while he was there.

Mark found the spot he and Marianne had shared and leaned up against the cenotaph, looking down at Abigail's grave. He tried to clear his mind and focus, but every little sound broke his concentration. The thought of shadowy figures coming out of the darkness made him nervous, and he now wished Marianne had left that part of the conversation out.

After a few more minutes of paranoia, he began to long for Jeremy's company.

Due to the lack of light, the statues had no definition. Most of them were just dark, unrecognizable blocks of stone.

Get a hold of yourself, he thought, chastising himself.

He decided to sit down on the ground between the two cenotaphs that flanked her headstone to help shield him from the breeze that had picked up.

No sooner had he sat down that he felt a hand rest on his right shoulder from behind.

His body just froze.

"Good evening, Mr. Banks," said a young woman's voice.

He began trying to fight off a panic attack. He could feel his heart racing faster with each passing second. He tried to turn and look at his shoulder, but he could not move.

The hand was not leaving his shoulder. He collected all the courage he could muster and let out a faint "Hello."

A gust of wind brought the familiar smell of vanilla, which seemed to calm him down enough to turn his head a little. He looked at his shoulder but could not see anything.

"You are Mark Banks, are you not?" she asked playfully from behind. He felt the slight pressure of her hand leave his shoulder.

"Yes. Mark Banks. That's me." Mark mustered the courage to turn around but could not see her.

"What a night to be alone in a cemetery. I would think someone of your age would have something better to do," she mused.

"I'm sorry, but I cannot see you, and I'm a little freaked out right now."

She gave a small laugh, and he could sense her move in front of him. He took a deep breath and focused on the spot where he thought she was. A small circle of light began to appear like the one he had seen on his previous visit.

"You need to relax, Mr. Banks, and try not to look at me with your physical eyes or I will remain just a ball of light. No need to fear."

Mark stopped trying to follow the orb and just relaxed his gaze on the whole area.

"Good. Once you get used to it, your eyes will pull in enough light to see me."

He tried to do what she said, but nothing happened.

What am I supposed to be seeing?

"My realm," she answered.

Did she just read my mind?

"Yes," she said, answering his thought again. "Due to our connection, I can respond to your verbal expressions or subconscious ones. Whichever model of communication you're most comfortable with. I need you to open our visual connection. To do that, I need you to fix your gaze on the spot where my voice is coming from. Not the bit of light you see moving in front of you."

Mark moved his eyes up a little and noticed the ball of light began to grow larger until the outline of a beautiful young woman appeared directly in front of him, about two feet off the ground.

"My name is Abigail Turnbow. But I guess you already knew that."

CHAPTER 23

UNCHARTED TERRITORY

Mark tried hard to follow her movement, which was causing her features to move in and out of focus. Once he stopped moving his head, her detail became sharper.

He marveled at how stunning her appearance was. She was wearing a brilliant, bright dress that looked to Mark like an ornate wedding gown. Her hair was a shade of red like he had never seen. When he finally caught her gaze looking right at him, it held him transfixed, and his eyes began to water.

"Now you are doing it, Mr. Banks." Her pleasant smile made him relax.

"You can call me Mark if you want."

"As you wish, Mark."

After several deep breaths to calm his nerves, questions started to bubble to the surface of his mind.

"If you don't mind me asking, what happened to you that ended your life at such a young age?" Mark asked, remembering her headstone said she lived only twenty years.

She did not answer right away but looked at him intensely with her brow furrowing. Mark chastised himself internally for asking such a personal question. It felt to Mark like she was looking into his soul with just her gaze. Suddenly a smile returned to her face.

"Your intentions are true, and I'm more than happy to tell you a little about myself. I was born in Dover, England, in the latter part of the nineteenth century. I moved to Maryland when I was in my twelfth year of age. Unfortunately, my temporal existence ended in my twentieth year from rheumatic fever. Would you like to know more about me or is that sufficient?"

"More, please."

Mark listened, mesmerized while she went into detail about her upbringing, her time in England, the reason for their move to America, her relationship with her family, and the young man who was courting her before her death. He noticed a pained expression when she went into detail about the agony she felt from succumbing to the fever but watched her mood lighten almost immediately when she began describing her transition to the other side.

When she finished, it again dawned on Mark that she was communicating with him both verbally and with her mind.

"It seems like you were using your conscious and subconscious to communicate with me. Is that right?"

"Yes, it is. For instance, you had a question running through your mind of what I wanted from you. This will be answered in due time. But first, why don't you tell me what I need to know about Mark Banks."

Not knowing how far back he should go, he decided to fill her in on all the events of the past year. The more they conversed, the more comfortable he felt in her presence.

"Earlier, you mentioned me being able to see your realm. What did you mean by that?" Mark asked, wondering what a realm was.

"Well, now that you are used to seeing me with your spiritual eyes, I want you to slowly look around me and tell me what you see."

Mark started to slowly look away from her image and noticed the cemetery beginning to fade from the view directly around her. It was replaced by a beautiful landscape. Bit by bit, the light started to penetrate the darkness that was all around, and it was becoming bright as day.

CHAPTER 24

A NEW LIGHT

The darkened cemetery was soon replaced by rolling meadows and majestic mountains in all directions. The scenery seemed to be illuminated by a light source other than the sun. There was also buildings Mark had never seen before. Many of them had unusual geometric shapes and angles. Everything he looked at was in pristine condition and in order.

He looked down to notice he was standing in a flowering meadow, surrounded by the most brilliant flowers and green grass he had ever seen. The yellow, blue, red, and green were very vibrant.

He then scanned the horizons again in both directions. The hills were covered with beautiful trees, plants, and bushes in full bloom and seemed to glisten.

The air he was breathing was pure, with no hint of pollution or toxicity. He also figured the temperature was perfect. Not too hot or cold but just right.

Mark looked at Abigail and noticed that she was thoroughly enjoying him taking it all in.

Mark looked around him again and could see other spirits moving all about. Some of them were in white robes, while others were dressed in different types of clothing from many different periods. They didn't seem to notice him or Abigail and passed by without a glance.

Mark felt like part of him was caught up in the air and was floating off the ground, even though he could feel the ground under his feet. He knew he was still standing in the cemetery.

"Abigail how is this possible?" he asked, trying to comprehend everything he was witnessing.

"Your gift allows you to see beyond the veil that blocks my realm from yours. I've been instructed to teach you how to use this gift to help us. I'm just glad we were finally able to make this connection."

Mark felt embarrassed he had not been more in tune with her earlier attempts. "I'm sorry that my concentration was broken so many times even though I could smell your perfume. Why is that?"

"I'm glad you asked that. Different senses can be more in tune with our realm than others at different times. The fragrance you noticed was my favorite during my mortal life and what I chose to identify with. My father had first purchased it for me before we left England. Sort of a peace offering for making our move. He would bring me a bottle of it whenever his business would take him back to England."

Mark was surprised that she corroborated everything the professor had mentioned in their last class.

"You mentioned that you needed me to help you?"

"Yes. I've tried to reach out to others who have your gift before but was not successful in accomplishing what was required due to some unfortunate circumstances. I must warn you to be very careful. Your gift can alarm a darker force if we're not careful. Unfortunately, it took trial and error on my part to understand how far we could take each training session before being discovered. This opened the door for some alarming events that have been put into motion recently."

It dawned on Mark that Abigail was referring to Marianne. Her explanation summarized exactly what Marianne had experienced and why she turned off her ability.

"But how do I use my gift to help you?"

"You just need to have enough faith in me to keep our channel of communication open no matter what happens. Each of our visits will be a stepping-stone to greater knowledge and understanding of what we must do next. Don't be fooled by the evil forces that are trying to obtain a path to our realms. They cannot mask the calm feeling you are feeling right now with me. Instead, they will invoke a very dark feeling. Do not try to engage them directly."

Even though Marianne had mentioned the shadowy figures that possessed her, Mark didn't fully understand what they were and if or when they would appear.

"Is there a way of hiding what we do so they cannot see it?"

Abigail smiled at Mark and cupped her hands to her chest. "Great question. That is why I'm here. My task is to train you to use your gift properly and not do anything that would notify them of what we are doing. If they find out you have the gift, they will use many different means to try to get you to help them. I'm praying they don't show up at all. But if they do, I'm more prepared to help you."

Her words encouraged Mark a great deal.

Abigail raised her arms above her head and began to move them down. The images of her realm began to close around them.

"I'm sorry, Mark, but our time for this visit is at an end. One thing I've learned the hard way is the longer we keep our channel open, the better chance they have of knowing about you and your gift. They have many eyes that are watching, and we must be careful. I pray I have not scared you off with what we have discussed tonight."

"No, not at all. I look forward to doing what I can. Do I have the ability to look into your dimension anytime I want?" Mark asked quickly, trying to get another question answered.

"You will be taught that in time. Instead of calling them dimensions, those of us here call them realms. You are currently occupying the third realm, and I, and those who have passed on like me, operate in the fourth realm. Just like you, not all of us who pass into this realm have the gift to work with those in your realm. I have been given a gift to work with you, and I will explain more very soon."

When she finished, the light around Abigail began to close in around her.

"It has truly been a pleasure getting to finally meet you, Mark. Goodbye for now."

Within seconds, her light closed into a small circle, and she was gone.

Mark sat there feeling the same way he did after his grandfather's visit. Although he felt completely exhausted, there was overwhelming joy and peace. On this visit, he had been allowed to get a glimpse of a new realm he had only heard about. He couldn't wait to share his newfound knowledge with someone.

It thrilled him to know that Abigail had backed up much of what the professor had been teaching him all along. The fourth realm was closer than he previously thought.

Making his way back to his car, he noticed it was almost midnight. The time difference was something he wanted to get to the bottom of in future visits.

During the drive back to campus, his body felt electric, and tears fell down his cheeks uncontrollably. He felt like he was experiencing all the happiest events of his life at the same time.

Even though Abigail's visit had added information regarding the afterlife for him, additional religious questions started to run through his head, and he knew just the person to ask.

CHAPTER 25

PUZZLE PIECES

Mark did not claim to be affiliated with any religion. He believed in God and would tell anyone who asked that he was Christian. His grandparents were Southern Baptist and took him and his sister to those services whenever they stayed with them. Outside of those visits, he enjoyed studying the scriptures on his own and arriving at his conclusions.

The person he could not wait to speak with the next day about his visit with Abigail was Kelvin Watts, the pastor of a nondenominational Christian church Mark and his friends attended Sunday mornings, located just off campus. He was a family friend of Mark's parents, who had gone to high school with them. He had also met Mark's grandparents many times and spoke very highly of them. This familiarity created an immediate bond between the two of them.

Mark liked the fact that the pastor did not try to persuade him to join any one faith. He encouraged him to do his scripture studying and answer his questions by asking the Lord in prayer, which fell right in line with what he was already doing. He told Mark many times that his office door was always open and to drop by any time.

After their Sunday-morning service ended, Mark waited for the pastor to retire to his office. He told Jeremy and Stacie he needed some counsel from the pastor regarding his supposed visit with his mom and would meet with them later. He hadn't had time to fill them in on what happened the night before and didn't want to be peppered with their questions while trying to get his own answered.

Mark felt nervous and excited when he knocked on his door.

"Brother Watts, do you have a second?"

The pastor walked over, put forth his large hand, and shook Mark's firmly. "Sure. It was nice to see you and your friends together on this beautiful Sabbath morning, Mark. What can I help you with?"

Mark settled into a chair across the desk from him.

"I have some questions for you about an experience I had last night that I need help understanding."

"If it is about any angry feelings toward our football team's embarrassing loss, those questions are natural," the pastor said, followed by a deep chuckle.

Mark knew the pastor was only half kidding. He had played defensive back for the university and often worked a win or a loss into his sermons.

He had confidence the pastor would listen sincerely since he had previously told him about his experience with his grandfather. Instead of doubting or trying to talk him out of what happened, the pastor believed him wholeheartedly.

Mark jumped into the events of the previous night, giving him all the detail he could. He also explained to him the feelings of pure joy he felt afterward.

Once he finished, he pulled a piece of paper out of his pocket that contained the questions he had and slid them across the desk. The pastor snatched it up eagerly and started looking them over. Then he started to thumb through a stack of scriptures on his desk without saying a word.

Mark was tempted to jump in and add a further explanation but kept his silence, not wanting to break his concentration.

The pastor finally looked up after tabbing several pages.

"There are reasons your grandfather and Abigail have reached out to you, and I feel you need to know a little more about what state they are in and how their world and our world are connected. Are you familiar with the event of Jesus's good friend Lazarus and what took place between them in the New Testament?"

Mark's mind began searching for the story and what had transpired. He knew he had heard the story before but had a hard time coming up with the specifics. After thinking about it for a moment, he decided to give it a shot.

"Well, Martha—or one of the Marys, I forget which one—went to tell Jesus that Lazarus had died, and it took him a few days to get to him after his death. Then he raised him from the dead."

Brother Watts smiled. "Not half bad. In the time between his death and when Jesus was able to get there, where did Lazarus's spirit go while his body was lying there?"

The pastor's question caught Mark off guard. The focus of the story was on the miracle of bringing him back to life, and Mark could not remember if anything had been mentioned in the scriptures regarding Lazarus's spirit. Since he had no answer, he shrugged his shoulders and couldn't wait for the explanation.

"By the expression on your face, it looks like I got you with that one. Let me mention one you might be more familiar with that deals with the same thing. While Jesus's body lay in the tomb for three days before his resurrection, where did his spirit go?"

This time, Mark was on top of it. His grandfather read the scriptures surrounding this event to him every year during Easter dinner, and they discussed it many times.

"Well, he told the thief on the cross next to him that he would be with him in paradise, so I would say he went to paradise," Mark answered, hoping he was right.

"Well done. Lazarus's spirit would've gone to the same place Jesus's spirit went. Those are just a few experiences from the scriptures that deal with our spirits leaving this life to go to the next. Lazarus's soul was not in limbo for the four days it took the Savior to reach him. His spirit had moved on to paradise and needed to be called back to his body for Lazarus to return to mortality. I often wonder about the shock that Lazarus must have felt, thinking he was done with this life and then suddenly being called back. Was he completely happy with the outcome or a little disappointed?" he asked with a deep chuckle again.

Mark laughed with him. "I wouldn't be."

"Let's look at some scriptures from both the Old and New Testaments that refer to our spirits."

Mark had never noticed that his Old Testament looked a lot different from his New Testament and gave him a confused look.

The pastor picked up on it. "I like using the Hebrew Bible, called the Tanakh, for my Old Testament study and the New Revised Standard edition for the New Testament. To me, they are the least translated forms of these books."

The fact that he used different translations for each Testament added to the many reasons why Mark loved his style of teaching so much. The pastor was not a conformist who felt everyone should use the same version of scripture. He had mentioned to the congregation many times how he had taken the time to read all the different translations of scripture and concluded that these were the best for him.

"Are you ready to stroll back a few thousand years with me?" asked the professor, leaning forward in his chair.

"Yes, please. Let's go."

CHAPTER 26

ROAD MAP

The pastor opened the very front of his Hebrew Bible and began to scan it. Mark leaned forward and noticed that each verse on the page was marked with a different color pencil. There were words and thoughts written all over the margins. He couldn't believe the amount of studying the pastor must have done over the years to make sense of everything that was on there.

"Let's go back to the earliest reference of a soul that Moses described in Genesis, chapter two, verse seven."

He turned the Tanakh around to face Mark and pointed at the verse.

"Go ahead and read the verses to yourself but tell me what you think they are saying."

Mark always felt intimated reading scriptures aloud due to the unusual way they were written and was glad the pastor didn't request he read them out loud. He looked down at the verse and read it.

> *And the Lord God formed man of dust from the ground, and He breathed into his nostrils the soul of life, and man became a living soul.*

Mark thought about it for a moment before commenting.

"Adam's body was created first, and he didn't become a living person until his spirit entered it."

"Great explanation, Mark. His matter was created here on earth, but his spirit was brought from elsewhere and put into his body. The scriptures teach that our spirits originated somewhere else and are older than our bodies. In essence, our bodies cannot exist without them."

The pastor reached over and thumbed to the next verse quickly.

"Take a look at Daniel, chapter eight, verses fifteen and sixteen. Tell me the interesting characteristic of our spirits mentioned in those verses."

Now it came to pass when I, Daniel, perceived that vision, that I sought understanding, and behold, there stood before me one who appeared like a man.

And I heard the voice of a man in the midst of the Ulai, and he called and said, Gabriel, enable this one to understand the vision.

"The voice called the spirit Gabriel that appeared to Daniel," Mark said, hoping he was right.

"You are correct yet again. When spirits manifest themselves, they appear just like these verses suggest, like a man, and they have names. They can be very tangible when necessary. Look at first Kings, nineteen, verses five and six."

He lay and slept underneath one juniper and behold! an angel touched him and said to him: Rise and eat.

And he looked, and at his head, there was a cake baked on hot coals and a flask of water. He ate and drank and again he lay down.

Mark thought for a moment but couldn't come up with anything regarding this event. He immediately thought back to feeling Abigail's hand on his shoulder. He looked at the pastor and shrugged his shoulders.

"These verses deal with the prophet Elijah. He felt an angel touch him. Just like Abigail touching you. You also mentioned that the smell of her perfume let you know when she was close by. I would call your experience with her a home run of spiritual interaction."

The pastor closed the Tanakh and opened his New Revised scriptures.

Pieces of the puzzling questions Mark had written down for the pastor started to fall into place. Each verse he had read shed additional light on the relationship between the body and spirit.

Mark could see the excitement in the pastor's face when he slid the New Testament over toward him.

"Jesus's apostles wanted to stress to the early Christian saints that knowledge of one's spirit was equally important as that of our bodies. Look at James, chapter two, verse twenty-six."

> *For just as the body without the spirit is dead, so faith without works is also dead.*

Mark didn't have a chance to say anything before the pastor continued. "Same thing we learned in Genesis regarding Adam, right? One more verse just popped into my head. Look at Hebrews, chapter one, verse fourteen. I didn't have a chance to tab that one, so go ahead and locate that one if you would."

Mark began to flip through the pages, and the book of Hebrews seemed to fall open, much to his relief.

> *Are not all angels spirits in the divine service, sent to serve for the sake of those who are to inherit salvation?*

Mark thought for a moment when the meaning suddenly hit him. "Abigail is reaching out to me to provide a divine service to those of us trying to inherit salvation in our current state." He was surprised that he grasped the concept so quickly.

The pastor smiled broadly and nodded his head in agreement, without saying a word.

"That brings up another question I just thought of. When I asked her what dimension she was in, she corrected me and said I was currently in the third realm, and she was from the fourth realm. Is there anything about realms or dimensions in the scriptures?"

"Glad you asked. There are many realms and heavens mentioned in the scriptures and other religious teachings. Let me show you."

CHAPTER 27

MANY REALMS

The number of books on the pastor's wall impressed Mark a great deal. He didn't think anyone could have more than Professor Windham had in his office but figured the pastor would win if he took the time to count them.

He could tell that Brother Watts's mind had kicked into overdrive by the number of books he was taking off his shelves. After several minutes, he had another dozen books piled next to his scriptures. From the smile on his face, Mark could tell the pastor was thoroughly enjoying taking him on this scripture hunt.

"Mark, there is a common thread in all major religions that deals with what theologians have termed realms, spirit worlds, or heavens that I think ties in with what philosophers and scientists have called dimensions. I believe they are all talking about the same thing. Now I want you to look at some references that come to mind from a few different religious books."

The pastor opened a page of a book that Mark did not recognize. He slid the Quran toward Mark.

"Look at these verses from the holy book of Islam that deal with what we have been discussing."

Mark's eyes went right to the verse the pastor had highlighted in yellow. The verse mentioned the seven heavens Allah had created. The pastor then had him read some other verses that spoke of the angels of these heavens being messengers, which corroborated the verses he had read previously.

Mark had never really thought of looking to other religious books to validate his Christian beliefs and was surprised to learn they were there.

The pastor continued to hand Mark different books. He had him read entries in the Samsara, a book that deals with the teachings of Buddha, that showed references to multiple heavens.

He read from a book on Hindu teachings that showed they too believe in seven heavens, or *lokas*.

Then he read from the books the pastor had that dealt with Greek and Roman polytheism that explained their gods resided in multiple dwellings in the heavens.

When he finished reading, Mark sat back in the chair, rubbing his temples with his fingers. Thinking about all the similarities of these religious teachings from around the world was starting to give him a headache. He was beginning to realize that the world, and all the people who inhabit it, did not seem so far removed or distant anymore. The commonality he felt with humanity was reassuring to him.

After he had a few moments to gather his thoughts, Mark realized there was a piece missing from his stroll through other theologies.

"Brother Watts, you mentioned that these other religions agreed with our Christian beliefs on multiple realms or heavens, but you haven't shown me any verses in our scriptures that touch on it."

Brother Watts shot him a look of surprise.

"That is right, Mark. I failed to show you those first, and I apologize."

He quickly grabbed the New Testament and almost immediately turned to the verse he was after. "Read John, chapter fourteen, verse two if you would."

> *My Father's house has many rooms; if that were not so, would I have told you that I am going there to prepare a place for you?*

"A room and a realm are the same things then?" Mark asked for clarification.

"Yes. The rooms refer to kingdoms, heavens, or realms if you will. Now look at second Corinthians, twelve, verse two."

I know a man in Christ who fourteen years ago was caught up to the third heaven. Whether it was in the body or out of the body I do not know—God knows.

Mark gave the pastor a blank stare.

"The apostle Paul was speaking about a Christian man he knew who was caught up in the third heaven. The concept of multiple kingdoms or heavens was not lost on the early saints like it is today. Like the experience of this early saint, who was able to witness another heaven or realm, I imagine your body must have had a change for you to witness Abigail's realm for yourself."

The pastor paused and looked him up and down for a moment. Mark figured it was to see if he could notice a tangible change in his appearance.

"You mentioned you felt like you were floating and that the visit with her turned out to be a lot longer than you thought. It seems that time is different in the next realm and must be part of the physical change. Going back to Lazarus, he probably thought he was gone for quite a while in the spiritual realm and would've been surprised when he was told he had been dead for four days."

The pastor reached over and grabbed the Tanakh again.

"I want to show you a couple of verses that deal with a few of the ancient prophets who experienced the realm you did. Go to second Kings, chapter two, verse eleven."

And it was that they were going, walking and talking, and behold a fiery chariot and fiery horses, and they separated them both. And Elijah ascended to heaven in a whirlwind.

Before Mark could comment, the professor turned to another section. "And now Ezekiel, chapter eight, verse three."

And it stretched out a form of a hand, and it took me by a lock of my hair, and a wind picked me up between the earth and between the heaven, and it brought me to Jerusalem in the visions of God, to the entrance of the inner gate that faces north, whereat was the seat of the image of jealousy that provokes jealousy.

"There are many different ways a man can experience this transformation to witness another realm or be taken to it," Mark said, amazed.

He realized his soul must have been caught up between the cemetery and the fourth realm to witness what he did.

The pastor continued. "You can see that Elijah was taken directly into heaven without tasting a mortal death in the flesh, and Ezekiel was allowed to access and view the realm that exists between earth and heaven in the flesh, just like you did."

"But you mentioned there was a tie-in with dimensions. How does that play in here?" Mark asked, trying to understand how they connected.

"Thanks for the reminder. Back to the great philosopher Aristotle, who lived about four hundred years before Christ. He mentioned dimensions in his writings on the heavens. The study of heavens and dimensions was done to understand where the gods dwelt and was likely one study by these early philosophers. Only within the last few centuries has the study been broken out between science and religion. I must admit that I'm a little jealous of the gift you have been given and would encourage you to meet with Abigail to gain more insight."

The pastor sat back in his chair and let out a deep sigh, putting his hands behind his head.

Mark realized the answers to his questions had always been there, and he was truly grateful for the knowledge that the pastor had. It would've taken him years to learn everything they had just discussed.

It wasn't just happenstance that he was here at this moment. His grandfather knew he needed to attend the University of Maryland to attend the only class that could teach him how to use his gift. Now that he had used his gift to open the channel of communication with Abigail, she had helped plant the questions in his mind that prompted him to meet with the pastor. The pastor happened to know Mark's family well, which created an instant connection of trust between the two of them.

The symmetry of it all confirmed to Mark that he was on the right path. He now felt he had the direction he needed for future visits with Abigail.

Mark noticed the pastor was giving him a strange look each time he turned to face him while returning the books to the shelves.

"What is it, Brother Watts?"

The pastor stopped and looked directly into Mark's eyes.

"Mark, it might be the lighting in here, but your eyes look different to me. They look like a lighter shade of blue."

The pastor walked over and adjusted the blinds that were hitting Mark directly in the face.

"Look straight at me."

Mark had a hard time keeping his gaze. It always made him uncomfortable to look directly at someone who was staring right at him. He did his best to keep his gaze.

"Yes, your eyes seem a lighter blue. How strange," was all the pastor offered.

Mark was too overwhelmed with what they had just discussed to start up a conversation about eye color, and he felt like he had taken enough of the pastor's time.

"Thanks for the time, Brother Watts. You've been a huge help." He stood up and was about to leave when the pastor reached into his desk drawer and pulled out a piece of paper. He placed it in Mark's hand.

"Here is a list of events in the scriptures that deal with our soul that I compiled years ago that might give you further insights. Hopefully I've given you the answers you were looking for. Whatever Abigail wants from you, have faith in God that he will lead you to understand and see it through. Just remember that you can get a lot of answers to life's questions by regularly attending church." The pastor chuckled again and walked with Mark to the door.

"Sure, Brother Watts. You know I love coming to your service." Mark gave him a fist bump and exited his office.

When he left the church, he turned his phone back on and noticed a text from Stacie that alarmed him.

"Mark, something is wrong with Paul. Meet us at his dormitory. Please hurry."

CHAPTER 28

UNSETTLING EVENT

Approaching Paul's building, Mark noticed Stacie running toward him with a look of panic on her face. Jeremy was close behind her with the same look.

"I'm worried something is wrong with Paul," Stacie said, giving Mark a big hug.

Mark's first reaction was to make a wisecrack that there were a lot of things wrong with Paul, but he refrained.

Stacie grabbed him by the arm and pulled him toward the entrance. He could feel the clamminess of Stacie's hands on his bare skin and knew something was worrying her.

They made their way to Paul's dorm room, which was at the end of the hall on the bottom floor. When they got to the door, Mark put one hand on the knob to try to open it and felt something unusual. The doorknob was unusually cold to the touch. He put his other hand on the door itself and noticed the same thing.

"How long have you been trying to get a hold of him? How do you know he's even in there?" Mark asked, looking back at her and Jeremy.

"We agreed to meet outside my building to study after church, but when I got there, he wasn't there. I figured he had slept in, so I came here to get him. When I knocked on the door the first time, it sounded like I heard him moan inside. I've tried knocking on the door, calling, and texting him, but I can't get a hold of him. His car is outside, so I know he's in there."

Jeremy nodded in agreement. "Stacie's right. I tried banging on the door but can't get him to respond."

"Where is his roommate?"

"Paul told me he went to see his folks for the weekend. I think he's in there and he's in trouble," Stacie said, placing her ear up against the door.

Jeremy reached over the top of them and began to pound on the door. "P-dog, you better be playing around, bro."

Stacie backed away, rubbing her ear from the loud sound of Jeremy's knock.

Mark backed him off and put his ear up against the door but didn't hear anything. He knelt again and reached his fingers under the door. He noticed the air on the other side was cold and wondered if he had an air-conditioning unit on full blast.

"I'm done playing his game. I'm going to go find someone to let us in," said Jeremy, walking off quickly.

Mark decided to see if he could see into Paul's room from the window outside while Stacie waited there.

When he got there, the window was a little taller than he expected. He stood upon the tops of his toes, but the blinds were shut tight, and he couldn't get a look in.

He had just rejoined Stacie at the door when Jeremy showed up with a college-aged superintendent who did not look very happy he had been interrupted.

The young man quickly unlocked the door and walked off without saying a word to any of them.

Although Stacie constantly vouched for Paul to be included in their friend group, there was something about him that Mark did not like. He didn't know what they would find upon entering the room.

Mark took a deep breath and began to open the door slowly. A blast of cold air hit him and brought shivers up and down his back upon entering the darkened room.

Mark noticed the outline of a body under the blankets on one of the beds. "P-dog, you all right?" Mark asked. There was no answer.

Mark reached along the wall to his right and flicked on the light. Paul was lying motionless on his bed, with only the top of his head visible.

Stacie rushed around Mark and kneeled by his bed. "Paul. Are you okay?" she asked, shaking his shoulders.

Jeremy then moved past Mark and pulled back the covers.

Mark was alarmed to see how pale he was but was relieved to see he was breathing. He sat down toward the bottom of the bed and noticed that his sheets were cold and a little damp. Looking around, he was surprised to see there was no air-conditioning unit in the room.

Jeremy joined Stacie in shaking Paul, and his eyelids opened just a little.

Paul slowly moved his arms up and wrapped them around himself, trying to get warm. "I don't feel good," he said, closing his eyes again.

Mark's initial thought was he must have partied too hard the night before and had a massive hangover.

"I'm going to call for an ambulance," Jeremy said, pulling out his phone.

While Jeremy and Stacie were relaying information to the emergency operator, Mark continued to scan the room for anything out of the ordinary.

It didn't take him long to notice a strange-looking object lying in between the two beds on the floor. At first glance, he thought it was a crude art project. He leaned over to take a closer look and noticed it was oblong and made from some sort of clay. It had some writings imprinted on it that started on an outside edge and worked their way into the center, where there was a red stone or jewel.

He reached down and picked it up.

Almost immediately, he felt a sudden surge of violent thoughts race through his mind regarding Paul. All the negative thoughts he had toward him over the past few weeks rushed to the surface of his mind. He quickly put the object on a desk that was at the end of Paul's roommate's bed. The negative thoughts vanished.

What was that?

The sound of the approaching sirens caught their attention, and Jeremy rushed out of the room to go meet the ambulance.

Within minutes, the room was filled with emergency personnel attending to Paul.

During the chaos, Mark turned his focus back toward the object, and he was about to pick it up again when one of the paramedics asked for all three of them to follow her outside.

The paramedic asked for a full recap of the events. Stacie went over her plans to meet up with him, and then Jeremy jumped in to explain the events leading up to their emergency call. They all vouched that they did not know of any medications or addictions that Paul had, and with that, they loaded him in the ambulance and drove away.

They made their way back to Paul's room to lock it up, and Mark could tell that Stacie was shaken by what had happened.

"He'll be okay, Stace," he said, putting his arm around her and pulling her close. "Has anything like this happened to him before?"

"No, I've never seen him like this. I don't know what could've happened."

Mark realized he had not filled them in on his visit with Abigail the night before, but he felt it wasn't the right time to bring it up.

All of them just stood there in silence for a few moments, looking around his room.

When Stacie and Jeremy walked over to make up Paul's bed, Mark's eyes were drawn back to the object again. For whatever reason, he had a feeling he shouldn't touch it directly and decided to use a couple of paper towels that were sitting on a microwave on top of the desk to pick it up.

He walked it over to his friends. "Have you guys seen this before?" Mark held the object out in front of them.

Stacie glanced at it. "No. Where did you find that?"

"I noticed it on the floor between the beds."

"I remember him saying his roommate was an art major. Maybe it's one of his projects?" Jeremy offered.

"I need to go up to the hospital and make sure he's okay," said Stacie, pulling Jeremy past Mark and out the door. Mark slipped the object into his jacket pocket and closed the door behind him.

The knob was not cold anymore.

Mark had a feeling the object he was holding played a part in what happened to Paul, and he needed to find out what it was.

CHAPTER 29

THE PATH IS SET

After relaying everything that happened the day before, Mark sat with wide-eyed anticipation while Professor Windham studied the strange object Mark held out in front of him. He had decided he couldn't wait until their class that coming Friday and was happy to catch the professor in between classes that Monday morning.

"I'm sorry to hear what happened to Paul. This is a most unusual object," said the professor, moving back and forth to view it from several different angles. "Whatever it is, the text looks to be written in Latin. Unfortunately, my one semester of Latin will do us little good here."

Mark was put off by the professor's response. He had gone out of his way to meet with the professor and thought if anybody would have an idea of what the object was, it would be him.

"Set it down here on my desk, directly under my light here."

Mark carefully sat it down on his desk under a bright lamp.

The professor took off his glasses and moved in closer. Mark in turn moved in closer and noticed something he had failed to previously. Under the bright light, the stone in the middle seemed to glow a brilliant red. He could also see some finger impressions on one side that suggested it was made by hand.

106

Mark broke the silence. "We thought it might have been Paul's roommate's since he is an art major. But Stacie found out from Paul at the hospital that he found it outside the library on the ground."

"Outside of the library?" the professor asked, keeping his focus on the object while stroking his chin.

"Yes. From what Stacie told me, Paul was walking home from a party Saturday night after the game and was passing the library when he noticed someone walking straight toward him. The person stopped about ten feet in front of him and placed something on the ground, then took off in the other direction. Paul walked over and picked up the object. When he began walking back to his dorm, he had a feeling that someone was following him. He kept looking around but didn't see anyone. He mentioned to Stacie feeling a strange coldness when he made his way down the hall to his room. Everything went black once he entered his room. The next thing he knew, we were in his room waking him up. I noticed the same coldness when we entered his room."

The professor looked up from the object and gave Mark a look of concern.

"What did the hospital say had happened to him?"

"The only explanation the hospital had was that he had suffered a severe panic attack. Paul said it wasn't a panic attack and told Stacie it was holding the object that caused all of it. Once he held it in his hand, he was not able to let go of it. While he was blacked out, he said he had the most horrible dreams that he could not wake up from."

Mark couldn't tell whether the look of concern on the professor's face was for Paul or something else.

"Mark, you need to find Marianne and explain what has happened to her," said the professor abruptly.

Mark thought his request was out of the blue and noticed the professor's reaction was like the one he had when he showed him Marianne's notebook.

Before he could ask why, the professor hastily folded the paper towels back over the object and handed it back to him.

Mark didn't turn to leave, hoping that delaying his exit would make the professor elaborate.

It didn't.

The professor grabbed his briefcase. "Please come see me before Friday's class if you can meet up with Marianne."

Without giving him a chance to ask why, the professor walked out of the office, leaving Mark there alone.

CHAPTER 30

CONVENIENT SURPRISE

Mark was making his way to his next class using a seldom-used shortcut. He kept wondering why the professor had wanted him to reach out to Marianne about the object he found and how he was going to do it.

He was lost in thought when he heard a familiar voice from behind. "It's good to see you are still a part of the living and have not crossed over to the other side."

Mark whirled around to see Marianne smiling at him. He was not expecting to run into her using the same shortcut.

"Yes, it would appear so." Mark patted his body with his hands, gesturing to her that he was real.

Marianne walked up to him and took him by the arm without saying anything, then continued walking in the same direction. Mark wasn't sure how he was going to bring up the subject of the object he was carrying or his experience with Paul.

Marianne moved closer to Mark to keep warm as the wind howled through the small opening between two buildings they were passing. Mark put his arm around her to pull her close. He could tell that there was no hesitation on her part anymore.

"What's that?" she asked, leaning against the object in his jacket.

Mark didn't say anything, surprised that she had even noticed it.

"Are you carrying a gun for protection?" she asked with a playful smile. She tapped the object with her knuckles a few times and laughed.

Mark felt like there was no better time to bring it up.

"Funny you should ask," he said, pulling the covered object out of his pocket. "I was just with Professor Windham, and you said the last time we talked that if I had any other questions about the class or weird things happening, I could reach out to you. Well, I found something yesterday that I wanted to ask you about."

Marianne scooped it out of his hand, and the paper towels fell open, revealing the object.

Mark was relieved to see it was not touching her directly.

"Do you know what it might be?"

Marianne looked down at it and stopped abruptly. She looked back up at Mark with a look of terror on her face. Suddenly, all the color from her face drained out, and she staggered back a little.

Mark quickly caught her arm and pulled her over to a nearby bike rack to lean against, where she hurriedly handed the object back to him.

He sat there confused about what was happening.

She buried her face in her hands and then looked up at Mark. "I can't believe everything is happening all over again."

"What's happening again, Marianne?"

"Remember I told you about my experience with the shadow people on my last visit to the cemetery? The night I had my experience with them, I noticed a small object on one of the cenotaphs next to me. It didn't look exactly like the one you're holding, but it was similar. I was holding it in my hands when I was attacked."

Mark noticed her gaze did not leave the object, and her whole body started to quiver.

"Mark, you need to get away from everything that has happened and get rid of that thing so no one can ever find it. I'm telling you that we are not meant to get involved with anything outside our path here in this life," she said, pleading with him. She grabbed his free hand and held it tightly in hers.

Mark could tell he better not push for more information and gave her a few moments to calm down. Although he was touched by her concern, it bothered him that she had given up on her gift and was trying to make him do the same. He felt she needed to know where he stood.

"Marianne, I can't just walk away and forget everything. I have so many more questions that need to be answered from the experiences I've had."

"Push those questions and experiences you've had far away from your memory. There is a battle that is going on for our souls that we are not equipped to fight. If you care about your family and friends, you'll stop involving yourself."

Her statement regarding a battle for souls confirmed the reason Abigail had reached out to them both.

Marianne turned away from him, looking in the other direction.

"I didn't realize the damage my ability was doing until it was too late. My involvement caused my roommate to withdraw from school."

"Do you mind telling me what happened to her?" Mark asked calmly, hoping he was not prying too deep.

Marianne turned to face him slowly and then looked up at him with regret. "The same night I had my experience in the cemetery, I came back to our room shaken and went straight to bed. I don't know how that object made its way into my book bag, as I clearly remember leaving it in the cemetery. She must have found it while I was asleep. I woke up the next morning, and she was gone. I asked around to see if anyone had seen her, and one of the girls down the hall said they had found her in the hallway the night before, crouched into a ball and unable to move, after hearing her scream. The only information they could get from her was that she was being attacked by something evil."

"Do you think they were the same things that attacked you?"

"I have no doubt. There is something to these objects that must call to them."

"Did they happen to mention any unusual coldness when they found her?" Mark asked.

"Yes. Yes, they did. When they went over to help her up, she was cold to the touch. They helped her to her car, and she said she was going to go home. I tried calling her several times over the next few weeks, but she never returned my calls. I haven't seen her since."

"What happened to the object?" Mark asked, hoping she still had it so he could compare them.

"I don't know if she threw it away or what, but I do know you shouldn't be walking around with it."

With all the similarities between what happened to her roommate and Paul, Mark decided to tell her about his experience of finding his. When he finished, she was shaking her head back and forth. She was about to say something when there was a silent buzz on her cell phone. She glanced down to read something.

"Mark, I've got to drive a friend to an appointment in five minutes, but I'm warning you to push all of this aside before it's too late. You see what these types of objects can do. I would get rid of it and pray no one ever finds it."

She gave him a look of concern and then walked off.

Part of him wanted to do what she said and get rid of the object before something happened to him. But before he did, he decided to ask one more person about it.

CHAPTER 31

TREPIDATION

Mark felt a little awkward dropping in on Pastor Watts again so quickly. Approaching his office, he heard him talking to someone on the phone in fluent Spanish. This gave him hope that the pastor would be able to decipher what the inscription said, at the very least. Mark had looked up the first couple of words on the way over and confirmed they were Latin. The pastor often talked about the importance Latin language had in religion and how it aided the spread of Christianity around the world.

Mark waited just outside his office. The ten minutes it took the pastor to conclude his conversation seemed like forever. When the pastor said goodbye, Mark quickly entered the room, much to the surprise of the pastor.

"Back so soon. Did you have questions from those verses I gave you?"

"I'm sorry, but I haven't. I need your help with something else I found yesterday after we spoke." Mark placed the object on his desk and opened it. "Be careful not to touch it."

The pastor looked at Mark and then at the object with a raised eyebrow.

"I can't explain it, but it fills your mind with terrible thoughts and images if you touch it directly."

Mark was happy to see that the pastor trusted him. He picked it up using the paper towels and studied it for a few moments. Mark wondered if he could sense its darkness because a strange look of concern crossed his face.

"It looks to me like a charm of some sort. Where did you find this?"

"From one of Stacie's friends. I was hoping you could read the inscription on it. One of my professors said it was written in Latin, but he couldn't interpret it."

The pastor held it closer and began to rotate it slowly while following the inscription to the center. The pastor suddenly stopped and looked at Mark with surprise.

"Mark, I can understand most of it, but the last part seems to be an incantation that needs to be read out loud. I feel impressed not to do that. However, I can write down most of it for you if you would like."

Mark agreed and waited eagerly for the pastor to write down the translation on a pad of paper. When he finished, he handed it to Mark.

> Endless are our days to rule and subjugate. Power and greater understanding are what will be bestowed to those who assist us in taking back what is rightfully ours. Open the door of eternal wisdom by repeating aloud—

Mark was amazed at the pastor's ability to translate it so quickly. "Why would someone leave something like this for our friend to find? I mean, there's no way he could've known what it said."

"I'm guessing whoever left this was hoping your friend would simply translate this on a computer and then unknowingly read it aloud. This is disturbing, Mark. What ended up happening to your friend?"

Mark relayed the events of obtaining it and spoke in greater detail about the evil thoughts he had when he touched it. He noticed the pastor jotting down notes while he talked. When he finished, the pastor stood up and took a large book from the top shelf.

"There are many kinds of spiritual or mystical charms out there, Mark. Most of them have a very specific purpose, and I believe you have what is called a portal key."

"A what?"

"Historically, it is an object used to open a door, or gateway. People through the ages have used all sorts of charms to try to open doors into other spiritual realms. The writings on this object suggest it was created to summon something evil into our world. I'm not quite sure what the gemstone in the center is for, but this looks like it was made quite recently."

The pastor started thumbing through the book and landed on a page with several artifacts. He turned it around for Mark to look at. Mark noticed many of the objects resembled the one he had brought.

"Even though the object appears to be made recently, the incantation that's written on it in Latin appears to be ancient in origin. Whoever placed it on the ground for your friend to find knew exactly what they were doing. The person who made this would have a good knowledge of the history of charms and how to use them. There also appears to be a specific curse placed on it, which would explain what happened to your friend—and you when you touched it directly."

The fact that someone had purposely been leaving cursed objects around made Mark sick to his stomach. It was starting to dawn on him why Marianne had been so forceful with her warnings for him to stop what he was doing.

Mark's attention was drawn back when the pastor started talking about the many types of charms and objects mentioned in the book that claimed to have mystical powers associated with them.

The pastor touched on the Hindu and Buddhist Cintamani stone, the alchemist philosopher's stone, and the Christian Spear of Destiny. Mark was surprised at the number of different objects that were out there.

"There are many religious artifacts in the world, and most of them have a spiritual and sacred meaning. Go into many of the holiest places around the world, and you will be amazed at all the symbolic objects. However, some organizations out there claim to be a religion for the good of mankind but have secret operations that are for evil purposes. They use these objects to conjure the wrong kind of spirit or spirits. It was no coincidence that you came into possession of this object, Mark. Someone knows about your ability, and that of your friends, and is trying to use your gifts to open a door that should not be opened."

Mark made a mental list of those who knew about his gift. He quickly arrived at the one person who was orchestrating all his moves over the past few months. Professor Windham.

Mark noticed the pastor staring at him, waiting for a response.

"Thanks for all of the information, Brother Watts," he said, glancing at his cell phone. "I'd better run. I promise to see you this Sunday and to look up those other verses you gave me yesterday."

The pastor walked around the desk and looked at Mark with deep concern. "Be careful, Mark. Wherever there is light, there is also darkness. Just remain faithful and prayerful that you will be protected. I will also pray for you."

Mark smiled at him confidently even though the pastor's words regarding the darkness worried him on the inside. "I will, and I appreciate your prayers for me."

Mark quickly wrapped up the object, put it back in his jacket pocket, and left.

During the walk back to his dorm, he noticed about twenty texts from Stacie and Jeremy, wondering where he was and if he wanted to go with them to visit Paul. He decided not to reply, realizing they had most likely left. Instead, he decided to get something to eat. He wanted some alone time to plan out his next steps.

Making his way past a wide opening toward the student housing, a stiff fall wind began to pick up that had a cold bite to it.

He put his hands deep in his jacket pockets to keep them warm. When he clutched the object with his right hand, he noticed something different. The object was warm to the touch.

Noticing he was alone, he carefully unwrapped it. The gemstone in the center appeared to be glowing. He looked at it from many different angles, assuming the last bit of light from the setting sun was hitting it just right. Mark didn't realize the paper towels had split open beneath the charm, and it was touching his skin directly.

A rustle in a group of bushes to his right caught his attention. He turned to let his eyes focus on the spot for a moment and noticed a dark shadow that began to take a human shape. The presence of the figure moving toward him kept him frozen in place.

The object was becoming uncomfortably hot. He tried with all his might to let go of it but couldn't.

Thick darkness enveloped him.

CHAPTER 32

AGENT OF DARKNESS

Mark could not comprehend what was happening. The darkness that had gathered around him felt heavy, like someone had put a thick, cold blanket on him. His breathing became labored. The electric feelings he had from his previous visits with his grandfather and Abigail were replaced by sharp pinpricks moving throughout his body.

Through the darkness, he could barely make out the campus. That scenery in every direction was soon replaced by a vast wasteland of charred earth and decaying structures. He tried to scream out, but his voice was muted in the hellish realm that he was trapped in.

He couldn't believe there was no one around to notice what was happening. The campus was usually busy this time of night. Realizing the full magnitude of his predicament, he mustered up the courage to speak.

"Who are you and what do you want?"

"It was you who summoned me," the voice said, coming from all around. The words sounded gargled and seemed to echo through the darkness. They didn't sound human.

"I didn't summon you. I have not repeated any of the inscription. Now, who are you?"

Within seconds, the darkness moved around Mark, and a portion of it condensed into a human form standing directly in front of him. He could almost make out a silhouette of a man, but the form twitched in and out of focus.

"I value your interest. I am one of the nameless. If you must attach an identity to my form, you may call me Koltar. It is you who will help me usher in a new beginning for those of my kind."

Even though the thought of continuing to converse with this dark being frightened him to his core, he knew he needed to buy some time to find a way out of his predicament.

"Why did you call yourself the nameless?"

"Let's just say the realm where I come from does not require an identity. With your help in opening the door to your realm, I will be able to wield an influence of change for the benefit of mankind," Koltar said assuredly.

Mark was in shock. "I don't understand what door I could've opened for you."

"You've had an encounter with someone from the fourth realm, have you not?"

How does he know about Abigail?

The thought that this being was aware of their visit made it even harder for him to breathe.

"There are a lot of things that I know about you. I've been monitoring the progress of your ability for quite some time, and there is no question you possess the gift. You have squandered it long enough. Let me teach you the true path of your ability."

The negative thoughts that he encountered when he first touched the object started to arise. The amount of focus it took him to keep them at bay was making his head throb with pain.

"I still don't understand why you need me."

"I cannot simply walk through a door that has been sealed shut by the ignorant. It must be opened by someone like you. You have the power to visit multiple realms, and that is a power that is not given to anyone in my state. We are relying on you to create the path for us. We can offer you the treasures of the world for your efforts if you assist us. Can the creator promise you the same?"

Mark's ears perked up when Koltar mentioned the creator, and he wondered if he was talking about God.

The struggle to maintain control of his mind was becoming too much, and he longed to end the conversation.

"I will not help you no matter what you promise."

"It is what I can do to you if you do not help me that you should be concerned with." Koltar's voice grew more menacing. "I know about your sister, mother, and friends. Now that I'm close to completing my charge, you will help me, or they will suffer for your impudence. What happened to your friend was only a taste of what I'm capable of."

Mark could feel the panic set in from learning that Koltar knew about all his family and friends.

"Just leave them out of it. They have nothing to do with this."

For the first time since their conversation started, Mark could tell he was able to move his arm a little bit.

"Only you can determine what happens to them. If you close off your ability and choose not to see your task through to completion, you will seal their fate."

The warning for him to not close his ability made him wonder if he was a member of the shadow people who possessed Marianne.

"Again, I don't know why you need me. You have someone creating these charms for you. Have them do it." Mark hoped to get more information on who it was that was helping.

"The person that created the object in your hand does not have the gift you possess. He is only responsible for setting these events in motion and will earn his reward. You can save me time by reading the full inscription on the charm. I will help you complete it."

Mark could feel his free hand reaching for the piece of paper the pastor handed him that was in his pocket. He tried to stop himself from grabbing it, but his hand pulled it out and held it in front of him. The longer he stayed trapped in this conversation, the easier it was for Koltar to control his actions. He knew the only recourse he had was to do what the pastor had instructed and say a prayer.

With all the sincerity he could muster, he prayed for divine help to be released from Koltar's power.

Within seconds of saying the prayer, he managed to slowly crumple up the piece of paper in his left hand and toss it to the ground.

Koltar bellowed out a loud moan, and Mark felt an intense pressure begin to build around him. All the pain he had felt in his life, including his parents' divorce and the death of his grandparents, welled back up within him. Koltar's form moved within a few inches of Mark's face.

"It is no use resisting me. You see the power I have over you. It would be a shame to destroy you now and make you waste your gift before you realize its true potential."

Mark fell to his knees and could feel Koltar's form exerting extreme pressure around his head, and he began to lose consciousness.

CHAPTER 33

TIMELESS BATTLE

Within a matter of moments, a light started to penetrate the darkness that swirled around Mark. It began to spread around him like a warm blanket. The cold darkness began to dissipate, and he could feel the weight on him start to lift. Koltar's shadowy figure started to jerk in several different motions and let out a very different kind of moan than before.

Mark regained control of his body and stood up quickly.

A familiar voice instructed him to throw the object on the ground. His right hand loosened, and he dropped it. Within seconds of the object hitting the ground, the light enveloped Koltar's figure completely.

"There is another way to open the door, and it will be to your loved one's ruin," screeched Koltar before fading from view.

Mark whirled around to find Abigail standing near him with a look of relief. She turned to him and pointed at the object on the ground.

"Mark, you need to get that portal key away from you."

Mark kicked the object off the walkway onto the grass and sat down on the opposite side, trying to regain his composure. It surprised him that she used the same term Pastor Watts used earlier.

He looked up and noticed Abigail was waiting patiently while keeping her gaze on him. From her expression, he could tell that this was not how she wanted to find him.

"How did you know I was in trouble?"

"Let's just say you have others who are watching out for you, and they informed me of your situation," Abigail said, a smile returning to her face.

Mark felt a peaceful assurance wash over him. "It was my grandfather, wasn't it?"

"Yes, it was. Your bond with him is still very tight. Although he could not intervene on your behalf, he moved quickly to alert me."

Abigail turned her attention back to the object.

"Thank you for being strong enough not to read the inscription on that portal key. I'm afraid they have an advocate in your realm who is helping them accelerate their plans, and we are going to need more help than I thought to keep them shut out. Since your realm has been compromised, we need to move into mine. Relax your mind, Mark, and follow me."

Mark calmed his mind, and within moments, the college campus faded from view and was replaced by her realm. However, this visit was different. In every direction he looked, Mark could see more souls than before going about the tasks they had been given. Many of them acknowledged his presence with a pleasant smile and appeared happy that he was there.

Mark enjoyed the feeling of joy wash over him. The thoughts of dread that had just held him captive faded from his mind. He was grateful Abigail gave him time to take it all in for a moment.

"Abigail, I'm so glad you showed up. I promise you that I didn't do anything to bring that thing here."

She moved directly in front of him and laid her hands on his shoulders.

"I trust you wouldn't. Please explain to me what happened."

Mark took a moment to walk Abigail through the events leading up to her intervention. He noticed that once he mentioned Koltar and his ability to see into its realm, she became even more alarmed.

"Mark, because of the power you have to travel to different realms, you must be extra careful. Yours is a very rare gift. You must find out who is placing these portal keys and stop them from creating more of them. I will try to find out how you can destroy them and stop what's coming.

Koltar's initial plan of getting you to read the inscription has failed, but I'm sure he has initiated another plan."

Mark looked at Abigail in shock. "What do you mean I have to destroy *them*? How many are there?"

"I would imagine this person is creating enough for your friends to find since they have your gift or at least a portion of it. I'm afraid I'm not privy to the exact number. Koltar will try to bring harm to anyone who will not help him, so time is of the essence."

Abigail's words overwhelmed him. Not only did he have to find out who was placing them, but he had to be on the lookout for multiple portal keys before his friends got hurt.

"I mentioned to you that Koltar pulled me into his realm, which I assume is the second realm. Do you know anything about that realm and who Koltar is?"

"His is not a realm of progression but damnation. He needed the portal key to pull you into his realm so he could communicate more readily and reveal more of himself to you."

Mark was surprised that she referred to Koltar as a male, even though he assumed that was the case.

"It is the curse that has been placed on it that invited him then?"

"Exactly. A being from their realm must be aided or invited to make themselves known to someone in your realm. They cannot do it on their own since they have been shut out. Their goal is to cause pain and misery to those of us who can progress. Due to choices made long ago, they will forever be trapped in their state and have been looking for ways to cheat their damnation since they fell."

Her explanation reminded Mark of Pastor Watts's sermon weeks earlier about a war in heaven mentioned in Revelation. He couldn't help but conclude that Koltar was one of the fallen spirits the pastor had talked about.

"Koltar is a fallen angel then?" Mark asked, hoping he was wrong.

"I'm afraid so."

CHAPTER 34

UNWANTED DISCOVERY

Mark cringed at the reality of going up against a fallen angel. His confidence and knowledge of his ability had been growing quickly over the past few weeks, but his run-in with Koltar had shaken him to his core.

"Abigail, you're telling me Koltar is an agent of the devil?"

"Mark, I do not want to understate the power of this agent of darkness. From what I saw happening to you, I would conclude that he is taking his orders from Lucifer himself."

Mark put his hands on his head and let her words sink in for a moment. He could feel himself falling on the inside and was glad he was sitting down.

"How in the world can I stop something like him?"

"To learn how to combat their plan, you will need to contact a special council from my realm. I've been told this council meets in the vicinity of Philadelphia to protect unauthorized access to our realms."

"Philadelphia?"

"Yes. Things are happening too fast for me to uncover on my own and then relay to you. I need to watch for events happening in this vicinity. Independence Hall would be a good starting point. They have been aware of the growing evil in the world and have come up with many interventions over the past few centuries to thwart the evil one's plans. The council is made up of some of the most brilliant souls that ever walked the earth."

"I don't mean any disrespect, Abigail, but since they're in your realm, wouldn't it be quicker if you met with them and I stay here on the lookout?"

"That does seem more logical, doesn't it? However, my understanding of these happenings is still growing, and the information they give you will be meant for you only."

Mark's concentration in the fourth realm was broken when he heard a few students coming near them. He froze in place, letting them walk by.

Abigail laughed, purely amused.

"When will you realize, unless they have the gift you have been given, they are unable to see us? You and I can continue conversing no matter how many people from your realm wander by."

Mark smiled back, a little embarrassed. He knew time was of the essence and steered the conversation back to the council.

"I will travel to Philadelphia to find this council, Abigail. You mentioned Independence Hall, but is there a starting point or anything I should be looking for?" Mark asked, hoping that finding them would be quicker than it was contacting her.

"I would tell you if I knew, but I only know of the council itself. I'm sure they are aware of the events that have been put into motion and will most likely be expecting you."

"I wish the council could just come down here for a visit." Mark realized how lazy his comment sounded once it left his lips.

"Oh, Mark, don't let your grandfather hear you talk like that," Abigail said with a teasing smile.

Mark was glad she did not take offense and took comfort that she mentioned his grandfather again. He looked around to see if he could see his grandfather nearby, but Abigail had already begun to close the portal to her realm around him.

"Please be careful and do exactly what they instruct. I will be here for you and do everything I can to help see your task through."

Mark turned his attention back to the person who was assisting Koltar with his plan. The realization that Professor Windham could be the agent assisting in this devious plan crept into the forefront of his mind and made him swell with anger.

"Abigail, what would I look out for in finding the person who's been helping them?"

"They would most likely have an ancient book of spells that would be unique in its appearance. It would be larger than your average book and stand out. The council should have direction on how to deal with them and break the spell that has been placed on each portal key."

Mark realized he must have been looking at Abigail with a frightened look. She reached out again and placed her hand on his shoulder. He felt her warmth and concern flow through him.

"Mark, you are a brave young man, and I am sorry this task has fallen squarely on your shoulders. This has turned out to be a lot more than even I imagined, and I am afraid I'm still learning ways to assist you. I do not have all the answers, but I will do my best to come better prepared for our next encounter. Until then, farewell, my friend."

When Abigail vanished from sight, Mark realized he had forgotten to ask her what he was going to do with the portal key lying on the grass across from him. He knew he could not be anywhere near it, nor could he let it be found by some innocent student.

He decided to bury it where only he would know where to find it. Noticing two uniquely cut bushes near the closest building, he carefully moved the object over with his foot and dug a shallow hole with his hands. Using his foot, he moved the object into the hole and packed it tightly.

Although he was anxious to get to Philadelphia to find the council, he had to find out if his hunch regarding Professor Windham was correct.

CHAPTER 35

SUSPICION

Mark could tell he was walking too fast for Jeremy to keep up on their way to their Spiritual and Psychic Phenomenon class. He could hear him breathing heavily behind him. He had spent the last few days devising questions to ask the professor that would reveal what he was up to, and he couldn't wait to get there. He didn't want to have another run-in with Koltar. If the professor was truly the one behind it, he was going to find out today.

He had spent most of his time studying everything he could about portal keys, charms, the occult, and any other subject he could find that could shed some light on what he was up against, but it only created more questions.

"Dude, what is your hurry this morning?" Jeremy said, gasping for air.

He slowed down a little to let him catch up. "I just need to get some things answered."

Mark had also spent that week dodging questions from Jeremy and Stacie. He tried to act normal around them but knew they could tell something was weighing him down. He was going to need their help at some point but decided to keep the information he learned from the past week quiet for now, even though it was killing him. He was worried about them finding a portal key of their own, but didn't have a plan in place to destroy them or stop what was coming. He figured the less they knew, the safer they were.

They had just entered the classroom when Mark realized he had not come up with a plan to keep Jeremy from joining his planned interrogation of the professor after class.

He was glad he didn't have to worry about Stacie. She had texted him to let him know Paul did not feel like attending the class and that she was going to stay with him. For some reason, she blamed the professor for what had happened to Paul and had sent additional texts with several questions she wanted Mark to ask him.

When they settled into their seats, Mark and Jeremy began to make small talk with the students around them while they waited for the professor.

Mark listened to everyone begin to one-up the other regarding their experiences with the unseen world over the past week. A few commented on their excitement capturing pictures of orbs with more cemetery visits. Another student mentioned she had some apparition follow her around the Smithsonian museums but could not make definite contact with it.

Mark was tempted to blow them all away with what had happened to him but thought better of it. Jeremy would kill him if he wasn't the first to know.

He watched Jeremy move in closer to ask the girl more questions about her visit to the Smithsonian and wondered why the professor was running so late.

Just then, the professor entered the classroom in a hurry.

"Sorry I'm late, students, but it has been a busy week," he said, out of breath.

I bet it was, Mark thought with contempt as he visualized the professor placing objects all over the campus with a sadistic smile.

Watching his every move intently, Mark could sense that the professor was a little more fidgety than usual while setting up the projector.

"I've got a special treat for you today, class," the professor said, scanning the class until his eyes landed on Mark. "Some things are happening around here that are very exciting and really beyond explanation."

Mark's heart began to beat faster, and he felt assured the professor was involved. He was tempted to start asking the questions he had prepared in front of everyone but decided to wait to see where the professor was going first.

The professor plugged his camera into the projector, and with a flick of a switch, an image of the campus at dusk appeared on the whiteboard.

"Earlier this week, I was just walking around campus, like I often do with my camera in infrared mode, to see what might show up. Like I've mentioned previously, spirits give off heat, which is why I use this camera to capture unusual sightings."

The professor paused when the sound of the wind in the camera mic echoed loudly through the classroom. He quickly adjusted the volume.

"I was just coming down one of the paths from the library toward the student housing when I saw this."

The camera slowly steadied on an area in the middle of a walkway that showed an unusual mass.

Mark's heart sank when he realized the professor was capturing his hellish visit with Koltar on his camera. He couldn't fathom how the professor's camera was able to capture what was happening but people walking by could not notice.

The professor began to play it in slow motion. Several gasps went up from the class.

"At first, I thought it was just the lighting and the shade from the trees due to the setting sun that was causing it," he said, pointing at the image on the whiteboard with his expandable pointer. "But watch what happens when I began to move the camera back and forth."

Mark noticed that no matter which direction the professor moved the camera, it did not affect the size or color of the mass.

"I knew it wasn't my surroundings that were causing it. It was truly a spiritual mass of some sort."

"You were the one who probably summoned it," Mark mumbled out loud. His angry look toward the professor caught Jeremy's attention.

"What is your deal?" Jeremy asked. "You've been looking at the professor like you want to smack him around since he walked in."

Not wanting to create a line of questioning with Jeremy, he changed his expression and shook him off.

The professor continued. "I have only seen this type of energy captured on film one other time. It was on some security footage from one of the girl dormitories over a year ago. Except it wasn't captured using infrared. It was a dark mass at the end of one of the hallways."

Mark realized the professor must have been given the footage of what happened to Marianne's roommate. His mind was caught up between trying to listen to the professor explain the difference between light and dark energy and what Marianne had told him about her experience. He didn't remember her mentioning an unusual mass.

After the video finished playing, the professor explained how rare it was to capture that kind of spiritual mass contained in a single area and how any number of light sources should have interrupted it.

Mark had a hard time buying that the professor had just happened upon him while he was trapped in Koltar's hellish realm. He concluded that the professor must have been following him after he showed him the object earlier in the day.

Thoughts of how long the professor had been orchestrating his every move began to race through his mind. He could feel his anxiousness about meeting with the professor growing.

The remainder of the class was taken up with other students asking the professor additional questions about the mass. Mark noticed he remained very vague, dodging most of them. He was determined to not let him dodge any of the ones he planned on asking.

CHAPTER 36

TURNAROUND

The first thing Mark had planned on doing was locating the book of spells that Abigail mentioned. He decided to wait to approach the professor in his office.

When he turned to give Jeremy an excuse of why he needed to stay after, he noticed him in full flirt mode with the girl who had visited the Smithsonian. He watched them exit together without having to say anything.

Mark waited patiently for the professor to wrap up his equipment and retreat to his office, then slipped in behind him quietly.

"Oh, Mark," the professor said, jumping back a little and noticing him in the doorway. "What can I do for you?"

"I need to talk with you about what you captured on your camera," he said with a serious expression, trying to keep his feelings of betrayal to himself for the moment.

Mark noticed the professor giving him a strange look.

"Sure, come into the light a little better, and let me take a look at your eyes," said the professor, walking around his desk to get closer.

The request caught him off guard, but he let the professor position him in better lighting.

"The coloring of your eyes is changing. You have the sight now, don't you?" the professor asked with an excited grin.

Mark was surprised to hear this observation regarding his eye color again. If the pastor and professor had both noticed, he figured it must have something to do with his visits with Abigail that was causing it.

"If you're asking if I've been in contact with someone from the next realm, I have. That's what I wanted to talk to you about."

"Sure, have a seat. I would love to hear about it. Give me a minute to put some of this stuff away."

Mark was happy to have some time to look around the office while the professor was busy, but it did not stop him from talking. The professor began explaining how the gradual translucency of the iris is a sign of those who have been given the gift to see beyond the grave.

He did his best to stay with the professor while scanning the bookcases behind him. He did not notice a book that fit the description Abigail gave him, so he decided to force the issue.

"Professor, you remember the object I showed you earlier in the week. I'm wondering if you would have a book that might explain more about what it is."

Mark focused on the professor's face to see his reaction.

"Gee, Mark, let me see," he said, without any surprise, and turned around to search.

While the professor was busy looking, Mark made a more thorough scan of the different stacks of papers and books the professor had scattered around the room. Nothing looked out of the ordinary.

The professor's hand landed on what looked to Mark like a more modern book, and he pulled it off the shelf.

"Here is an interesting book that talks about different charms used throughout history that might be of interest." He handed Mark the book. "Feel free to borrow it. Did you find Marianne, and did she have anything to say about it?"

Mark didn't know why the professor brought that up again. He decided against revealing what Marianne had told him and shook his head no just in case the professor was fishing for information on her whereabouts.

Mark looked the book over quickly and realized it was not the book he was looking for.

The fact that the professor knew nothing about portal keys ruined his first line of questioning. Had the professor expounded in detail, it would be obvious to Mark that he was involved in the creation of the objects.

He turned to his second line of questioning about the history of why the professor created the class in the first place to see if it would reveal a dark purpose. The professor was very forthcoming about his reason for creating a class that would bring people together to share their experiences and knowledge of the hereafter.

Realizing he was running out of time, Mark asked some follow-up questions he had regarding the strange mass the professor filmed, to see if he had been following him. The answers the professor gave showed it was nothing more than a coincidence he was there.

When all was said and done, Mark realized the professor was not the agent of Koltar he was looking for. He had conflicting feelings of both relief and disappointment surge through him. On the one hand, the professor had his best interests in mind and could be trusted again. On the other, it was back to square one on who the person could be.

Mark decided not to hold anything back and told the professor everything that had happened since they last talked. The professor listened in wide-eyed amazement as he covered Marianne's reasons for leaving the class, Abigail's visits to them both, and his visits to the fourth realm.

When he reached the point of telling the professor about his visit with Koltar, he had one burning question he had failed to ask during class.

"Professor, did you notice anything inside of the mass you filmed on Monday?"

"No, not really. Why do you ask?"

"Well, there was someone trapped in there. That someone was me."

CHAPTER 37

PATH DEFINED

The professor hastily grabbed his camera from the storage bag and pulled up the footage again. Mark watched him squint at the image on the small screen from several different angles.

"You were trapped in there?" the professor asked, turning the screen toward Mark with a still image of the large red mass.

"I was trapped in there with a dark being named Koltar."

The professor leaned back on his desk and just stared at him.

Mark explained everything that happened during his encounter. He also detailed Abigail's miraculous appearance at the request of his grandfather.

After finishing, the professor put the camera down and sat down in his chair. Mark could tell he was worried about something.

"Were you able to talk to Marianne about any of this?"

His question made Mark wonder if Marianne had said anything to him about the impending conflict.

"I haven't had a chance to talk to her about a lot of what I just told you. She told me in our most recent visit to forget everything before anyone got hurt."

"That is why I wanted you to reach out to Marianne when you showed me the object. It was her run-in with some dark beings that drove her away last year. I thought she could offer some counsel on how to avoid it before it happened to you. But the fact that you showed up to class today leads me to believe you are not rattled by what happened Monday evening and want to see this task through," the professor said with a look of hope.

"I guess so."

"If that is the case, I will not fail you like I did Marianne."

Mark felt relief knowing that the professor was offering his help but was nervous about what challenges lay ahead.

"Professor, Abigail informed me that the object I showed you is called a portal key, and it's used to open the door for those spirits from a hellish realm to enter ours. It was made by someone here who is helping Koltar, and the one I found is not the only one."

"Do you happen to have the object with you?" the professor asked hopefully, eyeing Mark's backpack.

"Not with me right now, if that's what you mean. Abigail told me to keep it hidden so someone wouldn't stumble on it. I've hidden it where no one will."

"That's best for now. I agree there are more portal keys out there, and that reminds me of something."

The professor picked up the book he had given Mark and thumbed his way to the middle. He turned it toward Mark and began flipping through several photographs of different objects.

"Since you don't have it in your possession, and I really can't recall the details of the object, which of these does it most resemble?"

Mark scanned the objects for a moment and was surprised he didn't notice them when he flipped through the book earlier. Some of them had ornate designs with many beautiful stones interlaid in different patterns. Others had writings inscribed on the top or sides of the object. After a few moments, one of them caught his eye. "This one here." Mark pointed to one that had a circular inscription that contained two gemstones in the middle.

"You're right, Mark. That does look like the one you showed me."

Mark thumbed to the section of the book that detailed its history and learned the style of charm dated back to the second century AD and was unearthed near Rome. The circular writing pattern usually signified the progression of souls from one life to another in many religious beliefs at the time.

"Now I wish you would've brought the object with you so I could get a closer look. Are you sure that the object is out of sight and only you know where it is?"

"Yes, it is out of sight. I know I was alone when I buried it. Would all the objects look like the one I have?" Mark asked, hoping the professor knew the answer.

"I believe they will. It looks like they are using a very ancient blueprint. It's important to find them before we have more instances like Paul's."

"Are you telling me if I don't find all of them, Koltar could start popping up all over?" Mark asked, alarmed.

The threat Koltar had given him regarding Stacie, Jeremy, and his family jumped to the forefront of his mind. He wondered if the other charms had already been planted for them to find and knew he needed to warn them right away.

"I know this is alarming, Mark, but I've recently learned of resources that might be available to you. Are you familiar with the First Continental Congress?" asked the professor. He reached for another book from his shelf and opened it to a picture of America's forefathers sitting in a small chamber.

"I remember reading about it in high school. Why?"

"These great men were not only founding fathers of our country and democracy, but they were involved in so much more. They were religious men first and foremost. Men of faith who had a love of God and felt it was their divine duty to make sure freedom of religion was respected and tolerated in the new government. Many of their journals talk about a secret group headed up by Benjamin Franklin that not only discussed matters concerning this life but also matters concerning our next phase of life."

Mark was astonished to hear him referencing the council Abigail had instructed him to seek out. He hadn't said anything about it.

The professor thumbed through a few more pages and showed Mark a page that had a symbol with a V and an inverted V connected with an eye in the center. Mark learned from the professor that the symbol was a representation of God watching over everything and that the group adopted the symbol to remind themselves of their duty, which was to protect and make sure nothing got in the way of our soul's progression.

"Do you know what this group is called and exactly where they met?" Mark asked, hoping he could fill in some of the details that Abigail did not know.

"I do. They call themselves the Vita-Mors Council, which translated from Latin means *death brings life*, and they still meet in Philadelphia."

Mark was glad to learn the name but was hoping for a specific location. "Anything else I should know about?" he asked.

"This council was charged with protecting our world from evil influences that would seek to destroy our freedom to worship God and understand his plan for us in this life. You're instrumental in helping to protect these freedoms for all mankind and ensure Koltar's plans are thwarted."

Mark took comfort in the professor's words. Instead of feelings of fear and worry that had been building recently, he suddenly felt a feeling of profound responsibility.

"Mark, I cannot tell you exactly what to do next, but I know who would." The professor pointed to the picture of the founding fathers again.

Mark's mind was swimming. It seemed like Abigail and the professor were somehow working together. Their instruction on finding this council was almost identical. He did not doubt that meeting with them had to be his next move.

Now that he had the name of the council and confirmed Benjamin Franklin was running it, he took one more chance of pinpointing where they met. "Where in Philadelphia would you suggest I start my search?"

"I would start your search at one of the oldest and most famous cemeteries there is, the Christ Church Cemetery, and work out from there. I will be visiting the Library of Congress this weekend with a friend who is in town, and I will look for what I can regarding portal keys that might help you."

It amazed Mark how quickly things could change. Just over an hour ago, he wanted to tear the professor's head off for lying to him. Now those feelings had been replaced with respect and appreciation for the information he provided and his willingness to help.

CHAPTER 38

PHILADELPHIA

Mark decided he would leave for Philadelphia the next morning. He had wrapped up his homework for the week and wanted to give himself the whole weekend just in case it took longer than expected to contact the council.

Mark felt a little guilty for leaving without bringing his friends up to speed as he intended. But how could he quickly explain that he was going to Philadelphia to find Benjamin Franklin and a secret council to discuss the next steps in fighting an interdimensional battle? It was almost too much for him to believe.

To make matters worse, Stacie had stopped by that evening with plans of how they could spend time with Paul over the weekend to lift his spirits. Although he wanted to be there for Stacie, he knew he couldn't wait another week.

For the second week in a row, he was able to convince his friends that he needed to visit his mom and sister and would be back by Sunday. He didn't know how long he could keep using that excuse, but they both supported his decision without questioning him.

Mark got up before Jeremy and left a note on his gym bag reminding him to not expect him back until Sunday. He did not want Jeremy calling and texting him the whole weekend.

It was a two-hour trip up Interstate 95 from the campus to Philadelphia. He contemplated his discussions with Abigail and the professor regarding their ideas on the best way to contact the council.

His confidence was beginning to grow in his ability to sense someone's presence from the fourth realm, and he felt it would not take long to make contact if he followed the same steps, especially if they were on the lookout for him.

Mark decided to start his search at the Christ Church burial grounds, as the professor suggested. He was hoping that his early arrival would beat the tourists who would soon be showing up to throw a penny on Ben's grave for good luck.

Upon arriving, he was happy to see that no one was around. The tours of the property didn't start for another hour. He didn't know if his proximity to Ben's grave, standing outside of the fence, was close enough to make contact, but he had no choice.

While he waited, he grabbed one of the tourist pamphlets and started reading. He was surprised to learn that the height of the church steeple made it the tallest building in America until 1856 and that George Washington, John Adams, and Ben Franklin all worshiped there.

While these facts and others started permeating his conscious mind, he let his subconscious mind relax so he could be in tune with any sense of contact.

He had no sooner started this process when he heard some movement coming from the other side of the fence near Ben's grave.

"You're looking for him in the wrong spot," a woman's voice said faintly.

Mark stayed relaxed and focused his gaze on the area the voice was coming from. "You know who I'm looking for?" he asked in the direction of the voice.

While he waited for a response, a cool rush of wind moved past him.

He turned in that direction and noticed the figure of a woman starting to form on the opposite corner across the street.

She beckoned for him to follow her.

CHAPTER 39

RUNNING INTERFERENCE

By the time Mark made his way across the street, she had moved over to the next corner and waved him on. Every time he seemed to be gaining on her, she would rapidly move away, keeping the same distance between them.

After following her for a few blocks, Mark realized he was jogging to keep up. It amazed him that she moved so effortlessly, hovering just above the ground.

Mark slowed down enough to catch his breath but not lose her. He followed her a few more blocks when he noticed her come to a sudden stop under a large tree in an adjacent park called Washington Square.

Mark began to walk cautiously toward her, hoping she would not take off again. He was grateful she stayed still.

Upon reaching her, he noticed that she did not have the same light around her that Abigail had. Her face showed a sad countenance.

"Good morning," he offered lightly.

The woman's countenance lightened a little.

"A good morning to you, fine sir."

Mark smiled broadly, recalling what she said at Ben's grave.

"You mentioned I was looking in the wrong spot. You know what I'm looking for?"

"It's not what you are looking for but who," she said with a full smile now. "Word of your impending visit has traveled to me quickly, and you are seeking a meeting with Ben Franklin, are you not?"

"Yes, I am. But how did you know that?" Mark asked, wondering why he had been contacted by her and not by Ben.

"It was your guide in my realm who disseminated the information through channels of communication to me. My charge is to arrange an appointment between you and the Vita-Mors Council."

She must be referring to Abigail.

"Why yes, I believe that is her name," the woman said after the thought crossed his mind.

Mark was amazed that she could read his thoughts like Abigail.

"The fact you were able to hear me at the church and then visualize my form so quickly proved to me you have the gift and are worthy of such a visit."

Mark wondered why he did not feel the same joy that he felt when visiting Abigail.

"I don't mean to pry, but why did you look sad when I first approached you?"

The woman looked at Mark in surprise. "In all of the time that I've been arranging these visits, no one has ever taken the time to ask me that. My name during my time in your realm was Hannah Campbell. I was a young woman with a bright future, working toward a life of service, when my mortal life was suddenly taken from me."

Mark was not expecting that response and was at a loss as to what direction he should take their conversation now.

"I'm sorry to make you talk about it, and please don't feel like you have to continue."

She looked around at the grounds that surrounded them for a moment, like she was being followed. She sighed deeply and looked back at Mark.

"You stand on a very sacred spot, Mr. Banks. Many souls perished and were buried here during the Revolutionary War." She pointed to a memorial that had been erected in the center of the park. "I was a very educated woman for that period, and it was an exciting time to be alive. Witnessing firsthand the birth of a new nation was amazing. However, the loss of life was very costly. I was a trained nurse and assisted in saving the lives of many Patriots during the conflict. I also helped bury many of these brave men in this very square wherein you stand. We did not have time to bury them properly, and many of the graves were very shallow."

Mark could tell this was a very dark chapter in her life, due to her pausing several times to collect herself. He kept quiet out of respect.

"Many years after the war, Philadelphia built a medical school adjacent to this square, and I enrolled to continue my studies in the field of nursing. I soon found out some alarming news from a dear friend and mentor of mine, that there was a group of students who were coming down to this sacred area at night and digging up the bodies of these brave men to use for their anatomy studies. After witnessing it for myself one evening, I informed some members of the school administration. I was appalled when they did nothing about it. So, I took it upon myself to lie in wait for many nights and ring a cowbell to chase them off. One evening, I was waiting for them to gather and was hiding behind this very tree when some of these students ambushed me from behind and beat me unconscious. I passed away a few days later from the injuries I sustained."

Mark felt awful when she began to weep. "I'm so sorry about what happened to you, Hannah." He was shocked that someone who had moved on was still carrying around so much pain.

"The sadness of my hopes and dreams being dashed so cruelly that night weighs on me now. However, I do not weep for myself but for those who ended my life. They will be judged for what they did and are currently paying the price."

Mark let her words sink in. He wished he had Pastor Watts there to elaborate on what happens to the spirits of evil people who die. He would have to follow up on that subject with him.

"Thank you for sharing your story, and I'm so sorry if you felt that was none of my business."

"Do not be sorry. It is healing to express my story with you. I have been charged to continue to protect this area from those who wish to disturb it, and it is this sacred duty that keeps me content and fulfilled. I appreciate your inquiry about me and my purpose here. No matter what realm you currently occupy, it is always nice when someone takes interest in your journey, whether it's past or present. But you did not come here to hear my tale of woe, did you? You have more pressing matters to attend to."

Mark noticed the light around her increase.

"You mentioned earlier that you oversee setting up meetings with the council. Where do you recommend I start?"

She moved around him quickly and pointed in the direction of an adjacent building.

"Located just around the corner of this building, on South Fifth and Chestnut, you will find the American Philosophical Society Museum. Mr. Franklin still makes his rounds to and from this area frequently, and that is where you should start."

"What time of day is my best chance for meeting him?"

"Time is of no use in our realm, and we do not live our lives using a clock anymore. The intentions of your heart will be more than enough to beckon him."

Mark smiled and nodded his head in agreement.

"May God bless your endeavors in assisting us in the protection of our realms." She clasped her hands together and gave him a slight bow.

"Thank you, Hannah."

Mark looked in the direction of where she had pointed. When he turned to confirm which building it was, she had vanished from sight.

Hannah's story made Mark think back to his conversations with Marianne and her decision to not involve herself in this conflict. He felt some disappointment in her for trying to get him to turn his back. It was apparent he had more people in his corner than he thought, and he hoped Marianne would eventually come around.

The streets were beginning to get a little more crowded with tourists when Mark made his way over to Chestnut Street.

Smells of freshly baked bread wafted through the air, and the thought of a Philly cheesesteak seemed so tempting, but he decided to ignore his hunger pains and head straight to the museum.

Mark could feel a charge of energy walking around the museum and the adjacent Independence Hall grounds.

When he arrived in front of the building, he read on a plaque that the American Philosophical Society was founded in 1743 by Ben Franklin and a few other scholars. It was an eminent scholarly organization for hundreds of years until it was designated a National Historic Landmark in 1965.

Noticing a small alleyway behind the museum, he turned down it and deliberately slowed his pace for some reason.

Just then, he noticed the sound of some rather loud footsteps coming up beside him. Turning to his right, he expected to see someone walking next to him, but there was no one there.

Continuing, he could still hear that the footsteps were keeping up with him.

Suddenly, the footsteps moved in front of him and veered off in the direction of what looked to be an inconspicuous entrance to the museum.

Mark followed the sound of the phantom footsteps up some old cement steps to the door, where he heard them stop abruptly.

He noticed a sign encouraging visitors to use the front entrance and that these doors were locked.

Just then, the doorknob clicked, and the shape of a small young man began to form in front of him.

"No time to doddle, Mr. Banks. We have a lot of work to do."

CHAPTER 40

ENLIGHTENMENT

Mark stood in awe when Ben Franklin gestured for him to follow and disappeared through the door. Mark had always liked studying about him in school and had chosen to write about him for his sixth-grade book report on famous Americans. It was a paper that his grandfather had declared a masterpiece after reading.

Remembering he had heard the door unlock, Mark grabbed the knob and opened it slowly. He looked back toward the alley to make sure the coast was clear and then slipped in quietly.

Mark followed Ben down a small hallway. He heard faint voices of building staff talking toward the front entrance. Even though he was trying to walk quietly, his shoes still squeaked a little with each step. He couldn't fathom how the workers did not hear Ben's heavy footsteps echoing through the corridor.

At the end of the hall, Ben made a hard turn to the right and again disappeared through a small door. The doorknob clicked again, and Mark entered.

In front of him was a very narrow spiral staircase that went up a few floors. It looked like some sort of secret passage that appeared to be very old. Mark wondered if anyone in the building had ever used it. Mark cringed at the racket they both made while climbing each metal stair. He gripped the railings tightly due to them swaying several inches with each step.

Mark followed Ben into a small office that was ornately decorated. The woodwork of the furniture was very intricate. Bookcases covered almost every inch of wall space and were full of books, maps, and manuscripts that looked to be very old. There were lots of strange-looking objects laid out on small tables around the room. A large desk was located near the only window in the room, with a large worn leather chair that was facing out the window.

While looking around, Mark wondered if the office he was seeing was real or if he had crossed over to the fourth realm. It looked exactly like the paintings he had seen in history books, so he assumed the latter.

Suddenly, the large leather chair swiveled around, with Ben looking up at him smiling. It was not the older Ben who was pictured in the history books. This was a younger, more vibrant version. He looked to be in his early twenties, and Mark wondered if all spirits in the fourth realm looked younger than they were when they died. His grandfather seemed to look younger even though he recognized him immediately.

"Mr. Banks, our realms are in trouble, and we need your help," Ben said, leaning forward with his hands clasped together on his desk.

The fact that he was conversing with Ben Franklin made him wish he could record it to show his friends later.

"Let me get right to the point. Most of the people who have inhabited the earth have gone on their merry way with little to no thought about what comes after death. Or what came before it, for that matter. However, there have been a select few who had the gift to see beyond this barrier between our realms. Unfortunately, many of them were labeled as crazy religious zealots and treated as outcasts or institutionalized. Their gifts were squandered by humanity."

Mark thought back to a girl in junior high who professed to see dead people and all the bad names she was called by him and his friends. A rush of regret ran through him.

"How does a gift like this help humanity?"

"Historically speaking, evil forces have been kept in check from having full-scale access to your realm by these people who were allowed to use their gifts. From time to time, these fallen angels figure out ways to try to get higher levels of access. Your run-in with one of these dammed souls has traveled quickly to us, and we have learned they are developing a plan to gain unabated access if successful. I have been anticipating your visit and have been meeting with the members of my council to come up with our next course of action to combat their entry. The members of the council are anxious to meet you."

"You and members of the Vita-Mors Council have been waiting for me?" Mark asked, astonished.

"Yes. I'm pleased to learn you've been informed about the name of our council and its purpose then."

Ben stood up, walked around the desk, and stood next to Mark, smiling warmly.

"Mark, I've been watching you since you visited my grave earlier this morning and was pleased when Hannah gave me the go-ahead to reach out to you."

"She told me about what happened to her, which was horrible. Does she work for you?"

"I guess you could say she works with me but not for me. Maybe she told you it was I who informed her about those grave robbers who ultimately took her life. I have carried so much remorse for what happened to her. We are bound to help one another fulfill each other's purpose in our current state. She only needs a positive outcome to this struggle, and then her task will be fulfilled. She will finally be able to move onto a different path that will advance her further."

Mark was glad to learn why they worked together and could feel the sadness that Ben continued to carry with him. Now he felt added pressure, knowing that Hannah's progression in the hereafter hung in the balance of the overall outcome.

A question popped into his head that he had wanted to ask since they entered the building.

"Mr. Franklin, I still don't understand how you can slip past everyone in this building without anyone noticing."

Mark could sense Ben's relief that he changed the subject, and a smile returned to his face.

"Good question, but please call me Ben," he said with a wink. "I've been coming and going in this building for well over two hundred years, and occasionally someone will stop in their tracks and swear to another coworker that they heard some footsteps or felt a sudden temperature change when I pass by, but that's been the extent of it. They do not see because they choose not to see, or should I say, they cannot see. You are indeed seeing my office in the fourth realm. If one of the workers here were to walk into this room right now, they would see an old storage room."

Mark decided to follow up on his earlier thought regarding Ben's youthful appearance.

"You look nothing like I thought you would, even though I know it's you, if that makes any sense."

"Of course, I don't. All we had at the time I lived in your realm were painters to capture my image. I wasn't of much importance historically until my later years. You are seeing me at the pinnacle of my mortal existence. I have the same energy and quick mind that I had at the age at which you see me now. I'm quick as a whip. But enough about my handsome appearance. We have more pressing matters to concern ourselves with."

Ben walked over, took an object off the shelf, and set it on the desk.

"I believe you are familiar with an object similar to this?"

Mark couldn't believe what he was seeing.

"Yes, that looks a lot like the portal key I found. How did you get one?"

"These objects have been left for others to find repeatedly through the centuries. This one was left for me to find during the War of Independence. That is why I need you to tell me all you can about your experience with your key, so I can fill in the gaps from what has been relayed to me so far."

Mark jumped right in, explaining everything he could recall. Ben's interest seemed to be piqued when he mentioned Koltar by name.

When he finished, Ben just stood there with his arms folded and a look of deep concern. Mark refrained from asking any more questions, as he looked to be deep in thought.

"This Koltar cannot open the door by himself and knows he must influence someone with your gift to do it for him. That is why you are of so much importance to them."

Ben turned his attention back to the object.

"I know Koltar cannot make these objects. Someone in your realm is making them for him. Do you have any idea who might be working with him?"

"I initially thought it was a professor of mine, but when I confronted him yesterday, he had a reasonable explanation for all my questions. I'm pretty sure he's not involved. He was the one who agreed with Abigail that my next step was to find you and the council."

Ben shot him a look of disappointment.

"Unfortunately for us, this person knows who you and your friends are. They now know the door has been unlocked and you are the only one who can help them break it down. We cannot let this happen."

Ben walked over to another door in the corner of the room that Mark had barely noticed due to all the clutter. This time, he opened the door instead of walking through it.

"They should all be gathering now. I think it's time you met the council."

CHAPTER 41

VITA-MORS COUNCIL

Mark made his way into a larger room that had four ascending platforms. He expected to see it full of council members and looked over at Ben, confused.

"Relax, Mr. Banks. Everyone should be gathering shortly," Ben assured him.

Mark began to hear voices from different points around the room. One by one, the council began to appear. Within moments, the room was full of men and women who were turned toward one another, conversing. He looked around the room in bewilderment. They were dressed impeccably in the clothing of whatever period they lived in. Some were dressed very plainly, while others were more ornate. Mark was amazed at the variety of people involved in the council.

Ben motioned for Mark to join him in the middle of the room.

"All right, settle down, my friends."

Mark moved next to Ben and then looked out at the group and noticed all eyes were on him. It felt to him like everyone was trying to investigate his soul for validation.

"Ladies and gentlemen, the Vita-Mors Council has been called to session to discuss the possibility of full realm access. I have invited Mr.

Mark Banks of Baltimore here today because most recently, an agent of Lucifer himself has confronted him. This agent informed him that a plan to open a door from their hellish realm to that of the third realm has been put into motion."

A few of the council members gasped, while others started talking to each other again.

"Ladies and gentlemen, please." Ben waited for them to calm down again. "This agent, who refers to himself as Koltar, enlisted someone in Mark's realm to create and place a portal key for him to find. It contained an inscription that if read aloud by someone with his gift, would've opened the door wide open. Fortunately for us and all mankind, Mr. Banks did not read it."

Everyone in the room clapped. Ben motioned for Mark to acknowledge their appreciation, so he nodded his head and waved.

"Now many of you can recall a time during which you lived when these dark souls acquired limited access, and great atrocities followed. However, this is the greatest threat we have faced to date."

It had not dawned on Mark that what was happening had occurred several times in the past.

"Does the council mind if I ask when this happened before?"

A hand rose toward the back of the room, and a woman who looked like she was wearing pilgrim attire stood up to address the group.

"My mortal period was during the time of the Salem witch trials. There were many rumors of strange objects showing up around our community, and within a short period, the whole town went mad. Many members of my family and close friends were falsely accused of being witches and then burned to death. The event lasted only a few short months in the year of our Lord 1692, and our community never recovered. People I had known my whole life, who I knew to be kind and levelheaded, changed into angry, accusatory souls overnight."

Mark noticed many in the room nod in agreement and begin making comments. She waited for them to finish and then continued.

"Unfortunately, the ones who I believe had the gift that you possess and could've helped to prevent it were accused themselves of being witches and put to death. I believe these damned souls caused our respected leaders to act devilish and filled their minds with bloodlust."

The woman sat down, and another hand shot up. The man was dressed in long, flowing robes detailed with intricate crosses. He began to speak in what Mark thought was Spanish, but to his surprise, he was able to understand every word.

"It was my time of the Spanish Inquisition when the hearts of many of my clergy were duped into false beliefs and judgments. Those skewed beliefs led to thousands of deaths by fire for so many innocent souls. These evil spirits only had limited access, but look at the awful suffering they caused throughout all of Europe. These fallen souls thrive and thirst for our destruction."

A subtle panic began building in the room and soon turned into an uproar, with everyone talking at once. Ben quickly clapped his hands, and they all came back to order.

Mark continued to listen intently while more council members discussed the different tragedies they witnessed during their lives. With each story, he could feel the heartache and gravity of what they were saying.

When they were finished, Ben jumped in. "The world, in its current state, is wicked enough with only minimal influence from these beings. Imagine what would happen if they were allowed direct access to the hearts of man. We need to give this young man direction on how to destroy these portal keys and deny their access."

Ben's comment about keys reminded Mark that he needed clarification on something Abigail had mentioned.

"I have found only one of these portal keys so far, but I need to find multiple keys that could be placed all around my campus and destroy all of them. Is that correct?"

Ben looked out at the group as several heads nodded and then back at Mark.

"That is correct. You will need to find all of them and then destroy them all at once to close the door for good."

"I don't know how I can handle multiple objects when it took only one of them to almost destroy me. Can't I just destroy them one by one when I find them?" Mark asked.

Just then, another hand rose from a distinguished-looking man in colonial dress, and he stood up.

"Tactically speaking, Ben is right. You cannot defeat this enemy bit by bit. It will take one swift blow to remove this threat. It will be made known to you how to destroy them once you have all of them in your possession. Just be ready for it. The other objects will soon make themselves known to you."

Ben looked at Mark, nodding in agreement.

"Brother Hancock is correct."

Mark shot Ben a wide-eyed glance and mouthed the name *John Hancock* to him. Ben winked back with a sly smile.

Mark couldn't believe that he had just received council from John Hancock. He now wished Ben would've gone around the room and introduced everyone at the beginning.

"You mentioned to me earlier about friends of yours who might have your gift. They could be a great asset in helping you locate the remaining objects. Never underestimate the importance of true friends," said Ben, smiling at the council members.

Mark didn't feel comfortable with the thought of involving Stacie and Jeremy after what had happened with Paul, but he knew he couldn't do it without them. The comments from Ben and the council confirmed it.

Mark listened closely while the council warned him that whoever had placed the portal key he found knew where to position the others, and it would not be done randomly. Each member of the council took turns wishing him well before they faded from view.

Not knowing who was placing them was beginning to weigh on him heavily. Now that the professor had been ruled out, none of the other people in his life seemed like viable suspects.

Mark followed Ben back into his office, where he assured Mark that Abigail would be the one who would provide instruction on how to destroy the objects once he gathered all of them.

"No one has told me the exact number yet."

"I would imagine there would be one created for each one of your friends who have your ability."

Mark guesstimated there would at least be three more out there, after figuring the one he found was intended for Paul.

Ben put his hand on Mark's shoulder, and a feeling of his concern rushed through Mark.

"I wish you all the good fortunes I can in your quest to see this task through. If you ever need me, you know where to find me," said Ben. He sat down in his leather chair and smiled warmly as he and the room faded away.

Standing alone in what was now an empty storage room, Mark noticed the sun setting outside the window. He realized his meeting with the council had taken up most of the day.

He felt drained when he exited the museum the same way he came in and noticed he still wasn't used to the physical exhaustion he incurred when visiting the fourth realm.

His stomach was growling like crazy. It dawned on him that he hadn't eaten anything since early that morning, so he decided to swing by a nearby sandwich shop for a cheesesteak.

When he got the footlong masterpiece with extra cheese whiz, he mindlessly ate it, still in shock from visiting with the council. Not only that, but they were relying on him to do something that no one else could. He prayed he was ready for it.

Looking down at the time on his phone, he realized he would not make it back to campus until late, and he could meet with Jeremy and Stacie in the morning.

In the meantime, he felt it was time to bring his mother and sister up to speed with everything. They needed to be warned about what was coming.

CHAPTER 42

VITAL VISIT

It was just after ten o'clock at night when Mark pulled up to his home. He could see that most of the lights were on, which did not surprise him. After the carbon monoxide accident with his grandparents, both his mom and sister had become paranoid and tended to stay awake well past midnight.

Mark had no feelings of apprehension about showing up unannounced anymore since his relationship with his mother had improved. His sister, Cassandra, reassured him of how much better she was doing through texts and phone conversations since he had been away at school.

Mark rapped a couple of times on the screen door, and another light turned on in the already well-lit living room. Cassandra opened the door just enough to peek out.

"Cass, it's me." Mark realized he had not called ahead to let them know he was stopping by. He pressed his face close to the screen so she could get a closer look.

The door opened a little wider, and Mark could see her whole face now.

"Thank you, sir, but we have enough towels," she said with a straight face and closed the door.

Mark banged on the door harder.

"Hey, Cass, let me in. I'm freezing."

She slowly opened the door and then burst through the screen door, attacking him with a bear hug that almost launched them off the porch.

"I thought I wouldn't see you until after your finals," she said, squeezing him even tighter.

"I decided to drop by and say hi," he said, carrying her through the door and into the living room while she clung to him.

"Where's Mom?"

"She's in the kitchen baking."

She moved around and jumped on his back for a piggyback ride. Mark walked into the kitchen with her on his back, which startled his mother, who had her headphones in.

"Oh, Mark," she said, putting down her oven mitts and running over to embrace him. "What a surprise to see you, honey. What brings you home so late on a Saturday? You and Jeremy calling it quits?"

Mark rolled his eyes. His mom always teased him about how close they were and how they argued like an old married couple most of the time.

"No, we didn't fight." Mark squirmed to get Cassandra off his back. "It smells good in here. What are you making?"

"Just working on a new cranberry muffin recipe I saw on TV."

She reached for one that was still steaming hot and slathered it with butter, handing it to Mark.

"Tell me if I used too much of anything since I know you will be brutally honest with me," she said, rolling her eyes the same way Mark had.

Mark could tell she wanted to impress him as her eyes followed the muffin up to his mouth. He took a huge bite and then took his time chewing it, letting the flavors dance around in his mouth. He had always been good at identifying what ingredients were in the foods his family made and was the go-to taste tester.

After a few moments, he could readily catch the taste of orange peel and hints of ginger. "Mom, these muffins rock. I love the orange and ginger mixed with the cranberries." He took another huge bite to finish it off, while crumbs cascaded from his mouth onto the floor.

"Heavens, child. Slow down and enjoy it," she said, pushing him down on a kitchen chair while placing another muffin in front of him. She sat down next to him and stroked his neck with her hand.

This time, Mark put the whole muffin in his mouth.

"You look tired, baby. What brings you up this way?"

"I'm on my way back from Philadelphia," he said through the mouthful of muffin.

"Philadelphia?" his sister and mom said at the same time.

"What in the world were you doing up there?" asked his mom.

Cassandra walked over and slugged him on the shoulder. "And why didn't you bring me a cheesesteak?"

Mark grabbed her and started tickling her over his lap. "I did get you one, but it was such a long drive I had to eat it." She wailed with delight.

Even though he had thought of everything he wanted to say on the way over, he couldn't decide where to start. He could tell his mom was concerned about his surprise visit. He released his sister and turned toward her with a serious look.

Suddenly her eyes lit up. "This is the look you gave me before you told me about Grandpa. Has it happened again?"

Her comment took Mark by surprise. He wondered what type of look could tip her off to that thought.

"Mom, you're correct. I feel I need to catch you and Cass up on what has been going on at school this semester."

"Did you see Papa or Nanna again?" Cassandra asked, sitting down across the table from him.

"Yes, dear, there is something different about you." His mom grabbed him by the shoulder, turned him toward her, and leaned in to get a closer look. "Your eyes. They look like they are getting brighter."

Mark was startled to hear this observation from his mother. Looking in the mirror the night before, he did not notice anything different and couldn't figure out why everyone was seeing it but him.

"Do you guys want to hear what's going on or just stare at my eyes?"

"Yes, honey, go ahead," his mom said, sitting up at attention and folding her hands in her lap neatly.

Mark recapped everything that had happened from his first trip to the cemetery up through his visit with the council earlier that day.

Neither of them said anything when he finished. He felt that maybe he shouldn't have gone into so much detail and that he must have lost them along the way.

"You know, Mark, this does not surprise me. Your grandfather knew you had the gift." Mark noticed tears welling up in his mother's eyes, and she hurriedly stood up. "I'll be right back."

Mark didn't know what he had said to set his mom off and looked over at his sister. She just shrugged her shoulders, not knowing what was happening either.

His mother returned with a well-worn book in her hands and sat down next to Mark.

"This is your grandfather's journal," she said, turning through the well-worn pages. "I read it cover to cover soon after he died to try to connect with him. A lot of what he wrote about you surprised me. He never shared any of the things he observed with me. You had this gift a lot earlier than you think."

CHAPTER 43

UNEXPECTED INSIGHT

Mark tried to subdue his emotions while looking at his grandfather's handwriting. Knowing that he took the time to chronicle things about his gift made him feel even closer to him.

"Here is one when you were five years old. Please read it for us. Cassie should know a little more about your gift."

He wiped away some tears that had welled up in his eyes and began to read aloud.

> Something very special happened today. I took Jack down to Cheltenham wetlands to see the birds today. After about an hour of feeding them, we got in the car to go get lunch when he noticed the veterans' cemetery on the other side of the wetlands. He said in an excited voice, "Papa, I want to go there! I want to go there!" We pulled into the parking lot, and he jumped out and ran straight into the cemetery, stopping suddenly and looking all around. I caught up to him and noticed he had a very unusual expression on his face while staring straight in front of him. I assumed he was worried about being there, so I explained that a

cemetery contained the bodies of people who had lived on earth, but their souls had moved on to a better place. He looked at me in all seriousness and said, "They aren't dead, Papa. They're right here." His response took me by surprise. I asked him what he meant by *right here*. He looked around the cemetery and said, "They aren't scary or nothing, especially him." He pointed directly in front of him, and then he turned around and went and got in the car. At lunch, I asked him to describe what he had seen at the cemetery. He told me that he saw several people walking around who were happy and smiling. At first, I thought he had an amazing imagination for someone his age, until he told me that one of them started talking to him and told him to tell me hello. When I asked who the person was, he said his name was Chipper and he was wearing a pink tie. I nearly choked on my hamburger when he told me this. One of my best friends growing up was Dale (Chipper) Washington, who was buried in that cemetery. He was well known for wearing a high-collared dress shirt with a pink bow tie. We called him Chipper because he lost a couple of tips of his fingers on his right hand while using a woodchipper in his youth. Mark has been blessed with a very special gift, and I will do everything I can to make sure he never loses it. What a remarkable child.

When he finished, Mark sat there for a moment while grabbing a napkin off the table to wipe his eyes. His mom and sister did the same.

To read about an event that happened so early in his childhood and his grandfather's promise to help cultivate it made him realize their bond went deeper than he thought.

Mark's mom closed the journal and then opened a manila folder that contained some old black-and-white photos. She began thumbing through a few of them and then stopped on one and slid it over to Mark.

It was a younger picture of his grandfather with his arm around another young man dressed in a high-collar shirt and bow tie. The caption written at the bottom read "Me and Chipper, all gussied up for the dance."

Seeing the man in the photo jarred Mark's memory. He realized he had seen his grandfather's friend many times while growing up, and he was always wearing the same outfit. Up until that moment, he had assumed he was a living person.

"Mark, I need to tell you about something else that I remembered when you were telling us about your run-in with Koltar and how you felt trapped in darkness," his mom said, reaching out and grabbing hold of his hand.

Mark looked at his sister, perplexed, and then back at his mom, wondering where she was going with this.

"What is it?"

"I believe Koltar has been watching you for a long time."

CHAPTER 44

MENACING WATCHER

Mark couldn't tell if the look on his mother's face was one of regret or concern. He waited with anticipation for her to continue, not having a clue what she was referring to.

"When you were young, on several occasions, you would come into my room just sobbing that someone was in your room at the foot of your bed, watching you. At first, your dad and I assumed they were night terrors and that you would outgrow them. But as you got older, you described a shadowy figure whose face you could not see. You would become such a naughty and unruly child for a few days following one of these events. After a few years, around your seventh birthday, we called Reverend Williams to come to give our house a blessing. You stopped having these episodes after that blessing, and I had pretty much forgotten about it. But when you mentioned your run-in with Koltar, all these memories came back to me."

Her comments brought chills throughout Mark's body. He sat there speechless, trying to process what she had just told him.

"Mark, honey, what can I do to help you?" his mom asked, pulling him in close to her and kissing him on the forehead.

"Mom, I don't know right now. I need to wrap my mind around everything you just told me and what happened today in Philadelphia. I also need to talk with Jeremy and Stacie to see if they will help me."

"Do you think Stacie will help you?" his sister asked. Mark thought her question came out of the blue.

Mark couldn't remember if he told her anything about Stacie that would give her that impression. "Why do you say that Cass?"

"She called Mom and me earlier this week. I asked her how she was liking school, and she said something terrible had happened to one of her friends and that she would most likely be dropping one of the classes she had with you. I know now that she was talking about Paul, so I don't know if she'll help you."

This information troubled Mark greatly. He was going to have to work harder than he thought in getting Stacie's help. He didn't want her to close him off and knew he would have to be sensitive to her feelings regarding Paul.

"Thanks for letting me know she called, sis. I want you two to promise me you'll be safe and call me if anything strange happens."

"As I said, baby, this house has been blessed, so there is nothing that can change that."

Mark stood up to leave and leaned over to give his mom a tight hug.

"I'm glad to hear that, Mom. Just wait until I figure some things out, and I'll let you know if there's anything you can do to help. I better get going. I want to get back and get some sleep before I talk to Jeremy and Stace. Hopefully before church."

Mark always mentioned he was going to his church services whenever he talked to his mom. That way, she knew he was attending regularly. She kept in touch with the pastor and liked to check up on Mark from time to time.

"That's my good boy," his mom said with an approving look.

"You'll be glad to know I haven't missed a week in over a month and a half."

Mark was making his way to the front door when his mother told him to wait for a moment while she packed up some muffins to take with him.

While waiting, he wondered what else his grandfather had written regarding his gift. He walked back into the kitchen and asked his mom if he could borrow the journal, and she agreed.

With the journal and muffins in hand, he kissed his mom goodbye and went to hug his sister. Before he could, she grabbed the muffins out of his hand and shot out the door, much to his mom's amusement.

Mark turned and smiled at his mom. "I love you. Thanks again for sharing that information with me tonight."

"I wish I would've told you sooner. Please be careful, and I love you too." She followed him to the door and waved goodbye.

When he got to his car, he noticed Cassie putting the container of muffins in his trunk. He met her at the back of the car for a private conversation.

"How is mom doing really?" he whispered.

"Mark, she is doing so much better, and there's nothing for you to worry about. Our relationship is tighter than ever," she said, leaning in to give him a tight squeeze.

Her news brought him some much-needed relief that this aspect of his life was on solid ground.

"I love you. Tell Jeremy and Stacie, I miss them. You might have the gift to see dead people, but I have the gift of being the most liked by your friends," she said, teasing him. Mark was often jealous that his friends always took her side of an argument and protected her like their own sister.

He let her comment go for the sake of time and got in his car.

Driving off, he felt some relief about his decision to stop and warn them about the threats Koltar made, and he took some comfort that the house had been blessed. If anything happened, he knew they would reach out to him.

He glanced in his rearview mirror and could see his sister running down the street, waving frantically. He knew she was in good hands now.

CHAPTER 45

THE FALLEN

There was no time to meet with both Jeremy and Stacie before church, and Mark could feel his anxiousness sitting next to them while Brother Watts delivered his Sunday-morning message. Stacie had informed Mark she would meet them there. He and Jeremy had slept in and made it just in time. He wondered how they were going to react to being kept in the dark for so long.

The pastor's comment about fallen angels brought back his mom's comments about Koltar being the one who tormented him early in his life. He made up his mind to ask the pastor about that after the service.

Mark told his friends he had a quick question to ask the pastor, and they both agreed to wait for him. He felt a little rushed when he knocked on the pastor's office door.

"Brother Watts, it's me again. Do you have a quick second?"

"I hope it's not a quick second. I'm beginning to enjoy your visits immensely." The pastor motioned for him to have a seat.

Mark sat down and noticed the pastor arranging his scriptures in anticipation of the question he had.

"To make a long story short, I had another experience yesterday with a whole council of spirits in Philadelphia. Including Ben Franklin and John Hancock."

Right after he said their names, Mark realized how crazy it all sounded, and he worried that the pastor was going to stop believing him. He watched his reaction, but the pastor's expression did not change.

"Mark, these visitations are starting to happen more often now, and I want to know if you're listening to the Holy Spirit for guidance on why you are receiving them."

His question caught Mark off guard. He hadn't thought about who was guiding the overall steps he had taken so far.

"I feel everything is happening for a spiritual reason, and I know I've felt its presence."

"Well, you should be protected from the adversary trying to thwart your mission then."

Mark knew he better tell him about Koltar. "Remember I told you what happened to our friend Paul with that object I showed you last time? Well, I had just left your office when I encountered a dark being that knew I was carrying that object. He called himself Koltar. He had me trapped in his realm for what seemed like hours."

The gravity of what Mark just revealed seemed to take the excitement out of the pastor, and he leaned far back in his chair, letting out a large sigh.

"Mark, I've been giving it a lot of thought and prayer regarding the reason you found that object. I was hoping the evil was isolated to the charm only. Maybe some kids just messing around with some black magic for the fun of it. But now I'm certain Koltar plans to usher in darkness. What else have you learned since we last spoke?"

Mark was glad he understood.

"I found out from my mother, after a visit last night, that this evil spirit has been watching me since I was a kid. Abigail and the council have given me some good information about what they are trying to do, but I need to know more about what they are. Abigail said Koltar was a messenger of Satan himself."

The pastor grabbed his scriptures. "Mark, you are dealing with a damned soul. You've heard me mention in many of my messages that there was a host of spirits that followed Lucifer and were banished to this world to torment man. They are jealous and evil, and their only goal is to see us go contrary to what we know to be right. I want you to look at Revelation, chapter twelve, verses seven through nine."

The pastor opened his copy of the New Testament and turned it around for Mark to read.

> *And there was war in heaven, Michael and his angels waging war with the dragon. The dragon and his angels waged war, and they were not strong enough, and there was no longer a place found for them in heaven. And the great dragon was thrown down, the serpent of old who is called the devil and Satan, who deceives the whole world; he was thrown down to the earth, and his angels were thrown down with him.*

Mark remembered reading those verses many times. They took on a whole new meaning now that he was involved.

The pastor continued searching for scriptures while he talked. "This is a war that has been going on from the foundation of the world. Satan is trying to blind all of us who want to follow God. I'm sure that is what Koltar is trying to do through you. A couple of other scriptures that jump to mind are second Peter, chapter two, verse four." This time, he read it aloud to Mark.

> *For God did not spare angels when they sinned but cast them into hell and committed them to pits of darkness, reserved for judgment.*

"These damned spirits are not at all happy with their current state and what awaits them. I can only imagine the horror you felt while looking into the pit of darkness he showed you. Jude, chapter one, verse six says this."

> *And angels who did not keep their domain, but abandoned their proper abode, He has kept in eternal bonds under darkness for the judgment of the great day.*

"Mark, these spirits only know darkness. They do not comprehend the light. That is why they operate in the shadows and no light can come from them. Light cannot penetrate them. That is why you were surrounded by darkness during your visit with Koltar."

Mark wished Jeremy and Stacie were in the room, listening. He was worried they had left.

"Let's look at one of my favorite passages from the Old Testament. Look at Isaiah, fourteen, verse twelve."

This time, he turned it around for Mark to read.

How you have fallen from heaven, O star of the morning, son of the dawn! You have been cut down to the earth, You who have weakened the nations!

A light went off in Mark's mind after reading that verse. "That's it. If they get unchecked access to our realm, they will weaken the nations by constantly deceiving us and making us slaves to the devil like they are?"

"Exactly, Mark. Once the door they are trying to open through you is closed permanently, it will cause them greater suffering to know that their chance for unlimited access has been defeated. That is why they've had their eye on you for quite some time."

Mark realized Koltar was trying to scare him so much in his youth to get him to turn off his ability before he even knew what it was.

"Mark, I feel I must warn you not to go looking for Koltar as your ability increases. There are plenty of warnings about doing this in the scriptures. Such as Leviticus nineteen, verse thirty-one."

Mark read it aloud.

Turn ye not unto the ghosts, nor unto familiar spirits; seek them not out, to be defiled by them.

"Now jump over to chapter twenty, verse six."

Mark turned over to the verse and read.

And if any person turns to ghosts and familiar spirits and goes astray after them, I will set My face against that person and cut him off from among his people.

"I believe these verses were warning the children of Israel to not go looking for these spirits that want to defile us and make us unclean in the eyes of God. The more interaction you have with them, the easier it is for them to tempt you to their cause."

The pastor took the scriptures out of Mark's hand and flipped to another book.

"Deuteronomy eighteen, verses ten and eleven say the same thing." The professor read this time.

Let no one be found among you who consigns his son or daughter to the fire, or who is an augur, a soothsayer, a diviner, a sorcerer, one who casts spells, or one who consults ghosts or familiar spirits or one who inquires of the dead.

"A lot of people have tried contacting their dead loved ones using the methods spoken in these verses, only to be fooled by evil spirits into following the wrong path."

Mark finally realized the dangers of having a gift like his after reading the verses. He had gone out of his way to contact a spirit from another realm and was grateful Abigail contacted him first. It also dawned on him that the person helping Koltar was consulting the wrong class of spirits. He wondered if they were doing it willingly or if they had been deceived.

Mark noticed the pastor had picked up the Koran and opened it to a particular page.

"I mentioned in our previous visit that there are some similarities in religions of the world. Look at Surah thirty-five six from the Koran here."

Indeed, Satan is an enemy to you; so take him as an enemy. He only invites his party to be among the companions of the Blaze.

"There are many more references to Satan in this book and many of the religious books behind me. Every religion in the world that I've studied mentions an agent of darkness that opposes the light. These fallen souls are the opposition. Religious concepts of what evil is and why it oppresses humanity might differ, but they all acknowledge it in some way."

A knock at the door startled Mark from behind, and Jeremy popped his head in.

"Sorry to interrupt, Brother Watts, but are you ready to roll, Mark?"

Even though he wanted to see where the pastor would go next, Mark felt like he had gained a better understanding of what to look out for moving forward.

"Thanks, Brother Watts. I appreciate all the info you gave me."

"It is why I'm here, Mark. Thanks for bringing me up to speed on your history of dealing with these dark souls—and be careful."

"I will. Thanks again."

Mark could tell Jeremy was confused with the pastor's parting comment when he exited his office.

"What on earth were you guys talking about?" Jeremy asked, nodding to Stacie to join them.

Mark didn't say anything. When Stacie joined them, he put his arms around them both.

"It is time that you guys know what is coming and how to help me stop it."

CHAPTER 46

HOPEFUL ALLIANCE

On their way back to their dorms, Mark decided to start the conversation by asking how Paul was doing. After learning what Stacie had told his sister about dropping their class, he didn't think it wise to jump right into what they were up against.

Stacie informed him that his appetite had returned, and he would be getting back to his schoolwork that upcoming week. But he was still jumpy and had a hard time talking about what happened to him.

"Stace, do you mind coming back to our place so I can talk to you both for a bit?"

"What's with all this cloak and dagger? You and Professor Windham starting your own ghost-hunting business and you need Stacie and me to be the guinea pigs?" Jeremy asked jokingly.

Mark ignored his comment and kept his gaze on Stacie.

"Sure. Your place is closer than mine, and I'm freezing. I can't believe I let you talk me into walking this morning." Stacie pulled her scarf tighter around her neck. "If it's more assignments from Windham, save your breath. I'm done with that guy."

Mark knew it was going to be a hard sell to enlist her help. He decided not to mention anything about the professor or the class and kept the conversation light until they got back to his dorm room.

When they entered the room, Mark had them both sit down across from him on Jeremy's bed. Noticing their alarmed looks, like they were about to hear some bad news, he immediately began to lay out the events of the past week. Even though he had purposely kept them in the dark until he figured everything out for himself, he could tell by their expressions that they were not happy with that move. Seeing that they were getting angrier by the minute, he pressed on without giving them a chance to comment. He concluded with the events in Philadelphia and the new information his mom divulged to him the night before.

Neither of them said anything. He could tell Jeremy was hurt by the look on his face, and he noticed Stacie's body language was closed off, with her arms folded and her eyes avoiding contact.

Mark was not prepared for what came next. For the next several minutes, Jeremy and Stacie took turns reminding Mark that when they first agreed to attend Professor Windham's class, they promised to share all their experiences, and they were disappointed in him for betraying that pact.

Mark knew his friends were right, and he humbly agreed with all the points they were making.

"This is why we all need to get out of Professor Windham's class. We did not sign up to get involved in some crazy battle for our souls," said Stacie, switching gears.

She stood up and began to pace back and forth in the small walkway between the two beds. Mark and Jeremy sat up against the wall to give her space to walk.

"Marianne's journal made it very clear how it affected her, and with what happened to Paul and to you meeting this Koltar demon, I don't think any of us want to be next."

Mark took his time in calculating his next response, knowing he was on very thin ice.

"Stace, you make some great points. I wish I could just forget what has happened and shut it all out as Marianne did, but I can't. I don't think any of us can deny the experiences we had that brought us all together to this school and to be in Professor Windham's class. It is clear to me that we are the only ones who can keep this awful thing from happening."

Mark slowly reached up and gently pulled Stacie down to sit next to him.

"The ability I have has opened a door for both good and evil, and now I have been asked to shut this door permanently to stop a very bad event from happening. I'm going to need your help in destroying the portal keys that have been created that can open this door."

"Wait, you mean to tell me we're on a hunt for a bunch of Horcruxes like in *Harry Potter*?" Jeremy asked.

His comment caught Mark off guard, and he smiled at the similarities with one of their favorite movie series. "If it helps you to wrap your brain around it, then yes."

He turned back to Stacie. She did not look amused and was again looking at the ground with her arms crossed.

"I know you have been struggling with what happened with Paul, but we have known each other a long time, and I would not ask you for help if I didn't think I needed you."

Mark held his breath, waiting for her reply. But her expression didn't change, and she didn't say anything.

"So our next move is to find more portal keys?" Jeremy asked, sitting up on the edge of his bed. "Can we get a closer look at the one you have so we have an idea of what to look for?"

Mark knew Jeremy was trying to indirectly involve Stacie without coming right out and asking her.

Stacie stood up with a look of regret.

"I'm sorry, you two. You know I love both of you, but ... I just can't," she said before walking out of the room.

Jeremy stood to go after her, but Mark pulled him back down.

"Let her go. I've dumped a lot of info on her, and she needs her space," Mark said quietly. He had not seen her outright refusal coming and was disappointed.

CHAPTER 47

CLOSER LOOK

Stacie's outright refusal to help made Mark wonder if she knew or could sense something about the professor that he couldn't regarding his motives. He began to second-guess his initial determination that he was not the person helping Koltar.

He took consolation that Jeremy was behind him and decided he had better show Jeremy the portal key again so that he knew what to watch out for. The campus was usually quiet on Sundays, and Mark felt confident he could uncover the object without bringing too much attention.

When they approached the area where his confrontation with Koltar occurred, Mark began to have sharp visions of the encounter race across his mind. They caused him to take a couple of deep breaths and close his eyes.

"You okay?" Jeremy asked, reaching out to hold him up.

"Yeah, I'll be all right. I just need a minute."

Once he got a hold of himself, he led Jeremy over to the spot where he had buried it. He was relieved to see it hadn't been disturbed.

Mark put on some gloves and then crouched down to remove the dirt carefully. Even with the gloves, paranoia began to get the better of him, and his heart started to beat faster. He looked around in all directions and was grateful he didn't notice anything unusual happening.

Mark unwrapped it and held it out in front of him.

Before he could warn him, Jeremy reached over and adjusted it to try to get a better look. Mark saw Jeremy's face go from a pleasant look to an angry expression in a matter of seconds, and he pulled it away from him quickly to break the connection.

Jeremy shook his head. "What in the hell just happened?"

"Remember what I told you. You can't touch it with your bare hands. If you physically touch them, your thoughts will be filled with all sorts of nightmarish images and feelings."

"I know. I felt a wave of them fill my mind. How long was I touching that thing?"

"Only a second or two," Mark said, bringing the portal key back up for Jeremy to study.

"It looks like a piece of cheap art you would buy at a county fair, not some mystical charm. Will all the objects look like this?"

"They will look similar to this since they are all made by the same person for the same purpose."

"Just so I'm clear on this. Someone has been placing these items around here to help open a door for these fallen angels. What does this loser get in return?" Jeremy asked.

"Koltar told me that the riches of the world were not hidden to them, since they have been allowed to observe human actions for a very long time. He told me he would show me where some of these treasures were buried if I helped them. I imagine this person thinks they'll get the same thing."

"You mentioned the professor wasn't much help in explaining what this is. I think we need to take it to him again. He doesn't get off this easy. He can't get us involved in all this supernatural stuff and just hide out in his office," Jeremy said.

"That's a great idea," Mark said, stuffing the object deep down into his backpack to keep it away from his body.

Mark agreed that taking the object back to the professor for a deeper discussion might help him uncover once and for all if the professor was helping Koltar.

"We should also meet with Marianne and let her know that I'm on board to help you. Maybe we can convince her to help now that Stacie is out."

Mark liked that idea too but wanted to clear up one more thing.

"Before we do that, I think I need to visit with Abigail first and see if she has any more information on how many there are and what we need to do with them."

"Do you think Abigail would meet with me now that I've agreed to help?" Jeremy asked in excitement.

"If she has already contacted me and Marianne, I don't see why she wouldn't. There's only one way to find out."

CHAPTER 48

NEEDED COUNSEL

Just before Mark and Jeremy planned to leave for the cemetery, Mark received a phone call from Stacie. She apologized for refusing to help and informed him that she was willing to help. Even though he was dying to know why, he simply thanked her and told her he and Jeremy were leaving for the cemetery after they grabbed some dinner. He invited her to come. Much to his surprise, she agreed.

When she showed up at their dorm, she immediately ran up to Mark and gave him a tight hug. She looked up at him with tears in her eyes.

"Mark, I'm so sorry. I met with Paul today and told him what has happened to you. He told me he didn't want it happening to anyone else, especially if there are more portal keys out there. As you said, we had our experiences for a reason, and we're at this school for a reason. Anyway, I'm not going to run from my ability and leave you shorthanded."

Her sincerity caught Mark off guard. All the feelings of why he dated her came flooding back, and he pulled her back in for another tight hug.

"Thanks, Stace. I didn't know what we were going to do if you weren't in."

"I want in on this before we go," Jeremy said, engulfing them both in his arms.

Mark was beyond ecstatic to have both on board now and spent dinner going over all the events of the past week in more detail.

On the drive over, Mark still wasn't sure Abigail would appear with his friends in tow but felt it was worth the gamble. He knew he needed to start introducing them to the same experiences he was having if they were to truly understand what he was going through.

There was nobody in the cemetery when they pulled up. A slight dusting of snow had fallen, coating everything in white, which Mark hoped would keep people away.

They all made their way over to Abigail's grave, and Mark began to get in the right state of mind to meet her. He started calling out to her in his mind and within seconds could feel her presence.

"You've been busy, Mr. Banks. And it seems you brought your friends along for some company."

Mark looked over at Stacie and Jeremy and realized they had not heard her. He decided to converse with her mentally for a bit longer.

"Yes, I did. Ben told me you could help get us prepared for what's coming. I hope that's okay."

"A friend of yours is a friend of mine. Before revealing myself, I want to have some fun with your friends, if you don't mind. Tell them that to see me, they need to verbally say my name in unison three times."

Her request was a side of Abigail Mark hadn't known existed, but he was more than happy to play along. He worked hard to keep a serious face as he turned to his friends.

"Hey, guys, I think Abigail is near, but to see her, you must say her name together three times."

"Who are we meeting? Beetle Juice?" Jeremy said, smiling.

Mark kept a straight face even though his comment cut him up on the inside.

They both started saying her name slowly in unison. When they finished, Mark could hear Abigail's laugh audibly, and she slowly began to appear.

Jeremy and Stacie gasped simultaneously and moved in closer behind Mark.

"Welcome, friends. I am Abigail Turnbow, and I'm pleased you have come."

They both moved around Mark and looked at him to see if it was okay to respond.

"She is ready to communicate with you but only if you finish saying her name. I think you only said it two times," Mark said, laughing uncontrollably.

"Very funny, Mark," Stacie said, irritated.

Jeremy shoved him playfully.

"I apologize to both of you. I know you did not come out on this chilly evening to be teased; you have more pressing matters to attend to."

Mark composed himself. "Abigail, how were you able to appear so quickly to them, but it took me a while to see you?"

"The channel had to be opened with your ability to see me with spiritual eyes. Now that it is open, I can make myself known more quickly to others who have at least a portion of your gift."

Mark could tell that her comment about Jeremy and Stacie having his gift put them at ease and made them feel validated in being there.

"It would seem the meeting with the council went well," Abigail said, turning her gaze toward Mark.

"Yes, it did. But we've only been able to locate one of the portal keys so far. Ben mentioned others would need to be found and destroyed all at once and that you would have more information for me."

"Ben is correct. Now that you are aware of their craftsmanship, they will be easy to recognize."

"If we don't find and destroy all of these objects, how many of these Koltar spirits are going to come through the door?" Jeremy asked.

"Good question. I've been informed the opening would be the largest ever opened and allow a whole host of these fallen angels through. They have been testing the limits of access for thousands of years and have finally figured out a way to breach the walls that have kept them at bay. It is up to all of you to stop it."

Mark could see the look of concern on his friends' faces when they realized what they were up against. He held his breath, awaiting their reply.

CHAPTER 49

SIDE DOORS

Much to his surprise, Jeremy and Stacie didn't flinch. Their looks of concern were replaced with looks of determination.

"Abigail, Ben said you would tell us how we can destroy the objects once we find all of them. How do we do it?" Mark asked.

"By the use of a side door to my realm. I'm excited to see if your abilities permit you to access them."

Mark was surprised he hadn't been told about side doors and felt unprepared, not knowing anything about them.

"Was I supposed to know about them?"

"I will show you. They are the portals or openings we use to access your realm. They can be opened several different ways, but I'll help you open the quickest way I know how."

Mark thought back to the handful of ways he had observed. His grandfather came through a square of light, while Abigail and Marianne's cousin had appeared out of a ball of light.

Now that Mark had the answer for how to destroy the objects, his other reaming question needed to be answered. "How many portal keys will Koltar need to come through the door?"

"I have learned that the host that Koltar plans to bring with him must come through an opening large enough to accommodate them. You have found the portal key that has propped open the door, but there are four more out there that they need to break the door down. There are three of you here, but you will need to enlist the help of two more who have your ability to assist you to slam it shut."

Mark was glad to hear that Abigail knew the number of keys they would have to find. However, the news that he needed to enlist two more people to help destroy them was another hurdle he hadn't planned on. He couldn't see Paul or Marianne helping him, with what had happened to them.

Mark looked over at Jeremy and Stacie to see if they could offer any names of the handful of other students in their class. They both looked back at him with empty stares. He now regretted not taking the time to get to know any of them.

"There's more. Once you have found all the objects, the five of you must bring them to a central location that will beckon the spirits to come through. Then you must enter through a side door to my realm and destroy them there. They will have too much of a negative influence for you to do it in your realm."

"You mean by shutting these doors, we will be able to keep them out for good?" Stacie asked.

Abigail smiled and nodded her head in agreement. "I believe so. You will have helped stop one of the biggest threats we have ever dealt with."

"Well, now that we know what we need to do, we should probably find out if we can open these side doors," Mark said, dying to know if he could.

"I agree," Abigail said, clapping her hands for them to pay attention. "A side door is a portal used to enter different realms, and the knowledge of how to use them is only shared with those who wish to use them for a noble purpose. I can think of no better purpose than the task you have been charged with, so let me demonstrate."

Abigail began to move one of her arms rapidly to one side in a circular motion while placing her other hand above the circle she was making. She moved into it and disappeared through the opening. Suddenly, an opening appeared in her realm. Stacie and Jeremy leaned over to get a better view.

"That is awesome," Jeremy said, slapping Mark on his back out of excitement. He cringed and shot Jeremy an angry look.

"Mark, you can see how much quicker these doors make it to access my realm. This shortcut can be very useful but also very dangerous. If Koltar and his host get through these openings before you destroy the objects, it could cause a ripple effect of untold suffering for both our realms. Do I have your word you will do everything you're told when the time comes?" Abigail asked with a penetrating look at each of them.

Mark and his friends agreed in unison.

"Thank you. I know your hearts are true, but I needed to hear your declaration. For this exercise, once you are in my realm, you will have the ability to visit any point of the past you wish. But you must stay focused on that point in time for it to open for you. I want all of you to try." Abigail moved over right next to Mark.

Knowing how competitive Jeremy was, Mark could see his disappointment in not being picked to go first.

"Mark, I want you to focus on a spot to your left and concentrate on that area only. Now start moving your arm in a circular motion like you're creating rings in water and think of the exact time and place you wish to appear."

Mark let his mind clear and started moving his left arm in a short, concise circle. He noticed Abigail wave her hand above his circle and say something he couldn't make out. Within seconds, a portal of light started to emerge.

"Good. When the opening is big enough, move into it quickly," Abigail instructed.

When he felt the opening was big enough, he jumped through. He felt a surge of energy shoot through his body, and he was transported to the last point in time he was at his vehicle, which he figured was about a half hour earlier. He stood there in awe, watching himself and his friends get out of the car and walk toward the area he had just left. Noticing the portal of light was still open, he jumped back through. In another surge, he was back in front of Abigail, feeling a little dizzy.

"Well done, Mark," Abigail said with a pleasing smile. "You have taken to that ability quickly. It has now been given to you to use when necessary. But I warn you not to abuse the privilege and only use it when it's safe."

"You mean I can open this side door whenever I want?" Mark asked in surprise.

"Yes, but I want you to promise me you'll only use it when necessary or prompted to."

"I promise."

"Now I will bestow this gift to the both of you," Abigail said, looking at Stacie and Jeremy. "Stacie. why don't you go first."

Again, Mark saw the disappointed look on Jeremy's face.

Abigail moved over in front of Stacie as she began to make her circle. With Abigail's assistance, an opening of light appeared. Stacie moved through it quickly and was gone.

Mark began to get worried when Stacie did not appear after several minutes. She was taking a lot longer than he had. He noticed a look of worry on Jeremy's face and was about to say something when she suddenly reappeared.

"What was that Stace? Where did you go?" asked Jeremy with wide eyes.

"I went back to my old room at my house," Stacie said with a look of amazement. "I wanted to see if I could go farther away than Mark did, and that was the first place that popped into my head. It was just like I left it. I knew that no one would be there because my folks are out of town this weekend."

"Nice job, Miss Wonders. You can see that you can visit any place you focus on, even the present. But even if your folks were home, they would not be able to see you. They do not have access to see you in my realm."

Mark thought back to what Ben had said about his office and the workers in the building not being able to see them.

Jeremy pushed his way past both him and Stacie to get closer to Abigail.

"All right, Mr. Kozlowski, your turn," Abigail said, amused by Jeremy's eagerness.

Mark could tell Jeremy was taking a moment to compose himself and then began to make his circle. It took him a while to start to open his side door, and it opened and closed several times. Eventually, it was big enough, and Jeremy jumped through.

Several minutes went by with no sign of him. Mark realized he was gone a lot longer than Stacie had been. He looked over at Stacie and could see her concern.

"I thought this might happen," Abigail said, disappearing through an opening of her own.

CHAPTER 50

NEXT STEPS

Within a few seconds, Abigail was back with a weak-looking Jeremy in tow. He looked up and smiled at Mark and Stacie and then collapsed to his knees.

"What happened?" Mark asked Jeremy while he and Stacie reached down to help him to his feet.

"I don't know. I thought I would try to go further back in time than you did. I decided to visit the last time I was at Rehoboth beach with my grandparents. I watched my interaction with my grandfather and could instantly taste my grandma's tuna fish sandwiches she would always bring. I just broke down, and the next thing I knew, Abigail was there, and now we're here," Jeremy said, wiping away tears.

Abigail smiled warmly at Jeremy and then at all of them.

"Here is another warning. I don't recommend visiting yourself or direct family members. You can lose focus rather quickly and get lost trying to relive a part of you that has already lived. You must stay focused on where you want to go, while keeping track of the portal, so you can return. I won't always be around to find you, and you don't want to get lost in time."

"Lost in time?" Stacie asked.

"Yes. My realm is a timestamp to all the different periods of man's existence on earth. There have been some who get lost in my realm, visiting different eras to escape their reality. Even though I've given you the ability to access them, I can also remove this access if I think you're abusing it."

Mark was anxious to try opening a side door by himself for practice, but he knew his time with Abigail was nearing the end.

"Abigail, if we can't find two more people with our gift, can't we just destroy them quickly in our realm?"

"That would be more convenient, wouldn't it? As I mentioned before, their influence on you will be too great in your realm. You must find two more to help you. I must figure out a way to create a barrier for you to have enough time to step through."

It continued to amaze Mark that Abigail was still learning one step at a time like he was and had faith she would figure it out in time. He took comfort that she was on a similar path of understanding her purpose in this conflict.

"Your only goal is to step through and destroy the portal keys all at once. I'm still waiting to learn the details of how that will be done as well."

"Will you need to train the other two people we find to open their side door?" Mark asked.

"Mark, I don't need to be the one to show them. You've seen the hand gesture I used to grant your access. Simply perform that on their first attempt and say the following blessing." She leaned down and whispered in his ear.

"Can we hear it too?" asked Jeremy.

"I'm afraid I'm not permitted to let everyone know what is said," said Abigail, turning back to Mark. "Just make sure you share with them the warnings we have discussed. This is all the information I can give you at this time, my friends. I wish you God's speed in finding those other portal keys."

Mark stood there taking in everything that had just happened and was grateful he had been given clear direction on their next steps.

"That was amazing. She was amazing," Jeremy said, rubbing his hands together and blowing in them for warmth. "I say it's time we try getting Marianne on board, and maybe the professor knows someone who might help us."

Mark agreed that Marianne had to be included. She would have the shortest learning curve regarding what was happening.

"Let's tackle this one step at a time. Let's meet with Marianne before we see the professor on Friday. She might be more willing to help me now that you two are involved."

"Deal," Jeremy said and then bolted straight for the car.

Stacie simply smiled and put her arm around Mark's waist, turning him toward the car.

"Thanks for not giving up on me."

"Never have and never will."

CHAPTER 51

MAKE OR BREAK

Mark spent the next few days trying to come up with a plan to get Marianne on board. He knew she had concern for his well-being from their most recent conversation, and maybe after hearing all that had transpired since then, he could sway her to join their cause.

He settled on a plan to have Jeremy and Stacie meet him at the entrance of the McKeldin Library during their lunch break that Wednesday. He knew there was a good chance Marianne would be there since she had laid out her schedule to him.

When they huddled that afternoon, Mark showed his friends the selfie Marianne had taken when she programmed her number into his phone.

"Okay, J, you sweep floors five through seven. Stace, you take three and four. I'll cover one and two," he said, pointing at the library floor plan at the front entrance. "Just so we're clear, don't approach her yourself. Just text me if you see her. Got it?"

Stacie rolled her eyes sarcastically while studying the picture of her on Mark's phone.

"What's up with all the *Mission Impossible* stuff? If she's here, we'll notice her. I don't know how we would miss a girl with hair like that."

Mark couldn't tell if she commented on her hair jokingly or with a little jealousy due to her picture being on his phone. He pulled the phone away from her.

"Anyway, I want to be the first to talk to her," Mark said with a serious look.

They both nodded in agreement and then scattered.

Mark started his sweep and carefully scanned the first floor but did not see her. The library was packed with students, with finals only a few weeks away, and he knew it would be a lot harder to spot her. He made multiple passes just to make sure.

Fifteen minutes went by without spotting her. He hadn't received a text from Jeremy or Stacie yet either. He knew he couldn't miss this opportunity to contact her before their class on Friday.

Giving up on the first floor, he made his way up the stairs to the second floor.

Within moments, he spotted Marianne getting help from another student at a help desk with her laptop.

He sat down in a chair that was within eyeshot of her. His heart started racing again, and he told himself over and over to calm down. He sent a quick text to Jeremy and Stacie that he had found her and to come down to the second floor and blend in.

It was hard for him to look inconspicuous while he waited. The more he tried to pretend he wasn't watching her, the more awkward he felt. Suddenly she turned and looked right at him. He hurriedly looked away and then noticed out of the corner of his eye that she was heading straight for him.

"Hi, Mark," she said with a smile, leaning down to hug him.

Her excitement to see him helped Mark relax.

"Hey, Marianne. What are you doing here?" he asked casually.

"I've got a massive physics assignment due next week ahead of the final, and I needed help arranging a bunch of documents on my laptop to study." She patted her oversized book bag that was hanging over her shoulder.

"I like what you've done with your hair," Mark said, noticing that it was a lot shorter than when he last saw her.

Marianne began to run her hand through her snow-white hair, looking pleased that he had noticed. His first impulse was to ask her out on a date from the way she was looking at him. But he quickly remembered the task at hand and pushed the thought aside.

He kept the conversation going while he waited for Jeremy and Stacie to arrive. Marianne went into some detail about her classes and crazy schedule while he talked about the stresses of being a new college freshman and his impending finals.

With each passing minute, Mark wondered what was taking his friends so long. He didn't know how long he could keep her there making small talk.

Marianne glanced down at her watch. "Oh, heavens, Mark. I've got a club activity over at the Cole I've got to get to. I better get going. It was good to see you, and if you're ever up by the golf course, swing by Mulligan's, and I'll hook you up with some food. I'm a server up there."

Mark realized he hadn't even brought up anything that he wanted to discuss with her.

"I'm headed up that way myself, if you don't mind me tagging along," he said, standing up and moving in beside her.

"Sure." She put her arm through his.

They were about to go down the stairs to the first floor when Mark noticed Jeremy and Stacie walking toward them, about to say something. With a nod of his head, he waved them off without Marianne noticing. They caught on and moved out of their line of sight quickly.

From her reaction of being glad to see him, Mark felt confident he did not need his friends' help and could handle it on his own.

On their way up Library Lane toward the Cole Student Activities building, Mark decided to take a chance and jump right in.

"Marianne, a lot of crazy things have happened to me lately, and I need to tell someone who understands where I'm coming from and won't think I'm crazy."

"Sure. What kind of things?" she said in a tone that encouraged Mark to continue.

The way she was looking up at him made it hard for him to begin. Her soft smile and ruby-red lips were a major distraction.

He quickly composed himself and hit the highlights of everything that had happened.

When he finished, he held his breath, waiting to see what her response would be.

To his surprise, she stayed by his side. He could tell she was processing all the things he had just mentioned. She stopped abruptly and turned to face him.

"Mark, I appreciate you telling me all of this. I've had something happen recently that you should know about. You haven't destroyed the portal key you found, have you?"

Her question caught Mark off guard and left him speechless.

CHAPTER 52

UNEXPECTED

Mark had no idea where she was going with her question. He hadn't gone into much detail about how many of them there were and what would have to be done to destroy them. It was pointless until he knew she was on board, but her question opened the door for him to bring it up.

"I still have it. I've got to find four more of them to keep Koltar and the dark beings you saw from entering our realm."

He hoped mentioning how many were still out there would drive home the gravity of his situation.

Marianne's face went expressionless, and her walk slowed. She didn't say anything for several minutes. Her body language suggested to him that she was battling an internal struggle with what to say next.

When they entered the Cole building, Marianne grabbed Mark's arm and pulled him over to a secluded area near the stairwell.

"Mark, you said you need to find four more of these portal keys?"

"Yeah. Abigail mentioned it will take five of them to open the door wide enough for them to come through, and I would need to find four more people who have our gift to close it."

"I only saw the one you had briefly. Remind me again what the charm looks like?" she asked.

Mark described it in detail and explained he had it well hidden, just in case she was worried he had it on him.

Upon finishing, Marianne began fishing around for something deep inside her book bag. When she pulled out a small object that was wrapped in printed cloth and tied with string, Mark's heart sank.

She placed it in the palm of her hand and began to untie it. It opened to reveal a portal key almost identical to the one Mark had.

He stood there in disbelief.

"Marianne, how on earth did you get this?"

"I found it the same day you showed me yours. I was leaving this building late that night and found it lying right outside. I thought of getting rid of it right away but felt I should keep it until I saw you again."

"You didn't touch it with your bare hands, did you?" Mark asked out of concern.

"I didn't. I had gloves on. Funny you mention that. I had an overwhelming feeling to take off my gloves and hold it. It was like I was hearing voices in my head. I didn't want a repeat of what happened to me in the cemetery with that other object, and I resisted the urge. I wrapped it up and kept it in my bag. I'm glad you know what to do with it now."

She held it out like it was contaminated. Her hand twitched suddenly, and the object rolled off.

Instinctively, Mark reached out and grabbed the object with his bare hand.

Just then, he felt a surge of negativity rush through his body, and within seconds, he heard a familiar voice coming from a darkened area to the right of the stairwell they were facing.

"It is all going according to plan. I hope you now realize that it is inevitable that you help us," Koltar said confidently.

Mark felt his body freeze while he tried to find the definition in the darkness where the voice was coming from. He could feel Marianne's nails dig into the flesh of his arm out of fear. He tried to release the object from his hand, but it was too late. He couldn't move a muscle.

"Once I find all of these, I'm going to slam the door shut," Mark said, channeling the anger toward Koltar.

The voice became louder and more threatening.

"Both of you will see that the pathway through our worlds is connected, or I will see that your bodies are destroyed and your rotting flesh—" Suddenly the voice was cut off, and Mark was released.

Bewildered, he looked over at Marianne, who was clutching the portal key in the cloth she had wrapped it in.

"Please tell me you just heard all of that," Mark said, breathing heavily.

"Yes. That is the main voice I heard in the cemetery last year," she said, trembling. "This is what I've been trying to warn you about. I'm so sorry, Mark. I should've destroyed this the second I found it."

She raised her arm and was about to throw it on the hard floor when he caught her arm with one hand and scooped the object out with his other hand.

She looked up at Mark in surprise and fell toward him.

He quickly wrapped his arm around her waist and walked her over to sit at the bottom of the stairs.

"Don't blame yourself, Marianne. You were meant to find one of these. That is why I need your help," he said sincerely.

Marianne looked at the object in Mark's hand and then back at him.

"I don't know, Mark. You see how quickly this can get out of hand. Why can't we just destroy the two we have and forget about finding the others. If we don't have all five of them, then the door cannot be opened, right?"

"I asked the same question but was told it is not that easy. The objects have a spell on them. If we don't find all of them quickly, these beings will continue to grow in power and could influence people to harm themselves. That is why I need your help. It is going to take five of us with our ability to close the door. If I tried to destroy all five objects by myself, their influence would overtake me. Luckily, Jeremy and Stacie have agreed to help me destroy them. They are the ones who were with me when I found your notebook."

After mentioning his friends, he noticed a look of relief shoot across her face, and he decided to keep going.

"All three of us visited with Abigail and learned that we will need to hold the portal keys in one hand and open what's called a side door portal to the fourth realm with the other hand. Once we step through, we will need to destroy them all at once. If you help us, we will only need to find one more person."

To Mark's surprise, Marianne stood up and forcefully grabbed the portal key out of his hand, shoving it back into her bag.

"I cannot hide from what's happening anymore. I will keep this one with me until you need it and me."

Her determination was a side of her Mark hadn't seen before. He couldn't believe that their temporary run-in with Koltar was the catalyst in getting her to help.

"Thanks, Marianne. I know you wanted to move on from all of this, but I feel our paths were meant to cross for this purpose, and I know I won't be able to do this without you."

She smiled at him bashfully and moved in toward him.

Mark was about to lean in for a kiss when a couple of students called out for Marianne to join them, and he quickly backed away.

"Thanks, Mark. I better get going. I promised to help get this place ready for a rally."

She swung her bag over her shoulder and then gave him a tight hug.

Mark remembered one other thing he wanted to ask her before she turned to leave.

"Marianne, would you mind coming with us to meet with Professor Windham on Friday?"

"Why?" she asked guardedly.

Mark did not divulge that he thought the professor could be the one placing the objects around campus and decided to go with Jeremy's suggestion.

"I believe he could recommend a fifth person to help us, and it would be nice if you, Jeremy, Stacie, and I approach him together."

Mark could tell she was processing his request carefully.

"All right, Mark, I will come for you. I purposely have not seen him in over a year and don't trust him. But I trust and care for you and what you are trying to do."

"Thanks, Marianne. See you on Friday."

CHAPTER 53

STARTLING NEWS

Mark arranged to meet Marianne at the front of the library about an hour before the Psychic Phenomenon class so they could talk to the professor privately. He could feel their relationship starting to grow from mere acquaintances to good friends and maybe more.

Their shared experience from Wednesday had opened a new channel of communication between them. Marianne had called and texted him multiple times over the past few days with different questions and more insights into what she had experienced.

Even though she had agreed to help him, Mark was still worried she wouldn't show up when he left to meet her.

"Jeremy, I'm heading out. I'll meet you at the psych class in about an hour," Mark said, grabbing his hoody and backpack.

"Do you think she'll show this time?" Jeremy asked skeptically, still in bed.

"Yes, she'll show."

"That's what you said last time, bro."

Mark left quickly, not wanting to get into another debate.

He had spent the previous night catching Jeremy and Stacie up on what happened to him and Marianne at the Cole building. They were excited to meet her, but neither of them wanted to go with Mark to meet her that early before class.

While walking to the library, he felt a little nervous bringing his portal key along, even though it was wrapped up tightly and stuffed deep down in his backpack. Just the thought of another encounter with Koltar made him feel uneasy.

A cold rain had started to fall by the time he got to the library. He noticed Marianne standing just outside the main entrance, holding an umbrella in one hand, and rubbing her shoulder with the other, trying to keep warm.

Mark ran up and tapped on her umbrella, causing a spray of water to hit his face. "You could've waited inside," he said, ducking under her umbrella. He wiped his face with the sleeve of his hoody with an embarrassed grin.

"The library is nuts right now. I thought it would be better for me to just wait here so you could have an easier time finding me. Plus, I have Gertrude here to keep me company."

"Gertrude?" Mark asked, looking around and seeing no one nearby.

"My umbrella," she said, tipping it down so Mark could see the pattern of an old lady holding an umbrella all over it.

"Nice. I thought you were talking about someone you could see on the other side."

"Ha-ha, very funny. It's large enough to share," she said, moving close to him and putting it over them both.

Mark put his arm around her, and they started walking in step with each other.

Not much was said on the way over to the psych building. They were laughing too hard trying to keep the umbrella against the direction of the sleet that kept shifting.

"Did you bring your portal key?" asked Marianne.

"Yeah, it's in my backpack. How about you?"

"I thought about not bringing it, but I figured the professor would want to look at it. Maybe they will help him remember someone else in your class who might have seen one. I wish we knew who's leaving them all over."

Her comment reminded Mark that he still needed to find out, once and for all, which side the professor was working for.

They made their way into the classroom and began drying off when Mark noticed another teacher he had seen in the building a few times before. He approached them from the professor's office, with a stack of papers in his hands.

"Have either of you seen Professor Windham? I have some information I wanted to drop off, but his office is empty."

Mark shot Marianne a confused look and then looked back at the teacher. "We haven't, but we came early to talk with him about a few things."

"Great. Do you mind giving these to him since you are waiting? I'm late for another meeting across campus, and I promised him I would get these notes to him before his class." The teacher didn't wait for an answer and pushed the papers into Mark's hand.

Before he had a chance to respond, the teacher moved around them and exited.

Mark shrugged, and he and Marianne continued to the professor's office.

The professor had sounded excited to meet with them when he called him the night before to tell him the good news about Marianne wanting to meet with him again.

Mark couldn't hide his look of disappointment when they entered the empty office.

"I guess he got hung up on something important," Marianne said, looking around.

"Let's give him a few minutes."

Mark pulled one of the chairs out for Marianne to sit in and sat down next to her. He looked down at the papers he was holding and began reading.

"Should you be reading those, Mark? Maybe it's official school business."

"How confidential could they be if that other teacher just handed them to us? Look at this," Mark said, leaning over toward her so they both could read the note that was written on the first piece of paper.

Miles,

Here is the information you requested I compile from the reports turned into the student services office. You were correct. Many students have reported catching glimpses of a dark mass around campus. A few of them even reported a dark personage walking by them and then vanishing when they turned to face it. All of them have reported having very violent thoughts during these encounters.

Here are all the letters I have received. I trust that you will investigate what's going on and get to the bottom of it with your experience in the paranormal. After reading them myself, I can't help but feel the suicides over the past few weeks and what's happening are somehow connected.

Let me know if I can be of any further assistance.
Regards,
Jeff

Mark was saddened and concerned to read about the suicides. He had been too busy the past few weeks to notice what was happening on campus.

"Mark, did he tell you anything about this, or did he keep this information to himself?"

Mark noticed the look on her face included both anger and skepticism.

"No, he hasn't said anything to me about other sightings, but he did catch my confrontation with Koltar on his camera and showed it to the class."

"That's probably why he went walking around with his camera. He doesn't care about what happens to the students, only what he can capture to further his own goals," she said disgustedly.

Her comments made the anger rise within him, and he couldn't wait for the professor to enter the room so he could give him the letters and confront him again.

Looking around the room, Mark knew he couldn't have gone far after noticing a cup of coffee sitting on the desk that was still steaming and a half-eaten bagel.

"He must have been here a few minutes before we got here and just stepped out for a while," he said, setting the papers down on the desk.

He was about to bring up the book of spells when a slight breeze began to pick up directly behind them.

They both turned around, startled, and Mark noticed a small circle of light beginning to appear. When it grew large enough, Mark could see that there was someone on the other side. Suddenly, the professor stepped through the circle, holding something wrapped in a plastic bag.

"Sorry I'm late, you two, but I always stay too long when visiting the other realm."

CHAPTER 54

UNKNOWN GIFT

Mark could not believe his eyes after seeing the professor appear through a side door. Not once had the professor mentioned them during his lectures or to Mark privately.

He glanced over and noticed Marianne was staring straight at him, totally confused.

Before he could answer her questions, he had to get to the bottom of what just happened.

"You know about side doors?" Mark asked the professor, barely getting the words out.

"Yes, I do. I'm glad to see you are familiar with them."

Mark's mind was reeling.

"You've been telling me this whole semester about how I had a gift that few people had. Never once did you tell me that *you* had it."

The professor moved around to his desk and sat down in his chair, breathing heavily. He picked up his coffee and took a long sip.

"I had to make sure you could make contact before I could explain what this ability is and how it's used. I wanted to meet with you earlier in the week, but I've been very busy. I figured Abigail would show you how to use them in due time, and she has."

He placed the object he was holding in his other hand down on his desk and carefully unwrapped it to reveal another portal key.

Mark could not believe how fast the portal keys were showing up, and he wondered if Stacie and Jeremy would find theirs on the way over to class.

The professor turned to Marianne. "Marianne, it is good to see you again. I never had the chance to apologize for what happened last year. I should've been more supportive. But it has taken me most of this year to understand what is coming and what I needed to do to help stop it. I'm sure Mark is grateful you have decided to help."

Mark could see her face soften after he said this, and she smiled back at him.

"Apology accepted, Professor. Mark and I experienced something on Wednesday that changed my mind about my getting involved. I also found one of those charms. But before I get into how I found mine, where did you just come from?"

"Mark has probably told you that side doors open a portal to the fourth realm. Once you're taught how to open them, you can access them when need be."

Mark knew he better elaborate on what the professor had just said.

"Sorry about this, Marianne. I will be able to teach you how to open yours now that Abigail has shown me how to do it. Jeremy and Stacie were able to open theirs."

The professor sighed in relief and smiled. "Both of them have agreed to help you then. That is great news, Mark. You're enlisting quite the A team. We've got some time before class, so why don't catch me up on everything?"

Mark caught the professor up on what the council and Abigail had instructed regarding the number of portal keys and how to destroy them. He also confessed and apologized for thinking that he was behind planting the objects.

Marianne reached deep into her book bag, pulled out her portal key, and placed it on the desk. Mark did the same.

The professor pushed his object forward and carefully opened the other two. They were almost identical in every manner.

"Mark, have you had any success in locating the other two?" the professor asked.

"Not yet. I have Stacie and Jeremy looking out for them. I can't believe two more have shown up so quickly. Since you have a portal key and have our gift, does that mean you're on board with helping us, Professor?"

"It would be my honor to help you."

Mark felt a huge weight lift off his shoulders, knowing that he had one person for each portal key they needed to find.

"Professor, how did you find your key, and how long have you known about the side doors?"

"The portal key is the strangest story. I found it just outside the building a few nights ago. Whoever left it knew that I'm the last person to leave on Tuesday nights, and it was just lying on the ground in front of the main entrance for me to find rather easily. Thank goodness you had shown me the one you found and warned me about touching them directly. I had this sack from my dinner that I brought and used it to pick it up."

Marianne said, "Whoever is placing these is acting quickly and must know a lot about our schedules."

The professor shook his head. "Things are happening at a rapid pace now. I reached out to my guide from the fourth realm later that night, and he told me to hold onto it until I had a chance to meet with you. The use of the side doors I've known about for quite some time."

"Wait. He? You're not working with Abigail?" Mark asked, assuming she was the only spirit assigned to help them.

"I'm not, but I would imagine they know of each other. I've been meeting with Nathaniel since I was in college. He was instrumental in helping me create this psychic phenomenon class to identify those who had my gift. Our guides from the fourth realm have their contacts from higher ones as well."

Mark was about to follow up on the professor's comment about contacts from higher realms when Marianne grabbed his arm.

"Once all of us have our charms and can open the side doors, then what? How do we destroy them?" Marianne asked Mark, looking a little annoyed.

Mark realized he had left a few things out regarding what needed to be done.

"The only way these objects can be destroyed is to take them into the fourth realm and destroy them simultaneously by five of us who have the gift to access it. That's you, me, the professor, Stacie, and Jeremy."

Mark noticed a look of remorse cross her face, and he wondered if he had said something wrong.

"I guess if I hadn't shut everything out last year, Abigail could've taught me how to use these side doors, and maybe I could've helped stop this sooner. Do you think people have died because of my choice?"

Mark knew he couldn't let her carry the weight of the recent suicides.

"I don't think the object you found last year in the cemetery was a portal key. You are joining this cause at exactly the right time, and I know you will be able to open your door when the time comes."

"I agree with Mark," the professor said, jumping in. "I bet it was some kind of test object that allowed those spirits limited access in possessing you, but it did not have the power to open the door for them to all walk through."

Seeing that their words had lifted her spirits, Mark turned his attention back to the professor.

"Professor, how were you able to come out of your door so quickly? It seemed like I got a little stuck crossing over from that realm back into ours when I tried it."

"It takes some practice. The first few times, you get caught up in the wonder of it all and fail to focus on keeping track of where you opened your door. You must think of the specific event and stay nearby. The door will not follow you."

Mark thought back to the warning Abigail gave to Jeremy when she had to go retrieve him.

"Have you gotten used to the time difference when visiting that realm?"

"Yes. The more you visit, the longer you will be able to stay. You can witness quite a lot and not miss a beat back here. I've gotten to the point where I can open a side door rather quickly, think of a place or time in history, take it all in, and then come back within minutes here."

"That's why your coffee was still hot," Mark said, smiling.

"Exactly."

"What do you mean witnessing history?" Marianne asked, trying to keep up.

"If you want to visit a particular event, you can." The professor pointed to a picture of Abraham Lincoln hanging on his wall. "If you want to witness the Gettysburg Address in person, you can." He then reached behind him and pulled a book off one of the shelves behind him that showed people running from a volcano. "Or the destruction of Pompei from Mount Vesuvius, although I don't recommend the depressing periods of history, as they can take a toll on you emotionally."

Thoughts of what places in time Mark wanted to visit began to flood his mind as the professor continued. "The events you can witness their can teach you so much about the purpose of this life."

"The fourth realm can help us understand our purpose now?" Marianne asked, looking enthralled.

Mark also wondered where the professor was going with his statement.

CHAPTER 55

PROGRESSION

Mark expected a conversation regarding the purpose of life with Pastor Watts, not with the professor, and was anxious to get more insight into what he believed religiously.

"Marianne, the purpose of this life is to gain as much knowledge and understanding regarding how our bodies, the world, and our universe operate. Our soul continues a journey of progression with each phase, teaching us things one step at a time until we arrive at our purest potential and a state of full understanding."

The professor reached behind him and grabbed a large rock from his shelf.

"Right now, most people in our world feel like this rock. Heavy, rough, and bound to this earth, with little knowledge of their true potential. This rock will at some point become a beautiful diamond. It is God's purpose to get our souls to reach a diamond-like state. By being able to access the fourth realm before tasting death, you are on a faster track in turning your rock into a diamond."

Mark took comfort knowing the professor was on the same page with him in believing God was behind each step. He was also happy to see Marianne smiling and nodding in agreement.

The professor's demeanor turned serious, and he leaned forward, looking directly at Mark.

"Mark, it is important that you find those other two portal keys quickly. The longer we have these three objects in our possession, the possibility of us making a mistake becomes more likely," said the professor, wrapping up his charm.

"I agree, Professor. I will make sure Jeremy and Stacie are aware that they are next and to watch out for them."

Mark and Marianne gathered up their charms.

Before leaving, Mark realized he hadn't mentioned anything about the notes he had been given.

"I forgot to mention one of the other teachers dropped these by for you," Mark said, sliding the notes over to him.

The professor's eyes lit up. "Thanks, Mark. Maybe one of them will mention the location of a portal key, and we'll be able to track one down that way."

Mark hadn't thought of that possibility, and he hoped the professor would find something quickly. It worried him to think that the portal keys could be changing hands around campus and causing other students to take their own lives.

Just then, he could hear his classmates starting to enter the classroom.

"I need to get ready for our class, and we all have a lot of work to do. Make sure you keep your objects secure and out of the hands of the innocent."

"Will do, Professor."

Upon exiting the office, Mark glanced around the classroom and spotted Jeremy and Stacie already seated and talking amongst themselves. He was a little irritated that they had missed the whole conversation and that he would have to fill them in again.

He turned his attention back to Marianne. "Do you want to stay for the class?"

"I wish I could. But I have a final to prep for in my English class," she said with a look of disappointment.

Before she left, he took the time to introduce Marianne to Jeremy and Stacie. They were more than excited to finally meet her.

Mark walked her up to the exit. "Thanks again for coming, Marianne. I will let Stacie and Jeremy know that the professor is on board and let you know once we find the other keys."

"Do you think I will be able to access these side doors all of you can access? I did a pretty good job of closing everything off last year."

Mark thought about her question for a moment and worried that if he failed to help her open her side door, she might get frustrated and give up.

He decided not to chance it.

"Marianne, I think it's time you reconnected with Abigail."

CHAPTER 56

A NEW FORCE

Now that Mark had everyone that he needed on board, he wanted to gain a better understanding of what was to be done with the portal keys once the five of them cross over. That wouldn't be possible if Marianne couldn't open her side door.

Mark had found some time in Marianne's schedule for her to come with him to the HCC the next morning. He hoped that Abigail would be able to get Marianne's abilities jump-started again and provide more insight.

It had been storming for the past few days, and a thin coat of ice had coated everything in the area, which made the ride out extra nerve-wracking. Even though they had dressed warmly, the cold cut right through them when they stepped out of the car.

"Are you sure she couldn't make contact with us from the comfort of the library?" Marianne asked, shivering through her smile. Now Mark understood why Jeremy and Stacie were so eager to decline his invitation to join them.

Mark stopped abruptly within a few feet of Abigail's headstone, sensing she was there waiting for him. Their connection continued to grow stronger with each visit.

He looked over at Marianne, whose pale skin was turning a light shade of red and blue. "You probably already know this, but in a few moments, neither of us will be cold."

A warm breeze began to move around them, and Mark noticed Marianne smiling with anticipation.

Abigail appeared before them with a welcoming smile. "I am overjoyed to see you two together," she said, clapping her hands in gratitude.

Mark noticed tears begin to fall down Marianne's cheeks.

"Hello again, Abigail," Marianne mustered in a high-pitched tone.

Mark didn't say anything while he watched them reconnect. It dawned on him that he didn't know either of them just a few months ago, and now he had feelings of love and concern for both. He couldn't let anything happen to them.

"Abigail, Marianne has found one of the portal keys. We also found out yesterday that the professor has one with him. He has been working with a guide from your realm for over thirty years."

"That is great news. I'm happy to learn there are more of us participating in this cause."

"We also found out yesterday that he knows how to enter your realm through the side doors and has agreed to help us."

"That makes three of the five keys that have been found in your quest then."

"You were right when you mentioned being on the lookout for them. I'm hoping to find the others soon."

"Remember, I told you that if you were worthy of the task at hand, they would find you."

Mark turned to Marianne and waited for her to bring up the main reason they were there. He didn't want to put any undue pressure on her by requesting help with opening a side door on her behalf.

"Mark mentioned you could teach me to use these side doors?" Marianne asked, looking unsure of herself.

"I would be happy to. Even though Mr. Banks is more than capable of doing it himself," she said, shooting him a stern look and then turning back to Marianne with a smile. "If you remember, the fourth realm does not operate like yours. You will have to stay focused the whole time you are in it. Are you ready?"

Mark could see Marianne's face become focused while Abigail raised her hands symbolically over her.

"Now why don't you start by focusing on the area right in front of you and slowly begin to move your arm in a circle. Don't be worried if you cannot open it your first time."

Marianne began to move her arm in a circular rotation in front of her with her right arm while holding onto Mark's arm with her left. He was surprised and relieved to see a ray of light start to appear almost immediately. Pretty soon, the opening became larger and larger until it almost encompassed him, so he moved out of the way.

"Now step through the opening in front of you and make sure you concentrate on a point in time you have always wanted to visit," Abigail instructed.

Marianne counted to three out loud and then quickly stepped through, inadvertently pulling Mark in with her.

Mark felt like he was caught between realms. He decided to move further into the fourth realm and could see Marianne appearing on the horizon of a beautiful orchard. She moved toward him quickly, hovering just above the ground. Within an instant, she ended up pushing him out of the opening onto the frozen ground of the cemetery. The opening shut behind them.

"What happened, Abigail?" Mark asked, looking at her, impressed.

"Marianne has some amazing abilities. I've never seen anyone from your realm move that fast through mine."

CHAPTER 57

COMFORT LEVEL

Marianne dropped to her knees for a few moments, trying to catch her breath. Mark held her arm to keep her from collapsing to the cold ground.

Marianne shot back to her feet.

"When I went through, I couldn't decide on one event to visit. Everything I wanted to visit seemed to take hold of me and pull me from one stop to another. I just flew through it, taking in all I could. I figured I was gone too long, so I decided to return and was pulled back to the opening. I'm sorry about that, Abigail," she said with a look of determination. "Let me try again."

"That's the spirit, Miss Bawley. This time, try opening it by yourself."

Marianne began to move her arm around again, and the opening appeared quickly. Mark noticed her reach out with her other hand and touch the opening for some reason. Before he knew it, all three of them were standing in the fourth realm.

"Marianne, you have just opened a bridge between our realms. It is a very special gift to be able to perform the same function that I can."

All Mark could do was nod in agreement while he looked around at the beautiful meadow and cascading mountains that appeared all around them.

"How did you do this?" Mark asked.

"I don't know. I was so embarrassed that I lost focus on my first try that I just thought about us all being together in this meadow I visited years ago on a trip to Switzerland. This is even more beautiful than I remember," Marianne said, taking it all in.

"That is because you are seeing it in its most perfect state. When you visit a certain place in time, everything will be sharper and more brilliant than you've ever seen it."

Mark noticed Abigail moving around them excitedly from being able to share this knowledge with them.

"Abigail, since Marianne was able to pull us through all at once, would she be able to pull all five of us through when we are ready to destroy the portal keys?" Mark asked, hoping that was an option. He didn't want to worry about any of them losing focus.

"I don't see why not. I need to do a few more exercises with Miss Bawley in this realm before I know for sure."

Mark was excited to hear it was a possibility.

Seeing that Abigail had some work to do with Marianne, he wondered if he could visit another place in time even though he didn't open the portal. There had been little time for him to practice visiting the fourth realm since Abigail had shown him how to open it.

"Abigail, do you mind if I take a visit while I'm here?"

"Yes. Just remember to keep your focus on this opening so you can make your way back. I don't want to have come looking for you." Abigail gave Mark a quick wink and returned to Marianne.

After finding a secluded spot, Mark began to recollect what the professor had told him about visiting any event in history he wished. He sat down in the field and decided to focus on Philadelphia during the time of the revolution. More specifically, the day the Declaration of Independence was signed.

Thoughts of all the paintings he had seen in books regarding the event began to fill his mind. Within moments, he felt the same rush he had experienced on his first attempt. The meadow and surrounding mountains were soon replaced with colonial buildings, horses, carts, and people milling about Independence Hall in Philadelphia.

Mark realized he was sitting near the front of the building and couldn't believe it had happened so quickly. This event in history was one of his favorite things to study in high school, and he knew he would've joined up with the early patriots to fight for the cause of freedom.

He stood up and noticed a group of people gathered near the entrance to the building and joined them. He could feel the energy of this group of people who were aware of what was happening inside and slipped through them into the building.

From his previous visits, Mark headed straight toward the large chamber where the document was signed. He could hear a lot of deliberation going on.

Upon entering the room, he decided to sit in one of the vacant chairs in the corner of the room to just observe. The comments from some of the senators from the different colonies moved him emotionally. Their passion and conviction for their cause brought tears to his eyes. He couldn't contain his enthusiasm and walked over to join a large contingent in the center of the room.

When the debate had ceased and they reached the final vote, he watched with pride while each one of them got in line to sign the Declaration of Independence laid out before them. Chills ran through every inch of his body.

He paid special attention to Ben Franklin and John Hancock. Knowing that they were part of the Vita-Mors Council and that they had his gift, he wondered how often they might've come back to witness this point in time.

The temptation to visit his past had crossed his mind a lot. It was one of the reasons he hadn't dared make any visits of his own. He was glad he had heeded Abigail's warning to Jeremy and came to this moment instead.

While standing over the desk and watching each representative sign the document, Mark felt Abigail's presence move up next to him.

"If you are done with your visit, it is time to go," Abigail said, looking down at the document with him. "Isn't it exciting to witness something like this? This was one of the first things I chose to witness after entering this realm."

Before he could request to stay a little longer, she grabbed his hand, and they moved back to the meadow.

Marianne ran up to meet them.

"Should I tell him?" Marianne said, looking at Abigail with an ecstatic look.

"Better yet, why don't you show him?"

Marianne reached out of the opening and picked up a stone that was on the ground in the cemetery. She laid it out on her palm and began to look at it intently for a moment. Suddenly the stone exploded into a fine powder.

Mark was dumbfounded and looked over to Abigail for an explanation.

"Mark, why don't you pick one up."

Mark reached through and picked up a larger stone. He could feel the coldness of the air in his realm hit his hand.

"Now hold it out toward Marianne," Abigail instructed.

Mark could see Marianne focusing on the rock in his hand, and within a few seconds, he felt some slight pressure on his palm, and the rock was obliterated.

"How are you able to do that?"

"I can hardly believe it myself. While Abigail was instructing me on how I should hold the portal key in my hand to destroy it, I just looked at the rock, and it was gone."

"Tell him what you were thinking," Abigail said, encouraging Marianne to go on.

"I thought about what these evil beings could do to others if they were able to access our world and the rock was destroyed."

Mark looked over at Abigail for clarification.

"I think Marianne has figured out the proper thought pattern that will enable all of you to destroy the charms simultaneously. You must not think of destroying them for yourselves but out of concern for others. She also can open the portal for all of you."

Mark breathed a large sigh of relief as they made their way back through the opening and into the cemetery.

Marianne turned to Mark and hugged him tightly.

"I'm very pleased with our visit today, and I'm grateful you both have a clearer understanding of what is required. Until the other two portal keys are found, feel free to practice accessing my realm and be ready." Abigail waved and was gone.

Mark just stood there; grateful he had made the decision to bring Marianne with him. He looked over at her smiling.

Marianne slipped her hand into Mark's and squeezed it tightly.

"Thanks for not giving up on me, Mark. I would never have realized my purpose in having my gift without you." She leaned up and gave him a soft kiss on the cheek.

Mark did not feel his feet touch the ground as they made their way back to the car.

CHAPTER 58

CRY FOR HELP

Days went by without locating the other two keys, and Mark was worried. Even though everyone in the group was looking out for them, he felt that Jeremy and Stacie would be the ones to find them. He checked in with them throughout the days and could tell he was getting on their nerves.

While he waited for the keys to turn up, Mark made several visits to the next realm. Some visits, like the Gettysburg Address, filled his soul with happiness, knowing that humanity could learn their lesson for the betterment of mankind. Others, like the attack on Pearl Harbor, would anger him for hours afterward.

Marianne was also visiting and practicing what Abigail had taught her.

Each of them broke down what they had experienced after each visit.

He was disappointed to learn that Jeremy and Stacie hadn't been practicing opening their side doors at all but took comfort knowing that Marianne could open an access for all of them.

Mark was in his room studying for his finals when his phone started vibrating on his bed. He picked it up and saw it was Stacie calling.

"Hey, Stace, I can't hang out right now. I've got to study for my science—" was all he could say before she cut him off.

"I'm not calling for that. I just got a call from P-dog regarding something he heard by the stadium. Is Jeremy with you?"

"I thought Paul went home now that he's done with his finals," Mark said, confused.

"He did for a few days but came back to enroll for the spring semester. But you didn't answer my question. Is Jeremy there?"

"No, he isn't. I think he's up studying at the library. I haven't seen him all afternoon." Mark looked around the room for his backpack and didn't see it. "His bag is gone, so he must be up there. Why?"

"Paul said he was passing by the stadium when he heard someone yelling at the very top of one of the stairwells. He said it sounded like Jeremy, but he couldn't get a good enough look at who it was."

"Come on. This must be one of P-dog's little jokes, and he's playing you," Mark said a little impatiently.

"I thought the same thing, but then I tried texting and calling Jeremy, and he didn't answer. He wanted to meet up with me to grab something to eat, but it's been over an hour since we were supposed to meet. You know how he is with food. I'm worried, Mark."

"He's probably buried in a book at the library right now and has his phone on silent. Let me check my phone."

Mark glanced at his phone to see if he had any missed messages from Jeremy, but there weren't any. This made him a little uneasy. It had been hours since his last text, and Jeremy always reached out to him when food was involved.

"Let me text him our code word. If he has his phone, he will reply to that."

"Code word?" Stacie asked.

"Yes. Growing up, we would use it if we needed to escape a situation we didn't want to be in or needed help."

"Like what?"

"I got in trouble for being late multiple times in one of my early-morning classes my sophomore year. I was in the principal's office, and he asked why. I came up with an excuse that my grandma was very sick, and I would visit her in the mornings. I texted J while I was in there, and he came into the office to ask the principal something and then asked me how my grandma was. After he explained how sick she was, the principal let me go and even gave me a note to use whenever I needed it."

Mark had never mentioned this to anyone else and didn't know how Stacie would respond.

"You two are such children. You better not have used it on me."

"No, not ever, Stace. Let me text him now, and I'll get right back to you."

Mark hung up before she could say anything, happy she did not ask him to elaborate. He quickly texted the word *SpongeBob* to Jeremy.

Mark waited for about ten minutes, but there was no reply. He started to get a sinking feeling in his stomach and called Stacie back.

"I didn't hear back. I think we better get up to the stadium, just in case."

"I agree. I'll meet you in front of the library in five."

Mark grabbed his jacket and raced out the door. When he was near the library, he noticed Stacie had started walking toward the stadium, and he caught up to her. He could tell by the look on her face that she was in full panic mode.

When they rounded the corner to the west side of the stadium, Mark noticed a rather large crowd of students had gathered and were looking up, pointing toward the top of the stadium. They both went to the front of the crowd to get a better view.

Mark's heart sunk when he heard the unmistakable voice of his best friend screaming random words laced with profanity from the top of his lungs, words that did not make any sense.

"What is he doing up there?" Stacie asked, distressed. She turned to the group. "Has anyone here called nine-one-one?"

A girl who appeared to be filming what was happening on her cell stepped forward.

"Of course we did. We've been trying to talk to him, but he doesn't answer any of us. He gets close to the edge and then backs away."

Mark cupped his hands to his mouth and raised his voice, trying not to sound too alarmed. "Jeremy, it's Mark and Stace. Why don't you come down from there?"

"Yeah, Jeremy! This isn't funny!" Stacie screamed.

There was no reply.

Mark noticed his whole body was moving back and forth.

He scanned the stadium for a way to reach him but quickly realized Jeremy had moved across a rather precarious platform to get to where he was. He surmised the ledge he was standing on was only a few feet deep; with one false step, his best friend could fall to his death.

Squinting his eyes, he noticed a darkened shadow behind him that seemed to be moving.

"Stace, look a little to the right of Jeremy and tell me what you see."

Stacie squinted for a moment and then looked back at Mark in shock. "Yes, I see it. There is someone up there with him."

CHAPTER 59

DESPERATE MEASURES

Mark pulled out his phone and zoomed in on where Jeremy was standing. He noticed a dark silhouette moving toward him like it was trying to push him over the edge.

He moved his phone down a bit and noticed Jeremy clutching an all too familiar object in his right hand.

"Stacie, Jeremy is holding a portal key," Mark whispered.

The threats Koltar had made of hurting his friends came flooding into his mind.

"How can you even see that?" Stacie asked, trying to look for it on her phone screen.

Mark reached over and showed her the image of Jeremy's hand he had taken. "How do we get him to let go of it from down here?" she asked quietly, her voice cracking with emotion.

"First, we need to get rid of these people. We don't have time to explain what's happening. Especially if the cops are on their way."

Mark moved in front of the group, not knowing what to say at first. After getting everyone's attention, a thought popped into his head.

"Listen, everybody, I just found out that my buddy up there is filming a video for one of his classes. He just texted me he will be down in a bit."

The group did not disperse.

Mark pretended to get more texts and raised his eyebrows at Stacie to play along. She in turn began to pretend to get texts, and they both started a dialogue about what Jeremy was doing that made the group believe they were in contact with him. A few kids mumbled what a waste of time it was as they slowly dispersed.

Mark noticed the girl who had called the cops was still standing there, looking at them both.

"I called the police, so I better wait for them."

"Don't worry. My friend is going to come down right now, and if the cops show up, we'll explain everything to them," Mark said, assuring her.

He then turned in Jeremy's direction and for added emphasis yelled, "You better get down here. The cops will be here any minute."

His ploy did the trick, and the girl rolled her eyes at them before walking off.

Mark turned to Stacie. "Now we need to get him down before the cops do show up."

Mark moved to a spot with the best line of sight between him and Jeremy.

"J, you need to drop the object in your hand now." He waved his free hand, trying to get his attention.

For a brief second, he noticed Jeremy glance down at him and then turn back toward the shadow behind him.

The thought of their secret word popped into his head. He started hollering, "SpongeBob!" over and over until he got Jeremy's attention.

"Mark?" Jeremy yelled down in bewilderment. "Help me. I don't even know how I got up here."

"You need to put the charm down now."

"I can't. He won't let me," Jeremy shouted fearfully. Mark saw him glance back at the dark figure that was beginning to take a more human shape.

Mark looked at Stacie. "You need to help me keep his attention on us until he has the strength to get rid of it."

They both started shouting, "SpongeBob!" in unison, which got Jeremy's attention back. Mark noticed Jeremy beginning to crouch down slowly.

"Do it now!" Mark shouted with all the power he could muster.

Mark watched Jeremy begin to pry his hand open with his free hand.

The shadowy figure seemed to move right on top of him at that moment.

"Now!" Mark and Stacie both shouted.

Jeremy's hand opened, and the portal key dropped out of his hand and bounded off the ledge, plummeting toward the ground.

Mark dropped his phone and darted under the falling object, catching it with both hands.

He looked up to notice the dark figure descending toward him. He quickly placed it on the ground and moved away.

Mark heard Koltar say, "We are one step closer," before disappearing into thin air.

"What just happened?" Stacie asked, startled.

"It was Koltar who was up there with Jeremy. We need to get him down."

Mark and Stacie spent the next few minutes helping Jeremy navigate down. They watched with bated breath as he barely made it back to the platform, jumping in midair.

When he reached the bottom of the stairs, they both tackled him in a big bear hug. Suddenly a flash of light hit all three of them.

"Which one of you called for the police?" asked a police officer, with his large flashlight shining on them.

Mark turned just in time to take the full brunt of it in the face but was too stunned to say anything.

"I got a call saying there was a kid threatening suicide at the top of the stadium. You kids know anything about that?"

Mark composed himself. "The girl who called you has left. She thought she saw someone up on the top of the stadium." Mark pointed above him. "But we've been here for a while now and haven't seen anything."

"Do you two agree with his story?" the cop asked Jeremy and Stacie, unamused.

"Yes, Officer. We've been looking up there ourselves but haven't seen anything. I think she was just seeing things," Stacie said, managing a controlled smile.

"Well, that's no laughing matter, and I will have to call that young lady back and let her know that." He turned and abruptly walked away.

Jeremy collapsed to the ground. Mark helped him up to a sitting position.

"Jeremy, how did you end up holding that portal key on top of the stadium?" Mark asked, staring at the object lying on the ground a few feet away from them.

Jeremy just sat there staring off in the distance. Mark waited patiently for him to answer while Stacie rubbed his back.

Jeremy slowly wiped his forehead with his hands and cleared his throat. "I was on my way to the library when I noticed someone was following me. He followed me from our dorm to the front steps of the library. I turned to go see what he wanted when he took off running toward the stadium."

Jeremy stood up and used his hands to retrace where he had come from by pointing in several directions.

"When I got here, I noticed him reach into his bag and place the portal key on the ground. Then he took off running again. He placed the writing and stone side facedown, which is why I picked it up. I tried to drop it when I saw what it was, but it was too late."

Mark could feel Jeremy tense up the more he talked.

"Every bad experience I've ever had bubbled to the surface of my brain, and I just wanted to end my life. The thought of jumping off the stadium would not leave my mind, and the next thing I knew, I was being forced to climb up there. It was Koltar who was trying to persuade me to help him. Every time I refused; I could feel him trying to force me off the ledge. Next thing I knew, you two were shouting my name and our secret code."

"I thought we were going to lose you," Stacie said, leaning in to hug him tightly.

"That sounds a lot like what happened to Paul. Did you get a good look at him?" Mark asked, pressing for details.

Jeremy rubbed his temples with his fingers and then looked at Mark with a sudden realization. "You know what? He was dressed just like that caretaker guy at the HCC we ran into a few weeks ago."

"Pete?" Mark said in astonishment.

"Yes. It had to be him. I knew I recognized him but couldn't place it until now," Jeremy said, perking up.

"You mean to tell me he's been the one putting all of these portal keys all over campus for us to find?" Stacie said in disgust.

"Pete the caretaker. That makes total sense," Mark said, letting the realization set in. "He could've followed us home after any of those nights we visited the cemetery to learn where we lived and our routines. Who else would even know what we've been up to?"

Mark took off the jacket he was wearing, walked over, and wrapped up the portal key. "I think we know where to find the last charm," he said, holding the jacket at arm's length like it was hazardous waste.

"Do you think he hasn't placed it somewhere on campus already?" Stacie asked.

"I doubt it. It has taken him weeks to place the four we've found, so I assume he has a plan to follow you around next. I don't want to have another experience like this with you, Stace. We have the advantage of knowing who he is and where to find him. It's time to bring this battle to him."

CHAPTER 60

SECRET AGENT

Back at Mark's dorm room, the three of them filled the professor in on the details of what happened to Jeremy over Mark's phone. The professor was thrilled to learn they had discovered who it was that was helping Koltar.

Mark was grateful when the professor arrived at the same conclusion of looking for the final portal key at the cemetery and confronting the caretaker if possible. He had a hard time selling the idea to Stacie and Jeremy on the way over to the dorm, but once they heard the same suggestion from the professor, they both agreed to go.

"Mark, take a look at the portal keys you and Jeremy have in your possession and tell me if you notice anything different about them," requested the professor.

Mark retrieved his backpack from the end of his bed and pulled out both keys he had stuffed in there. When he unwrapped them, Mark noticed both stones in the center of the objects were glowing bright red.

"They're glowing, Professor. What do you think that means?"

"I think we need to get Marianne and get over to the cemetery with our keys right now. The time to slam the door shut has arrived. I'll be right over to pick you kids up," the professor said emphatically and then hung up.

Mark called Marianne quickly and was relieved he got a hold of her. After explaining the day's events and their plan of action, she agreed to meet them out in front of their building with her key.

When Marianne arrived, each one of them who possessed a key took turns explaining to Stacie what they could do while they waited for the professor. Mark knew the challenge they faced once they held them directly in their hands to destroy them.

The professor pulled up, and they all piled into his car. They all agreed to put the portal keys in Mark's backpack so they could retrieve them quickly when the time came.

On the drive over, they devised a plan for how they were going to approach Pete and get the final portal key from him.

They pulled in near the caretaker's utility shed and noticed there were no lights on, and his truck was not in the parking lot.

While they waited for Pete to arrive, Mark went over what they needed to do once they possessed all five portal keys.

After a half hour went by with no sign of Pete, Mark talked them into searching the shed for the last key instead of waiting any longer.

Mark led everyone toward the shed and looked through the clouded glass pane in the door. He noticed a dull blue light from a portable lantern in the corner of the room. He knocked on the door but didn't hear any movement inside.

Mark reached down and turned the rusty doorknob slowly. He was surprised to find it unlocked. "He must be somewhere nearby. Be ready for anything," Mark said, entering the shed cautiously.

Once inside, he was astonished by what he saw. Hanging all around them were pictures of all sorts of different charms. Many of them were very similar to the ones they had brought with them. There were several drawings and sketches and a small pottery wheel in one corner.

"Be careful while looking for the key in all this mess. It's most likely not out for us to find in plain sight," instructed the professor.

Mark went toward a corner that had a large stack of papers on a workbench. He carefully turned over one piece at a time, and one caught his attention. It was a map of the campus that had some markings on it.

He reached over and angled a small lamp that was nearby, clicking it on to see the map better.

227

Five circles spanning a large portion of the campus formed the shape of a cane. Each circle was connected by a line. The circle on the top of the crook was around the School of Public Health. The next one circled the stadium. He followed the line down to the Cole building. Then the library. The last circle was around the south campus dining building near his dorm.

Trying to comprehend what they meant, he quickly realized four of the five circles were areas in which a portal key was found. A chill shot down the back of Mark's neck. "Guys, I don't think the fifth charm is here," he said, glancing at the others while holding the map out in front of him.

"What do you mean?" said Jeremy, grabbing the map out of his hand. The rest huddled around to look.

Mark didn't say anything and watched each one of them come to the same conclusion after studying all the marks on the map.

"Mark's right," Stacie said, disappointed. "Why would he have placed my charm there? That's nowhere near my building."

"I agree, Stace. Something doesn't add up," said Mark.

"That's it," the professor interrupted with a large smile on his face. "That is how we need to be aligned to destroy the charms."

"These points are far apart, Professor. If each of us goes to these spots on campus, how will we know when all of us are in position?" asked Marianne.

The professor grabbed the map excitedly and began to trace the circled locations with his finger.

"This is not a map of exact distance but a map of position only. Pete simply had to place the charms in these vicinities for us to find. They must be tied to the ritual he was instructed to complete to prepare the door. My guide told me to be on the lookout for the proper alignment and I would know it when I saw it. This must be it. We just need to make sure to put ourselves in this shape once we enter the next realm. I would imagine we can be very close together."

"The shape of a candy cane? What's the significance of that shape, Professor?" Jeremy asked.

"The symbol of the cane, or staff, is one of the oldest symbols known to man. It signifies authority, power, and social prestige, which are all things these damned souls crave. There is a saying in ancient Buddhism that describes the importance of this symbol that just dawned on me. Let me see. *With this staff in my hand, I can measure the depths and shallows of the world. The staff supports the heavens and makes firm the earth. Everywhere it goes, the true teaching will be spread."*

The professor looked around at each of them with contentment. Mark could tell he was amused he was able to remember the quote.

"I didn't know you were Buddhist," Marianne said innocently.

"I'm not, but I love many tenets of that religion. Even the Bible references the walking staff as a symbol of dignity and high office."

Mark was about to comment about something he had read in his history class regarding the cane when they were all startled by the sound of metal hitting the doorframe behind them.

CHAPTER 61

CORNERED

They all turned around to see Pete standing in the doorway, holding a shovel menacingly. He flicked on a switch that illuminated a single light bulb above them and eyed each one of them up and down.

While the others stood there in shocked silence, a surge of anger raced through Mark. It was all he could do to hold back from charging right for him. "We know what you're up to, and it's too late. We will not open the door. You've failed."

Pete did not acknowledge Mark's comments. "I see you found my map," he said, keeping the shovel in front of him and blocking their only route of escape.

"Yes, we have. We know all your secrets now," Mark said in a mocking tone, keeping an eye on the shovel.

"You haven't found all of my secrets." Pete reached for the top of a cabinet to his left and pulled down a large black book that had no writings on the outside but was ornately decorated.

Mark realized it was the book of spells that Abigail had told him to look for. His mind began to race for a way to get it out of Pete's hands when he noticed a strange look began to form on Pete's face. Even in the dimly lit shed, Mark could see his pupils dilate until there was very little color left in his eyes. His facial features became hardened and expressionless.

Pete lunged at Mark with the point of the shovel headed toward his head.

Before Mark could react to defend himself, Pete's momentum was stopped by Jeremy's fist, which landed squarely on his right cheek and sent him crashing to the floor.

Mark noticed the shovel at Stacie's feet and shot her a glance to pick it up while he went for the book. She quickly reached down and grabbed it while the Professor and Jeremy jumped on top of the stunned caretaker.

They rolled him over onto his stomach, holding each arm.

"Marianne, hand me some of that rope hanging there, and let's tie his hands," the professor said, applying additional pressure on the arm he held, causing Pete to moan with pain.

Once they had him subdued, they rolled him back over into a sitting position.

"Where is the last portal key?" Mark asked impatiently. He observed Pete's facial expression change instantly to a frightened look.

"What do you mean the last key? They have all been placed."

"Don't lie to us. We have found all of them on your map except the one by the dining hall," Mark said, holding the map within inches of his face.

"It doesn't matter. My job is done. You cannot win this battle."

"That's why you are going to tell us exactly where it is and what we need to do to win," Stacie said, holding the shovel inches from his face.

Pete looked down for a moment. When he looked back up, Mark noticed he had a darker countenance again.

"I cannot wait to see whatever plan you think you have made fail miserably," said Pete. He licked the blood from a cut that had opened on his lip and began to laugh maniacally.

Marianne moved over closer to Pete. "Why are you doing this?" she asked while pushing the shovel in Stacie's hand down away from Pete's face. "I don't understand why you would want to help these beings bring so much pain and misery to innocent people."

The anger that was on Pete's face suddenly turned to fear, and he shook his head back and forth quickly. Mark couldn't tell if he was trying to clear the cobwebs from the blow he had received from Jeremy or if something else was happening to him.

"We are still waiting to hear why you are helping them," said Mark with a little more force.

"You can't understand how convincing he can be," said Pete in a low whisper, scanning the room with a frightened look.

"Who can be convincing?" Jeremy asked.

"Koltar. He's right here."

CHAPTER 62

DIVIDED

It dawned on Mark that Koltar was moving in and out of Pete, and he wondered if anyone else in the group had picked up on his personality swings.

"How did you come into contact with Koltar in the first place?" Mark asked, knowing he was speaking directly to Pete now.

Pete looked up at all of them with a humbled look and began to answer in a hushed tone. "A few years ago, I found a Ouija board at a yard sale. I brought it back here for me and a couple of my buddies to mess around with. We began to ask some yes or no questions and didn't think much of it. But when my buddies left, the eyepiece began to move on its own." Pete stopped talking and again began to scan the shed again.

"And then what?" asked Jeremy, still holding him tightly.

"I asked who was moving the eyepiece, and it spelled out K-O-L-T-A-R. When I said the name out loud, he appeared right in front of me. He said he had heard my call and needed my help in ushering in a new age of rectification for mankind."

This was the first time Mark had heard the conflict called this.

"The rectification?" Marianne asked calmly.

"I didn't understand it at first, but Koltar laid it out for me. He explained that there was a reason I had reached out to him that evening. He said that he had knowledge and understanding that mankind didn't have, and he wanted to rectify that and share it with us. He said that the most powerful people on earth, through the ages, were helped by his kind, and I was promised wealth untold if I helped them open the door."

"How's that working out for you now?" Jeremy said mockingly. "You're tied up on the floor of a utility shed in a cemetery."

Almost immediately, Pete's facial features twisted, and his eyes turned coal-black again. "You are lucky we need you to open the door, or I would've pushed you off the ledge yesterday," Pete said, his voice changing to a deep growl. "He doesn't have the treasures now but will have them soon enough. Then he will be in a position of power over all of you."

Jeremy shot Mark a look of surprise, wondering how Pete knew about his altercation on the stadium ledge.

"Not if we can help it, Koltar," Mark said, looking directly into Pete's dark pupils.

"It's too late for you. When you all take hold of the portal keys, I will be able to lead a host through a door that will never be shut again." Pete's body began to rock back and forth while he giggled to himself.

Mark could tell the others were starting to realize what was happening to Pete. Just then, he started to let loose with a string of foul language directed at the group. The professor grabbed a well-worn rag and wrapped it around his mouth to keep him quiet. Pete's eyes rolled to the back of his head, and he went silent.

"Where do you think that last key is?" Jeremy asked.

Mark rested the map on the book of spells and traced the point from the top of the cane down to the last point near their dormitory building again. He tried to remember if he missed recognizing any strange objects over the past few weeks but couldn't come up with anything.

"You guys don't remember seeing anything strange near the dining hall?" Mark asked, looking at each one of his friends. They all said they hadn't.

Mark looked down at Pete, who had come to again.

"All of the keys are accounted for except the one by our dormitory." Mark reached down and put the map in front of Pete and yanked the rag off his mouth. "You said all of them had been found. Where is that one?"

"That was the first one he placed. He put it in the trunk of your car."

Mark looked at the others in disbelief and then back at Pete. "My car. But how?"

"It was quite easy. Once we learned you and your friends were in Professor Windham's class, we followed you two to that restaurant and then back to your campus. You didn't even notice us pull right up next to you in the parking lot. You should know better than to leave your car unlocked," Pete said, sneering at them.

Mark could feel his temper starting to increase just by talking to Koltar. He took a deep breath to control it. "You're lying to us. I've found nothing in my car. Now where is it?"

"You will find it soon enough. We couldn't have done it without *all* of your help." Pete looked up at them with an evil grin.

Jeremy lunged toward Pete to strike him again. This time, Mark intervened and pushed his arm away, deflecting the blow.

"Jeremy, that's enough. This is what he wants. We're not dealing with Pete here. It's Koltar that's speaking through him."

Jeremy backed away, with Stacie holding onto his arm to calm him down.

"We need to get back to my car and hope that it's still in there," Mark said, looking at the professor.

"I agree," the professor said, pulling his keys out of his pocket.

"What should we do with him?" asked Stacie, pointing down at Pete.

"He got himself into this situation. He can get himself out," said the professor, stepping over Pete toward the open door. "We have more important matters to attend to."

Mark motioned for the others to follow, and they all exited the shed.

"Hey, you can't just leave me here with my hands tied behind my back!" Pete yelled. "He'll kill me."

"Just a second, everyone," Mark said. He went back in and grabbed Pete and walked him out the door.

"We're not bringing him with us, are we?" Stacie asked in disbelief.

"Nope. Since this is where our friendly neighborhood caretaker built the keys and all his blueprints are in that shed, I'm going to make sure he cannot do anything like this again," said Mark while handing Pete over to Jeremy to hold on to.

Mark went back inside the shed. He grabbed a gas can he noticed near the entrance next to a trimmer and a box of matches that were located on one of the shelves, then returned to the group.

"What are you going to do with those?" asked Marianne.

"I'm going to burn down this shed."

"You wouldn't dare!" Pete screamed. His body convulsed, trying to get out of the grip that Jeremy had him in.

Mark began to open the gas can lid and remove the spout. The others moved back without a word of opposition.

"Go ahead. My work for him is complete, and we are no longer in need of the book of spells. I have other business to attend to." Pete's body quickly relaxed.

Mark made a quick trip around the shed, splashing the gas all around the foundation, and then bent down to strike a match near the entrance.

Pete shook his head and looked at Mark in horror. "Please don't burn it down. I have maps of hidden treasure in there. I will share it with all of you," Pete said desperately.

"Too late for that, Pete. Your actions have inflicted enough damage for one lifetime. You cannot be trusted, and nothing you say can change that."

Mark carefully dropped the match and moved away. Within a matter of minutes, the whole shed was in flames.

Pete suddenly broke loose of Jeremy's grip and ran off with his hands still tied behind his back, screaming for help.

Jeremy moved to go after him, but Mark held him back. "Let him go. There's nothing he can do for or against us anymore."

The group hustled over to the professor's car and pulled out of the cemetery just as they heard the approaching fire truck.

Mark could not wait to get back to his car. He didn't know how he could've missed finding the first key that had been planted.

His anticipation was interrupted by his phone vibrating in his jacket pocket. He pulled it out and looked down to see that it was his mom calling. He let it go to voice mail so he could join in on the discussion with the others. His phone started to vibrate again. This time, he picked it up.

"Hey, Mom, can I call you back in a little while?" There was no immediate response. "Is everything okay?"

"Mark, you need to come home right away," said his mom in a panic. "There is something wrong with Cassie. I heard her door slam a few minutes ago, and she won't answer me."

"Okay, Mom, just settle down. Is she mad at you for some reason?" Mark asked, trying to keep her calm.

"No. She said she had something of yours that she wanted to give back and went into her room to get it to show me. That's when I heard her door slam. I've yelled and banged on her door, but she won't answer."

Mark could sense his mom was at her breaking point by the sound of her heavy breathing between each word.

"All right, Mom. Let me call her. She always answers my call, and I'll call you back."

"Okay, honey. Hurry."

Mark hung up and dialed his sister. The phone picked up, and he heard his sister mumbling incoherently on the other line. A deep fear took control of him as he made out the words *help me*.

"Professor, I know where the fifth key is. We must get to my house immediately."

CHAPTER 63

FORCED PREDICAMENT

When they pulled into the driveway of Mark's home, his mom came running out to meet him. Mark jumped out to meet her, and she wrapped him in a huge bear hug.

She was startled when everyone started piling out of the professor's car behind him, and he quickly introduced Marianne and Professor Windham.

Mark hurriedly led everyone inside, and they followed him down the hallway to his sister's bedroom. He knocked on the door firmly. "Sis? It's Mark. Open up." He waited for a moment, but there was no response.

"Let me try. She always liked me best," Jeremy said, pushing his way past Mark. "Cass, it's J. We have some important things to talk to you about," he said in an easy tone. Still no response.

"Mom, did you try to open her lock with anything?" Mark asked.

"Yes, I've tried a couple of times but could not get the doorknob to open." She opened her hand to reveal several broken toothpicks.

Mark reached up along the doorframe and located the small screwdriver he had placed there years ago that his mother knew nothing about. He pushed it in through the small hole of the doorknob and moved it around slowly until he heard the click of the lock release.

When he went to push open the door, it wouldn't budge. Confused, he looked down and turned the knob in the other direction. He leaned in and exerted everything he could, but it still wouldn't budge.

"Mark, open the door," Stacie said impatiently.

"I'm trying, Stace, but it feels like someone is pushing on it from the other side."

Jeremy and Stacie began to push with him, and the door opened slightly but then slammed back on them.

"I have a bad feeling about this," Marianne said, falling to the side. The professor quickly grabbed her by the shoulders to help support her.

"I agree, honey. What is going on?" Mark's mother asked, her voice shaking with fear.

Mark looked at his mom with a determined look and leaned into the door again with all his might. His friends grunted as they pushed with him. Just then, the door opened a few inches.

Instead of the light from the hallway entering the room, Mark noticed it was even darker than when they entered Paul's room.

Mark jammed his foot in the opening they had created to brace it, and all three pushed it open enough for Mark to walk through. He noticed a distinct drop in the temperature when he entered. He also heard several distorted voices chanting something toward the far corner of the room in the direction of Cassie's bed.

"Who's in here with my baby!" Mark's mom yelled, coming into the room behind him.

"Mom, stay back," Mark said, reaching out in vain to try to grab her. Suddenly, an unseen force pushed his mom back outside the room, with the door slamming shut, leaving Mark in the thick darkness, unable to see anything.

Mark reached out in the direction of the door and grabbed ahold of the knob. Before he could attempt to open the door, the chanting stopped.

He heard Koltar's voice through the thick darkness. "The rectification is at hand. Your sister will be a sacrifice if you do not do what I tell you."

Mark whirled around, swinging his fists into the void in desperation and anger. "Leave her out of this! She has nothing to do with it." His voice echoed off the walls of the bedroom, and he could feel himself slipping into Koltar's hellish realm again.

"She is fine and is resting comfortably. She has quite conveniently stumbled upon the portal key that was intended for you. It is the last piece of an ancient puzzle that will be solved tonight."

The chanting began again.

Mark tried his best to hold off the horrible negative thoughts that began to bubble to the surface of his mind. He closed his eyes tightly.

When he reopened them, he noticed the darkness, and his sister's room was replaced by a rocky bluff surrounded by a deep mote on all sides. Thick black clouds were briefly illuminated by shots of jagged lightning, but he couldn't tell what was giving off the faint light source around him.

As his eye's adjusted, he could make out several dark silhouettes surrounding his sister's bed at the top of the bluff. He moved closer to the group and noticed his sister clutching the glowing portal key in her hand that was hanging off her bed.

"It is me you want! Not her!" Mark yelled toward the group with rage. He began to realize that each word of their chant was driving him further and further toward madness.

"Yes, it is you we want. You and your acquaintances will open the door for us by holding the keys in your hands before entering the fourth realm, or I'm afraid your sister will remain a tortured soul in our control," Koltar said. His figure moved from the group toward Mark.

Mark now knew why Abigail wanted them destroyed in her realm. It would buy them enough time to destroy them so Koltar's host would not have as much influence on them.

Now he needed to get his sister to release the key she was holding to break the connection.

With each step he took toward his sister, a dark shadow would leave her side and move through Mark. It felt to him like they were attacking his soul with each pass. He could feel their torment, and his head felt like it was going to explode.

While Koltar continued spewing threats toward him, Mark strained his eyes and observed the faint reddish glow that was coming from the center stone. He knew he only had one shot to dislodge it.

Mustering all the strength he had left; he lunged in the direction of the bed and slapped the object in her hand.

CHAPTER 64

FACE-TO-FACE

Mark heard the key hit the ground with some force and watched the evil beings and darkness in the room centralize around Koltar's figure.

"We'll be waiting," he cried before trailing off into the darkness that was imploding on itself.

The sudden brightness from the lights in Cassie's room burned Mark's eyes for a moment, and he could hear her gasping for air. He rushed to her side just as the others came bursting into the room.

Mark's mom pulled Cassie up and held her tightly in her arms while Mark wiped beads of sweat from her forehead. She looked up at them with a look of relief.

"Hey, Mom," she said groggily and then turned to Mark. "When did you get here, and what's everyone doing in my room?" she asked, looking at everyone, alarmed.

"Sis, you were under the power of that dark being I told you about, but they're gone now, and you're safe."

Mark introduced the professor and Marianne. Cassie gave them a faint smile and then nestled into the arms of their mother, clearly exhausted.

Mark turned his attention to the key that was lying near their feet. He couldn't fathom how it ended up so far from campus.

"Cass, how in the world did you find this key?" he asked, picking it up with one of her beanies that had been lying nearby and showing it to her.

Cassie sat up a little, rubbed her eyes, and just stared at the object for a few moments.

"When you came by last week, I was putting those muffins in the trunk of your car and noticed it. Your car was a mess, and I was about to throw it away with some of the other trash I put in our can. I forgot that I put it in my pajama pocket and thought I better hold onto it just in case. I put it on my desk and forgot about it until today."

Cassie stood up slowly and walked over to her desk.

"I wish I hadn't kept it. I'm sorry, Mark," she said, turning back to face him with tears in her eyes. "I should've called you and told you I had it, and maybe none of this would've happened. I thought I was going to die."

"It's okay, sis. I'm sorry you were the one who found it. We didn't even find out it was in the back of my car until tonight. You had a pretty good hold of it, and I had to knock it out of your hand hard to break the spell you were under. What made you pick it up tonight?"

"I noticed a light coming from the center of it, and I picked it to see how it was glowing. Suddenly I felt a force grab me from behind and pull me toward my bed. That's when everything went black. It felt like I was in a deep sleep and unable to wake up. I tried to scream for Mom but couldn't. I felt like I was trapped in a horrible nightmare where you, Mom, and everyone I loved were standing over me chanting. It was horrible."

She walked back over and sat down, putting her arm around Mark, and laying her head on his shoulder. "Thanks for waking me up."

Mark kissed the top of her damp head. "That's what big brothers are for."

He reached over and handed the key to Stacie. "I believe this is yours now."

"I think it's time to take care of this once and for all," said the professor anxiously.

"You mean to tell me there are more of these objects you have brought?" Mark's mom said with a look of true concern directed at Mark. "Honey, I don't want to be rude, but I want all of you to take these objects and get them out of my house."

"Your mom is right, Mark," Marianne interjected. "I think it would be safer for us to take these objects back to school and destroy them there."

"I think that would be best, and I pray you know what you are doing, Mark." Mark's mom reached over and touched his cheek.

He grabbed her hand and kissed it tenderly. "I know what needs to be done now."

"Good." She turned and put her arm around his sister. "Come on, baby. Let's get you a drink of water."

While he watched his mom take Cassie out of the room, he said a prayer of gratitude in his heart that he was able to get there in time to help.

"Marianne's right. We need to do this somewhere else." Mark stood up and led them out of the room.

Approaching the living room, Mark noticed his mom and sister clutching each other and frozen in place while looking out the front window.

"Mom, Cass, are you okay?"

Mark rushed over and looked out the window. A countless number of dark, shadowy figures were glaring back at them from the front lawn.

"It's too late," said the professor. "We don't have time to get back to campus."

"Then it's over. The door is opened, and we failed?" Marianne asked with a pained expression.

"We're not too late," Mark said, keeping his eyes trained out the window. "Remember, Abigail said they cannot do anything in our world until we are all physically holding the keys. The fact that all five keys are here has brought them to this spot, but they cannot be unleashed unless we fail to destroy them. Please tell me someone brought my backpack into the house and did not leave it in the car," Mark said hopefully, noticing the professor's car was surrounded by the dark host.

"I saw that you did not grab it when we arrived, so I brought it in," Marianne said, pointing toward the front door.

They all shot one another a look of relief.

Mark slowly turned behind him to look out the sliding glass doors in the kitchen and did not see any figures in the backyard. "Looks like we will need to open our side doors in the backyard and destroy them there."

Mark motioned for Jeremy, who was closest to his backpack, to grab it.

Jeremy walked over and picked it up gingerly. Mark watched all the heads of the host follow Jeremy's movements, sensing a move was being made toward the keys.

Mark instructed his mom and sister to stay in the front room. He knew nothing would happen to them once they took the charms to the backyard.

The five of them moved slowly into the kitchen.

Suddenly, a small breeze picked up near the back sliding door, and a bright light appeared. Within seconds, Abigail was there.

"The time is now, my friends."

CHAPTER 65

TIPPING POINT

Although Mark was relieved to see Abigail, the thought of disappointing her and all that could happen if they failed in destroying the portal keys worried him. Everything that had been building over the past several weeks was now upon them.

They had no sooner stepped outside when Mark heard his mother holler from inside the house, "Mark, they're moving around the house!"

Jeremy quickly handed each one of them a portal key.

"Now that all the portal keys are accounted for, you will need to make the shape of a cane. Mark, you take the first position at the top of the cane here." Abigail moved over to the exact spot she wanted him to stand.

Mark wondered how she knew about the shape but pushed all nonrelevant questions out of his mind.

"Professor, you're next. Right here." Abigail moved to the next position. She instructed Stacie to stand in the center, then Jeremy, and finished aligning Marianne at the end.

Once they were in place, Mark quickly scanned both sides of the house and could see the dark images moving toward them from both directions. They began chanting again. Instead of the faceless forms he had witnessed before, he could now see their grotesque and twisted features.

Abigail clapped her hands for everyone's attention. "Never mind them. All of you must pay close attention to what I'm going to say." She moved back and forth between the five of them to make sure all eyes were on her. "There is not enough time for each of you to open your side door. I'm going to assist Marianne in opening a large enough door to my realm for all of you to step through. Once inside, I want you to immediately take hold of your charms with your bare hand and repeat the following citation to destroy them."

"Wait a minute," Jeremy said, interrupting her. "I thought Marianne was going to be able to destroy all of them for us."

Mark shot back impatiently, "Apparently, this is the only way. Now shut up and listen."

Abigail looked at Mark. "Please, Mark, no negativity."

She looked over at Jeremy. "Marianne has indeed been given the gift of divine focus, but she will only be able to destroy them once everyone says this phrase to aid her, which is *clauses foribus facere*. Make sure you pronounce the phrase correctly."

Mark glanced around the formation and could see everyone mouthing the words over and over. He realized while rehearsing the phrase that if just one of them failed to do what Abigail instructed, it would all be for naught.

"But what about them, Abigail?" The shadowy figures had moved within a few feet of Marianne at the end of the formation.

"My glory will keep them at bay momentarily but not for long. You need to enter, repeat the phrase, and hold them out for Marianne to destroy them."

Abigail started to move her arms above the spot Marianne was rotating her right arm. A massive side door opened to their right.

"The time is now, my friends. Jump in and Godspeed," Abigail said, moving back to the end toward Marianne.

Mark watched her brightness increase and blight out the shadowy figures, which kept them from advancing.

Mark jumped through the opening and was suddenly in the meadow that Marianne had opened for them at the cemetery. Looking down the line, he was relieved to see they were still in the proper alignment.

He quickly opened his key and held it out flat in his hand.

A feeling of panic shot through his head when his mind went blank trying to remember the phrase.

When the others started to say the verse, he immediately recalled the phrase and said it quickly enough for them to finish in unison.

He expected the key to explode, but nothing happened.

Mark glanced over into the backyard on the left and could see Abigail struggling to keep the dark mass at bay. He noticed the darkness beginning to encroach into the opening.

He looked down the line at Marianne, who had a panicked look on her face, and he could tell she was doubting herself.

"Marianne, you got this. I love you. Let's all try it again."

They all repeated the phrase, and Mark noticed a look of confidence on Marianne's face that he had never noticed before. One by one, the portal keys started exploding in their hands.

With each explosion, Mark could hear the figures bellow out in misery as the darkness began to retreat.

Upon crossing back over, the horrible sounds of the dark souls screeching, and moaning caused Mark and the others to cover their ears.

The dark host began to encircle Abigail, and she cried out in agony. Mark wanted to help but didn't know what to do.

Marianne rushed into the dark mass to try to help Abigail but was violently thrown back to the ground.

Mark ran over and helped her up.

"Someone has to help her!" Marianne yelled with tears streaming down her cheeks.

Within moments, the darkness had completely consumed Abigail. She cried out, saying something that Mark couldn't understand, and disappeared along with the dark host.

Shocked at what they had just witnessed, they all stood there without saying anything for several minutes.

"Where did she go?" Stacie yelled, breaking the silence and running over to the spot where Abigail had been. Jeremy and the professor joined her, while Mark held onto Marianne, who had her face buried in his chest, sobbing.

Mark's mother and sister came running from the back door and encircled him and Marianne.

"Is it over, Mark? Are they gone?" his sister said, looking up at him.

"I believe they are," he said, looking over at the professor for confirmation.

"They're gone," said the professor, stooping down to take a closer look at a large burn mark on the lawn where the struggle had been.

"What about Abigail? It's not fair if anything has happened to her," Marianne said in anguish.

Extreme guilt began to consume Mark. Not only had he put his friends and family in danger, but he let Abigail down in her time of need. Overcome with emotion, tears began to stream down his cheeks. Everyone moved in around him into one giant support circle. He could tell by looking around that everyone felt his pain.

While the group was giving him words of encouragement, they were interrupted by a voice from behind.

"What is happening here? This should be a joyous occasion. You did exactly what was required."

They all turned around to see Abigail with her hands clasped together and a look of pure joy on her face.

"We thought you had been dragged down to wherever they came from," Stacie said, wiping her eyes.

"Heavens no. You had your jobs to do, and I had mine. You were responsible for closing the door to your realm only. I had to allow them to take me to their realm so I could seal it shut from there. My guide from the fifth realm instructed me on what needed to be done."

Mark was caught off guard by her mentioning her guide from the fifth realm again. He looked directly at the professor, and they both mouthed the words *fifth realm*.

"My friends, all souls that progress from your realm to mine, and have lived a life of love and service to others, are on the same path to further enlightenment that I'm on. There are advanced levels of progression that I look forward to obtaining after I learn what I need to here. This experience has gone a long way in advancing my knowledge and spiritual understanding. You have witnessed just a glimpse of the powers you have. Just have faith in your abilities, and you will learn to expand them."

Mark could not comprehend how he could expand what he had already learned regarding the fourth realm, let alone access any others.

"For now, be very satisfied in the great service you have done for the souls in both of our realms. Many of them are singing your praises. The knowledge of this event is spreading like a wildfire of relief to all realms," Abigail said warmly.

The awful feelings they had all just experienced were soon replaced by relief.

Finally being able to feel the weight that had been building lift off his shoulders, Mark's heart was filled with contentment. He moved back while the others gathered around Abigail to talk more about what happened. Abigail in turn thanked each one of them for what they had done, which left all of them beaming with pride.

It dawned on him that his meetings with her would be finished now that their task had been completed. The thought of it made him hold back from joining the group so he could prolong her visit.

When she moved in front of him, Abigail put both of her hands on his shoulders. He could feel her concern and love for him touch his soul deep down inside.

"This is not goodbye, Mr. Banks. There is much more you need to learn, and you never know when your assistance will be needed again. I must attend to other duties, but I will always be available for you if you ever need me."

Abigail moved back to address the group. "I consider all of you my dearest friends. I wish you nothing but the best," Abigail said, waving to them with both hands before disappearing.

Mark looked over and noticed a confused look on his mother's face.

"I don't understand everything that just happened here, but did any of you kids get any schoolwork done this semester?" she asked with a serious look thrown in Mark's direction.

Her question made Mark break out laughing. Within moments, all of them were laughing with him.

The lighthearted moment seemed long overdue.

While the professor, Stacie, and Jeremy gathered around Mark's mom, assuring her they had, Marianne pulled Mark aside.

"I have a question for you. When I was doubting myself in being able to destroy the portal keys, did you mean what you said, or did you say it in the spur of the moment?" she asked with a sheepish grin.

Without saying a word, Mark grabbed her by the waist and pulled her in close for a passionate kiss.

Which also seemed long overdue.

The End